To Red:

Hope you enjoy it! :)

Jake Paul Shannon

The
Perfect
Portrait

by John Paul Shuman Jr.

DORRANCE
PUBLISHING CO
EST. 1920
PITTSBURGH, PENNSYLVANIA 15238

The contents of this work, including, but not limited to, the accuracy of events, people, and places depicted; opinions expressed; permission to use previously published materials included; and any advice given or actions advocated are solely the responsibility of the author, who assumes all liability for said work and indemnifies the publisher against any claims stemming from publication of the work.

All Rights Reserved
Copyright © 2023 by John Paul Shuman Jr.

No part of this book may be reproduced or transmitted, downloaded, distributed, reverse engineered, or stored in or introduced into any information storage and retrieval system, in any form or by any means, including photocopying and recording, whether electronic or mechanical, now known or hereinafter invented without permission in writing from the publisher.

Dorrance Publishing Co
585 Alpha Drive
Pittsburgh, PA 15238
Visit our website at *www.dorrancebookstore.com*

ISBN: 979-8-8868-3073-6
eISBN: 979-8-8868-3933-3

Table of Contents

Prologue vii

Part 1- A Troubled Heart
    Chapter 1 - Awakening 3
    Chapter 2 - Remembering 9
    Chapter 3 - Serena 15

Part Two - Family Ties
    Chapter 4 - A Father's Lament 23
    Chapter 5 - Explanations 29
    Chapter 6 - Finding Him 33
    Chapter 7 - Decisions 47
    Chapter 8 - Voyage 57

Part Three - The Visions of Old and New
    Chapter 9 - The Journey 65
    Chapter 10 - Detour 71
    Chapter 11 - Reprieve 75
    Chapter 12 - A Meeting of Minds 79

Part Four - Discovery
    Chapter 13 - The Purffect Village 87
    Chapter 14 - The City of Akoran 103
    Chapter 15 - Serena's Christening 115
    Chapter 16 - An Evil Emerges 121

Part 5 - A Philosopher's Question
    Chapter 17 - The Quest for Truth 135
    Chapter 18 - A Religious Resistance 145
    Chapter 19 - Pardon 153
    Chapter 20 - One More Member 165

Part Six - A Light in the Darkness
    Chapter 21 - Serena Reborn 175
    Chapter 22 - The Skies Turn Dark Again 181
    Chapter 23 - Return to Sumurka 191
    Chapter 24 - Back to Rhodam 209
    Chapter 25 - A Call to Arms 225
    Chapter 26 - Special Delivery 235
    Chapter 27 - My Perfect Portrait 243
    Chapter 28 - The Ultimate Battle 249
    Chapter 29 - Jay's Awakening 257

Epilogue 261

Dedicated to my Kitty.

Prologue

A Mother's Distress

My works were never highly sought after by many people in the area of Darbyshire. I was the type of person some came to for favors of the spiritual sort. However, this wasn't a plea for repentance or salvation. No, this was a mingling of the very fabric of nature, a twisting of the boundary between life and death itself.

On one particular night, I found myself in the presence of a woman. She looked to be in her early to mid-thirties, hair the color of autumn leaves, and eyes as brown as the wood that lit the fires in my chimney stack. Something was troubling her, for her aura was in disarray, a dullness I had been accustomed to seeing in those who were suffering from loss. She was dressed in a burgundy sweater and a loose pair of denim jeans, far from fit on her slender frame. "May I help you?" I asked her. She looked around my shop at various trinkets, and jewels, and at my collection of tapestries from across various corners of Europe.

"You may help me," she said, "but the question is, can you help me?"

"That depends on the degree of help by which you are seeking."

"Then consider this a degree of the highest importance."

She sat down in front of me and continued to look around. "Something is troubling you," I said.

"Yes, there is. Are you the one I have heard about from the locals? The one who practices in, how should I say it, binding?" I took a minute and lit a candle before answering her.

"By what do you mean binding? If you are afraid you will come off as sounding crazy, then put that fear aside."

"I am sorry," she said. "It's just that not long ago, I had to lay my infant son to rest. So young was my boy, and losing him took a part of me with him. I haven't been able to concentrate on my work or my life. Hell, I even lost my marriage. So yes, I am highly distraught. I feel it's not right that someone so young and innocent should be taken away."

"The fabric of life and death is mysterious, sometimes obscure. I can only serve as a bridge between the two, a go-between if you must say."

"Can you bring back lost souls?"

"Ma'am?"

"Serena. Serena Vega."

"Ms. Vega."

"Just call me Serena."

"Serena, as I said, I am only the bridge to help ones cross to see their loved ones. I can't simply bring back the dead."

"Then maybe you can link me to his spirit. My son Jay that is. My son deserves a chance."

"Hmm, you want me to awaken a resting spirit?"

"Yes."

"You know that is pushing serious limitations, Serena."

"Can you do this or not?" she said on a sigh.

"Yes, but I will need a few things."

"What's that?"

"First, I will need something of his." Serena reached in her pocket and pulled out a pendant.

"All I have is this," she said. "It's something I had made to give him when he was older. As for hair or anything like that, forget it." I took the pendant and observed it. Red, green, white with an inscription.

"This inscription," I asked.

"I personally came up with that. I always wanted to be linked with Jay in some way."

"I can use this. Now, I will need something of yours."

"My hair? Oh, sure."

"No, not that. If I am to bind you two and awaken this lost soul, I will need life sustenance."

"My blood?"

"Yes."

"Very well."

I reached over to another table and retrieved two vials and a pin. "Why two vials?"

"You will see shortly. Now prick your finger and then drain some in one, then the other." Serena took the pin and pricked her finger, allowing her blood to fill the two vials. I took them both, sitting one aside, then wiping some of the blood on the pendant from the other. I wiped the blood across the face of the pendant, then held it over the flame of the candle.

"Why did you do that?" Serena asked.

"Purification. Jay's soul, any soul, will be restless upon being disturbed. This is to purify him, a cleansing of his essence, and a hardening of his spirit."

"Oh, so you're strengthening him?"

"A weak spirit can't survive in any realm, Serena." After the blood had bonded into the pendant, I sat it between us. "Now, Jay's spirit is fortified, purified, and renewed."

"So he is alive?" Serena asked.

"Only spiritually. The blood will give him life and allow him to live."

"Perfect." Serena went to reach for the pendant.

"No!" I said, pulling it away.

"No? Why? That's mine!"

"It's Jay's now, Serena. Don't be so caught up in your own sorrow that you forget why you came here. This will be given to him when the time is right."

"Fine! How much will this cost me?"

"Money is not required."

"Then what will?"

"You have already paid me," I said, pointing to the second vial of blood I had set aside. "I now have a piece of you both. As I said, I am only the bridge by which you two meet. However, I must warn you, tread lightly, for I will not allow you to tarnish this agreement."

"What do you mean by that?"

"Let's just say agreements can be revoked. If at any point you stray away and use this link for evil, just like the bridge, I will no longer support you and you will fall."

"Is that a threat?"

"It is a term of the agreement, no more no less."

"Well, I guess once I cross that bridge, I will never look back."

"DO NOT CROSS ME, SERENA!"

Serena was obviously shaken by these words. She gathered herself and left saying I had no power over her, yet I knew I was a bridge she would inevitably cross and ultimately would never be able to see the light of the other side.

For the next twenty-two years, I watched as Jay's spirit grew. I grew to care for him, to love him as a child I never had. I taught him as best I could, most importantly about life. Tucked away, unbeknownst to Jay, were the terms of that agreement Serena and I had made over two decades ago. I knew she would be coming for Jay, what mother wouldn't. Yet I also knew Serena would lose sight and cross over, but saddest of all, the bridge would give way under both of their feet.

PART ONE

A Troubled Heart

Chapter 1

The Awakening

I had never believed in fate or chance. I didn't even believe in free will, people, or even myself. I was a ghost, a drifting soul without a purpose, a soul whose life was changed at the lake...

I opened my eyes to find myself lying in leaves. The area around me was quiet, cold, and still. The leaves were wet as if it had just rained. The pendant was still around my neck, the fateful words still etched in my mind. I got to my feet and examined the area. There were many trees about from pines to spruces. I did not see any animals. No squirrels, bugs, nothing. "How did I get here?" I said. I walked towards the edge of the woods and saw an old man digging in the ground with the shovel. He was dressed in a gray coat, head down. "Excuse me," I said to him, but he ignored me. "Excuse me!" I said louder, still nothing in response. Maybe I was a ghost. Maybe I was really dead.

One thing I noticed in this unfamiliar world was the lack of color. Everything from the leaves on the trees to the dirt, the sky, was all a dull shade of gray. The only sound was the meeting of the old man's shovel hitting dirt. I decided to leave him and began to explore "the gray world" more. Around the old man were headstones upon headstones. However, instead of names, there were only blank spaces. Who were these graves for? Was I next?

"I had the same look on my face," said a voice. I looked to see it was the old man.

"Now you notice me?" I said.

"I already knew you were here. I knew you were in the woods as well. The hourglass of life will teach you many things."

"What is this place, and who are you?"

"To take the lesser path first, I am a gravedigger. I guess you could say I sat the palate for death."

"Palate for death?" I said. "The tombstones are empty, and it seems there is no one else around. This place is quiet, too quiet."

"What do you expect in a world where things are not always as they appear."

"That doesn't make any sense."

"Your world doesn't make any sense either. I lived in that world. Trust me, it will drive a man to an early grave."

"So why are you digging graves for people that may never show?"

"Everyone needs a death bed. I have seen so much death. I have grown use to it. I will not tell you now, but you will learn in time."

"Well, I haven't the time for riddles on life or sagacious lyrics. I need to get out of here. Don't make me laugh because I don't believe in that crap."

"You don't believe in anything, I can see. However, this world teaches you to believe in something. The woman that brought you here doesn't just choose anyone."

"Woman? What woman?"

"You don't remember, boy?"

"No, I don't. I just woke up here in this hellhole, and what woman are you…?" There was one thing I remembered. Before I blacked out, there was a woman in front of me. How could I forget those piercing black eyes. "Yes, I do remember."

"That's all you need to remember. Most do."

"I am not the only one?"

"No, you're not. There are others. Those that angels choose for their grace."

"Oh goodness! Enough with the fairy tales!"

"You will be a believer in something, boy."

"I will be a person who leaves this world. I believe in that."

"I thought you didn't believe in yourself."

The Perfect Portrait

"Okay, I am leaving."

I started to walk away, but then I got this feeling. Someone was coming. The old man turned to me. "There is a church nearby over there. Hide there."

"From what?"

"Divine personified."

"What?"

"Just hide in the church, boy!" I looked and saw a church nearby. It looked old, and in ruin, just as it did in my dreams. "Go!" At the ready I ran to the church, which was a few feet away. Upon its doorstep I saw it had stone columns leading to the door. There were fountains, rusted, cracked, and near collapse. The floor was cracked, with weeds growing in them. Two gargoyles, both of stone, guarded the entrance. I hid behind one of them and watched the events unfold.

Her eyes were pitch black. Her wings were black as well, yet deep inside her soul was hope. She carried her sword in hand and cast her gaze upon an old gravedigger, who awaited her arrival. She landed just a few feet from him, their eyes meeting. The old man took a pipe from his coat pocket and lit it. "So, you have come," he said to the angel. She said nothing and walked over to him.

"You're late with them as usual," she said.

"I am an old man, you'll understand," he said. The angel raised her sword to his throat.

"One more smart remark and I will have your head."

"You won't do it. Ah, young people." The angel pressed the blade against his throat.

"Filthy is what you are. I had it fit that you serve me, you lowly wretched composite of flesh."

"And I helped create you, you self-righteous bitch." The angel was taken aback by this. Never had a mortal been so collected yet daring with her.

"You haven't changed. You never will."

"I was sixty already when you brought me here. Twenty years later, nothing's changed. I am surprised you didn't kill me the last time I was late with these graves."

"I gave you one chance, that's all. Yet I see you choose as you will. I can't take that from you. There is much work to be done, an awakening for all.

Don't mistake me for weak. I am not a little helpless mortal girl anymore. I have transcended. I am perfect."

"You are full of yourself." The angel withdrew her blade. "You waste your time with me. Aren't you looking for someone?"

"Yes, I am. Several souls in fact."

"Have you found him?"

"No, but I feel I am close. Yet, why am I telling you anything? You were against our joining." The old man took a puff and looked the angel in her eyes.

"You know why," he said.

"Yes, I do. However, it matters not. I am rebuilding everything. As for you, I expect these done immediately."

"Of course." The angel went to walk off but stopped. She stood there and sniffed the air.

"Another lives," she said.

"Come again?"

"Don't play stupid! There is another soul in this realm."

"It's just me, that's all."

"No, there is another. The one I bore. Where is he?"

"I haven't the slightest idea who you mean?"

"Listen to me, you worthless old fool! I can sense him. I know he is here in this realm. If you refuse to tell me, then I will show you just how much of a bitch I can be!"

"Why does the boy matter to you?"

"Are you serious? Has your time in this place warped what little sense you had? I intend to rebuild my family and I will not allow this opportunity to waste! I may have been cheated by your so called 'God,' but in this realm, I am above all."

"Strong words from someone who sold their soul."

"Unlike you…Father, I care about my family. Now before I kill you, where is he?"

The old man looked up at the sky and saw someone approaching. From the gray came another angel. Unlike this angel's wings, his were smoky grey.

The Perfect Portrait

Upon him was a black cloak, a mask covering his eyes. In his hand was an elongated spear. "Lady Serena, we have the whereabouts of the one you seek," he said, walking over and kneeling before her.

"Good," Serena said. "Broun, you certainly have lived up to my expectations. I commend you."

"Yes, my lady." Serena looked at her father.

"I must make haste, gravedigger. However, you will see me again, make no mistake. Remember, you may have created me, but I am the one who destroys. I will not forget this, and when you sleep, I will be watching. Your days, although long, are numbered." With those words, she and Broun flew off. The gravedigger stood there smoking his pipe.

"Pain can motivate, yet Serena's temper prevents even that from happening. She seeks to undo it all even at the cost of her soul. Yet saddest of all, it is I who bares the cross of these sins in my old age. I can only hope she can find it in her heart to forgive me, for I haven't forgiven myself."

To leave my child behind
The only one I bore
To be so blind
By the trappings at my door
My daughter cried tears
Yet I did not
She remembered
When I only forgot
Now in these days I prepare
Final rest for a world in despair
Strike me down, my child
I deserve it all
Yet fear for your soul
For the mightiest tend to fall
Take heed on your wings for they will fail

Chapter 2

Remembering

I was shocked what just occurred before me. "Were those angels?" I said. The gravedigger was still tending to his graves. He looked up and motioned to me all was clear. I came from behind the pillar that provided shelter for me and went back to the graves. "What was that all about?" The gravedigger stopped, took out his pipe, and lit it.

"Where should I begin?" he asked.

"You tell me. Who was that woman and why was she upset with you?"

"That woman's name is Serena, and she is my daughter."

"No way. Your daughter is an angel?" He nodded. "I can tell this isn't the real world."

"She's trying to rebuild the family that she lost."

"Wait, don't steer clear of the main topic at hand. You have a lot to discuss with me." The gravedigger took a puff and looked in the distance.

"It's true, boy. She carries a lot of hate, anger, and disgust at the world, at me."

"Wait a minute! That woman that appeared before me in the other world, that was her?"

"Yes."

"I don't see why she appeared before me. I was only enjoying myself at the lake."

"Apparently she found you in your world. How did she not find you here?"

"I was carefully hid."

"No, I meant how did she not sense you? I was certain she would have spotted you with you being…" He paused and looked at me.

"Me being…?" I said.

"Never mind. She has tasked me digging these graves. I should get back to this."

"There's something you're not telling me. First of all, what is this world we are in and who are you?"

"You didn't hear our discussion?"

"Did you see how far that church was? Of course not."

"This is the realm of the forgotten."

"It's a graveyard, so I can imagine."

"It's more than that. It is a place of silence, isolation, and regret. The sun never shines here, and everything is tinted in a pale gray. It is devoid of hope, and I am the only soul here, left to wither."

"So your daughter brought you here?"

"Yes, rightfully so in her eyes. This world is a manifestation of her despair."

"Despair at what?"

"I can't say."

"Why not? You know it helps if you talk about these things. Also, is there anyone else around here?"

"No, it's just me. Serena holds the most anger at me."

"Why?"

"You're a very curious child."

"I am twenty-two."

"You're still a child."

"Thanks for the encouragement. You know I was overlooked mostly in life. To be honest it seemed to be for the better. I was a loner, yet I never got into trouble much. I had my own doubts about the world, about this realm of existence. I had one woman who I loved as a mom, but I knew she wasn't. No matter how much I tried to love her as such, I knew deep inside she wasn't."

"Strange," said the gravedigger.

"What?"

"You had little memory of your world when you first arrived here."

"I did, but…something about seeing your daughter is bringing things back to me. I want to say I am just imagining all this but…"

"That pendant around your neck."

"Oh, this? I actually found this in my closet back in the other world."

"May I see it?"

"See it? You can have it. Ever since I touched it, the words engraved and the letter that came with it have been playing tricks with my head."

"Letter, you say?"

"Yes, it went something to the effect of saying 'I'm sorry for the life you never got to experience and for our family being torn apart.' It was signed by someone claiming to be my mom. However, the woman I was staying with, who I viewed as my mother, had neither written the letter nor gave me the pendant." The gravedigger looked at the pendant. Once he saw the engraved words, his eyes widened.

"What? It can't be!" he said, astounded. "These words…"

"Mean absolutely nothing to me."

"They should, to me at least they do."

"Why?"

"These words." The gravedigger thought. "Serena said these words the day before it happened."

"What happened?" I said.

"Wait, you read my thoughts?"

"Yes, I know, this pendant is weird. It's like it has a connection from the author of these words to me, weird, huh? You can keep that thing."

"No," said the gravedigger, "you should keep this. It truly belongs to you."

"If you say so. Anyway, I need to find my way out of here."

"That's not happening."

"Why not?"

"Serena knows you are here. She won't let that intuition go. Besides, there isn't a way out. I have tried but to no avail."

"What does your daughter want with me?"

"To that I can't say. You must figure that out for yourself."

"Well, I guess that beats the sham of a life I was living before. I tell you, having no purpose is a fate worse than death."

"I will be finished with these shortly. In the meantime, you could explore a bit more."

"You actually have a place of residence here?"

"Yes."

"Interesting. Do what you must. I am going back to the church."

"I highly advise against that. I only sent you there to hide."

"Well, now I am hiding out in the church. I need to see the inside of this bullshit for myself."

"Son, I—"

"I am not your son." The gravedigger shook his head.

"Take this." He tossed the pendant back to me.

"If you say so."

"What's the worst that could happen?"

Our father
That is not in Heaven
Hollow is thy soul
The kingdom that has not come

Give us this day
And for me a slice of bread
And you can forgive me trespassers
But their ass is mine

Don't try to lead me
For I can do that on my own
And I will be the evil they dread

For the power, the glory

The Perfect Portrait

And the sight of their heads on a stake

A-fucking-men

"What the hell?" I said, looking at the inscription on the door. I couldn't help but be shocked and laugh a little on the inside. "Some church this is. I didn't think anyone would go this far with contempt." I reached for the door and instantly pulled my hand back. "Hot?" I said. With the area around me being cold, there was no rhyme or reason why the handle should be this hot or hot at all. I took my shirttail and grasped the door handle. "Shit!" I said. "Apparently I am not going through the front." I decided to go to the back. The ground was covered with pieces of the façade that had fallen off, chips of brick and a piece of the back door had fallen to the ground. Nearby was a fountain of an angel with a book in her hand. "You must be the angelic comedian. Impress me." The statue, which was cracked with no water to bear, remained silent. I put my hand on the knob…cold. I turned the knob and went inside. The congregational area was in shambles. Water damage on the wood, the seats chipped and rippled as well as the floor. "So this looks like hell came here." I closed the door behind me, leaving faint light to come inside.

I walked to the front and saw a box sitting in front at the altar. "Strange." I took the box and sat it in a nearby chair. "Let me check…no angels flying around. Time to open this." As I went to open it, I stopped. I felt this strange sensation come over me, causing me to feel as if I wasn't alone in the place. I brushed the feeling off and attempted to open the box, but once again stopped. "Okay, this is bullshit!" I turned around and saw nothing but dead space. "Cracked windows, chipped façade, gargoyles on the front, and here I stand actually feeling a bit of fear. Am I going crazy or is there more to this and I just refuse to see it? My final answer is this is a joke. I don't know why I am here. I stopped again. Wait a minute…what did I just say?" I felt a burning sensation coming from the pendant. It felt like heat was coming off of it, which was strange. "Those words were not mine. I usually don't put my doubts about the church out there like that." Something was not right here. Then, a thought manifested in my mind…

She was twenty-eight years old at the time as her feet stepped foot in these hallowed halls. A radiant smile was adorned on her face as she gazed at the people with her dark brown eyes. Upon her was a body was as pure and white as the sun itself. At the front was her man, her knight in shining armor. Tears of joy were already forming before a word was said. The people, friends, and family mostly sat and adored her, yes, Serena was so happy that radiated the intense feeling. Sunlight beamed through the windows and, for a moment, it felt like an angel truly had descended from Heaven. Serena, twenty-eight, the girl with auburn hair, dark brown eyes, and a heart full of joy. Such was it on this day, a joyous holy day…

I stood there, my mind snapping back into reality. "I have had enough of this place. I need to get out of here. I need to get back to normal life, if there is such a thing."

Chapter 3

Serena

If words are power, then pictures are infinite. The ability to put a face on thoughts, to give a body to a shallow form. I have painted many pictures in both my own time and in this world. Yet the one picture, the perfect portrait, is still out of my grasp.

Serena

Being lost in the madness of your own mind is one thing, yet combining anger with that is something completely different. For Serena, life was, as it is now, never black or white. In the other world, she was a wealthy woman who aspired to be great in the world of art. "Art is one of the few activities that allows you to be God of your own world," she would say. Growing up, her upbringing was, for lack of a better term, a portrait of success. Her mother was a successful veterinarian in the city of Javele. She had a natural talent with animals and that connection made her first on the call list if anyone needed a pet tended to. At thirty-four, with short red hair and pale skin, she was often referred to as "the vampire woman who could give life." She was married to Mitch Vega, a successful traveling insurance agent. Mitch was thirty-seven, with short gelled black hair and a fit physical appearance. He was the portrait of a bright career. "He could sell a dog back his own shit," many would say around the city. Vega was a busy man, however, and his job would often lead him to spending days away from home. Serena, being just a child at the time, often wondered why her father would be gone for weeks at a time. Although she was told it was work, she felt there was another reason.

To pass the time, Serena would often draw. In her mind she envisioned a world where she was in charge. "To see to it that all were equal," her character would say. "No one is poor and everyone has." Her drawings were mainly childish at the time, with stick figures and bubbles symbolizing thoughts and expression, yet the message was far beyond her young years. It wasn't until she was in her early teens that she fully explored her abilities. After school, she would go to the art museum for drawing classes. There her tone began to change as she learned the world wasn't as willing and forgiving as she had hoped. The first detailed drawing she did was called "3 Monks and a Ferret." In the drawing, she explained that on a quest for knowledge, three monks came to a fork in the road. The first monk suggested they take the first path, the second suggested they take the latter. The third one, who was blind, suggested they take neither. The other two, looking puzzled, asked why. The blind monk smiled and pointed to a ferret that had appeared from a hole in the ground.

"Follow me," said the ferret. "My way is safest." The sighted monks laughed, suggesting that there was no way such a small and minute creature could lead them down the right path, yet the blind man suggested they listen to the ferret. The other two monks laughed and decided to take different paths. The blind monk followed the ferret, listening to his small feet. The path the ferret was on was long and arduous, but the blind monk followed. Eventually, they came to a stream and rested. "Why did you trust me?" asked the ferret. "You are blind and can't see, lost in darkness."

The blind monk patted the ferret and said: "Although blind, I still listen to truth. This path, although long, was well rewarded."

"Yet there are no riches here, no gold. Just a stream."

"My fellow brothers took a short path to riches that were fleeting. The knowledge they sought was for only their own gain. This stream, whose water is music to my ears, represents true knowledge! Ever flowing and meant to be shared. Therefore, I share the waters of this stream with you."

The Perfect Portrait

To be so young, Serena had captivated even the most expert art critiques. She had a way with putting her inner feelings into visuals on paper. She wanted to believe the time her father spent away was as the blind monk for a higher cause, yet even at eleven years old, she felt something was off. Serena's high school years were fairly normal. Having been gifted with artistic talent, she excelled in English and art classes. At the age of seventeen, her class took a trip to England. There, she was instantly drawn to the spectacular churches and how deep and dark even religion could be. While attending Mass, she noticed a particular statue. The statue depicted an angel holding a baby. Serena felt something with seeing that, and a spark inside had been ignited.

Returning home, Serena kept the image of the baby being held by the angel in her mind. Her drawings in turn became more religious in nature. She bore witness to her angelic visions in paintings. "To give an angel life by mortal hands," she would often say. She loved her new take on life, but an old feeling had returned. The feeling something was off with her father.

At twenty, Serena was enrolled in the Hughton School of the arts. As of an angel herself, she has spread her wings and was living in an apartment. Her mother was now forty-seven and starting to think of her waning years. It was a muggy Mother's Day night as the two of them had dinner at their family home. "My art career is going very well," Serena told her mother.

"That's very good," she said. "I am glad to see you're doing well for yourself."

"It's like Dad says, seize the success while young." Her mother's eyes darted away.

"About your father…"

"That is odd. I have not seen him that much lately. He even sent a card for my graduation. I figured he would have at least shown up for that. He must be real busy. I always wondered what he was so busy doing all the time, with hardly any down time."

"I have been told worse."

"What do you mean?"

"Lately, I have been hearing rumors from the staff at the office about him."

"What rumors?"

John Paul Shuman Jr.

"You know, Serena."

"Really, Mom? Twenty years of marriage is hard to throw away, at least I would see it that way."

"You wouldn't know unless you were with someone. I mean I am forty-seven now and the years are catching up to me."

"Come on, Mom! I am sure Dad wouldn't."

"If you have been having the same feelings as me, then surely you have asked yourself the same question."

"I have, but I would like to think he had more integrity than that."

"Being in my profession, I have learned to look beyond the surface, and from what I have seen, it's not pretty. The last time we spent a meaningful time together was when you were ten. Ten!"

Serena could see the doubt in her mother's eyes. Maybe Vega was doing more than selling dogs back their own shit. Maybe another one was in heart and he was jumping. "I am sorry."

"No, it's okay. Have you talked about this with him?"

"He is heading back from New York Saturday. I will discuss this with him then. Don't worry."

"Angels can't help but worry when something's wrong."

"I will sort this out. You have got your own to deal with."

"You're my own too, Mom."

Serena never could understand why she harbored the seeds of contempt for a man she rarely saw. Perhaps it was the fact the world wasn't the same as her works portrayed, or maybe it was the fact that she felt her mother's worry. Despite the fact her mother told her not to worry, Serena felt the need to confront her father, but at the same time, paintings would not finish themselves and dreams could not come true without action. Even Serena could not understand why this feeling would not leave. "Do not worry about me," her mother said. Not wanting to ruin the moment, Serena pushed the thought to the back of her mind, but the damage was done. The angels were angry.

Just as the world around her changed, so did Serena's work. Not every picture is perfect, nor ending happy. Serena would not just "not worry about it."

The Perfect Portrait

By now she was finishing her work for final exams. "Personal matter," she said to Dr. Adams in his office. He was forty-four, bald headed, and always wore a suit, just to teach class. His face was well kept for his age.

"The artist must be as desirable as his work," he would tell his class, to which he would always slide his glasses up on his pencil like nose.

"I know. I just need some time."

"You realize everything has a deadline?"

"You realize that deadline can kiss my ass. This is personal." Dr. Adams was not surprised.

"Very well, Serena. Only because you are one of my more dedicated pupils do I grant this."

"Thank you."

"Don't get too far ahead. You are twenty, and I am sure you know this world is less forgiving. I will give you one week extension. By five p.m. Friday of next week, I need that portrait."

"Yes, sir," she said.

Sometimes the mind needs to rest. Serena took delight in walking through the front door of the family home. Her mother had a bittersweet look on her face. "I thought I said..."

"No worries, Mom," Serena said. "I needed a break from my work anyway." Her mother put on some coffee, and the two of them sat at the table.

"I have seen your works," her mother said.

"Really?"

"Yes. I never knew you had such an imagination."

"Thanks to you and the trip to England. I couldn't have done this alone. I have a connection with angels, and you have one with your works. It flows."

"Your father will be in tonight. I figured we could at least talk as a family."

"Mother, stop with the inner doubt. I really believe you know more than you're letting on. I have never known you to be this withdrawn."

"I just don't want you to be worried."

"I am in this fight as well. If none of this is true, at least we confront the worry. Besides, I haven't seen the man in years and for someone to have little time off is puzzling."

"You always had a way of certainty, Serena."

"What can I say? Candice Vega, the life-giving veterinarian vampire, is my mom."

"I didn't know I had earned such a lengthy title."

"You deserve it, Mom. I wouldn't and couldn't have asked for a better mother. I love you and always will. You are my most important inspiration."

PART TWO

Family Ties

Chapter 4

A Father's Lament

I had been absent for most of my daughter's life. Hell, I had my put job ahead of my own family. The constant plane rides, the endless days, the checks that were being deposited left and right. I wanted to believe I was a working man, but deep inside, I was wrong to be so absent. Candice had filled me in over the phone concerning recent events. Her planning to resign, Serena's success as an artist, and my absence from a portrait that was supposed to be perfect. She had told me she was worried with my constant trips, forgetful on any anniversaries and birthdays that passed. I had left Candice to raise Serena. I had not been a real man.

    I would often drown my guilt in worldly pleasures, making good money I could afford to. Being lost in other women yet lying to her saying I had to make a quick stop to make in this city and that, never thinking I was adding to her worry. It was approaching six-thirty as I came back into the city. I myself was worried as soon as my feet touched familiar ground. I knew I had some explaining to do for the lost time.

    At last, without stopping to even take a piss, I was home. I would have much to piss out in the face of my family. I stood in the yard of 430 Sycamore Street. Candice, despite being busy herself, had taken the time to tend to a house I rarely saw. The grass was neatly cut, the flowers well nourished. I was home but my heart raced at the thought of what awaited me. How does a man look into his wife's and child's eyes after being absent for nearly fifteen years?

"You can do this," I said as I walked up the concrete steps. I took one final breath and put my key in the door. To my surprise, it still worked. I opened the door, briefcase in hand, sweat accumulating around my collar. I opened the door, the sound of the television playing in the family room. I put my briefcase down and walked towards where they were sitting. As I stood in the entrance, I saw them. Candice, the woman I have been married to for twenty years, and my daughter, my, how she had changed. Her dark red hair was in a ponytail. Her green sweater fitted nicely upon her body. She looked like a woman. No, she was a woman.

Candice's red hair had lightened somewhat over the years. Yet, even at forty-seven, she was still the woman I loved, or at least thought I did. Serena turned her head to me. "Well, look who it is," she said, getting up and walking over to me, arms outstretched. I hugged her and saw she wasn't a little girl anymore. As I held Serena, I saw Candice only look at me. I could hear the "Where have you been?" and "What were you doing?"

"It's been a while, Dad!" Serena said, looking at me.

"Business," was all I could manage to say.

"I am sure your life has been busy. Please, let's go the table. I made pizza." Serena walked into the kitchen, and I stood there, looking at Candice. She stood up finally and looked at me, not saying a word. I could see the anger building inside. If she was going to slap me, I deserved it.

"You sicken me," she said in a low, barely audible voice. "Why in the hell were you gone so long? And please don't say it was strictly business. Do you know how many birthdays, anniversaries, our daughter's graduation, you missed?"

"Candice, listen, I…"

"You what? Were you messing around in New York? Banging the El Chicana in Dallas? What, Mitch?"

"I know fifteen years is a long time."

"No, you don't know. You think simply shooting me money in the mail could replace the fact that you were not here for special moments? I even did some looking and came to find out that you were not working! Yes, your friend, one of many, Andrew Banecky told me! So, I will ask again! What the fuck were you doing?"

"I had last minute stop in…" Before I could finish my sentence, Candice's hand quickly landed across my face.

"You lying son of a bitch!" she yelled. "I am done with you!"

"Hold on, Candice, let's not jump to conclusions."

"I have got plenty of evidence to back up my conclusions!" Candice went to a desk and retrieved an envelope. "Pictures of you with another woman! The six-month extended stay in Georgia. Oh, I am sure Georgia's been on your mind all right! Then in Tampa, oh, what lovely sunshine has some twenty-five-year-old woman's ass had to bestow on you!"

"They are clients, Candice! Nothing more!"

"Please, Mitchell! This photo shows more than just a client! It's no wonder you were gone so much."

I couldn't believe what I was hearing. However, I had been wrong. The woman in Tampa was more than a client. In fact, several extended payment terms had been arranged. I was caught red handed. "Okay, all right! I fucked up! You want to hear me say it? I did! I needed a break from it all!"

"From it all? Twenty years, and a successful wife and daughter was 'all' you had to get away from? Have I not been loyal to you from the day I first met you? Was I not patient when you fed me bullshit lies? I even lied to our own daughter, telling her you were away making a future for her! I waited for you to come home, waited to feel like I was loved by more than the people I worked with. I was called many things in my time in this world, but what kept me going was that at one time I would come home to you and our daughter. I was busy many days too, but I didn't lose sight. Is it because I am not as young as I used to be? Is it because I am wanting to take the future I actually worked for and enjoy it with my family? What is it, Mitchell?"

I was less than a man. In fact, I felt like that shit I could sell back to a dog. Yet there was no selling this lie to Candice. "You know, Mitchell, the saddest part is that I lied to Serena. I carry the burden of your sins. Yet despite all that she felt, she forgave you. Know this, however, and I promise you this, the day will come when you have to look in her eyes and explain this to her, and by that time, forgiveness may be too late."

Candice left the room and went upstairs. I felt horrible, less than that. I went into the kitchen. Serena was finishing a slice of pizza. She stood there back to the sink, legs crossed, facing me. "How have you been?" I said.

"I have been fine, Dad. You know, exploring the world. I must say, my paintings have shown me a side to human nature you would not believe."

"You aren't going to chew me out as well?"

"You're not worth the words. Besides, I will chew you out when the time is right. The worst punishment is the one your own mind can give you. That being said, I could not waste a breath from this delicious pizza to throw up words on you. The kick in all this is that I have seen none of what you did with my own eyes, yet I saw it all through mother's. It's odd, like a chain; shake one end the other's feel it. To top it all off, a person can't choose for or against this. It just happens. I wonder if I will ever have a child like that someday. Anyway, it seems the chain has been rippled enough. Please…have some pizza."

That night I hardly slept. To be more specific, instead of kissing the lips of my wife, I was kissing the cover of a pillow on the sofa. Ironically, Serena sat in the family room with me, laughing at the TV and cutting her eyes at me. It was sad to say, but I was truly scared of my own daughter. I lay with my face turned towards the TV, afraid to turn my back. The weirdest part of all was that as soon as commercial breaks started, she would just look at me with those soul-piercing eyes. Even in the light only given off by the TV, I could see the contempt in them. She had her mother's deep brown eyes, and I knew she wanted to lay into me. Four a.m. came and still she and I were awake.

"You might as well try to rest," she said. "Ease your mind for the storm ahead."

"That's what I am afraid of," I said.

I have been afraid since that fateful day. Even in this place of existence. I find it hard to sleep at night. I am constantly haunted by my wife's words of contempt and Serena's eyes staring blankly at me. Candice did not have to say anything for me to know what was about to happen next. I figured that house being left to her would be some type of solace, but nothing could take back what I had done. Although I was like a ghost, I still went to see my daughter's works when I could. I was little more than a sight looker now. Even now as I dig these graves, I still feel her watching me. Maybe this is the punishment she referred to. My only regret is that Death can't come fast enough…

Chapter 5

Explanations

Finally, the gravedigger, or more specifically Mitchell Vega, had finished the graves. He took out his pipe and lit it. "I never smoked in life," he said. "The knowledge of death approaching will drive people to most anything." He looked up to see the boy approaching. "I take it you went inside the church," he said. The boy only shook his head.

"What the hell is this place?" he asked Vega.

"What did you see?"

"To hell with what I saw! I felt dread, mixed with a former memory of happiness."

"I know exactly what you are talking about."

"So have you been inside?"

"Why should I go when I experienced it?"

"So that was your daughter Serena who was married that day?"

"Yes. Although I was not allowed to be in her life, I still observed when I could."

"You must have done something really bad to get her to despise you this much."

"Trust me, son, I deserve it."

"Why does everyone keep calling me son? Do I know you or vice versa?" Vega only smiled, not giving a "yes" or "no." "Just when I thought this world could not get any stranger."

"Things are not always as they seem. I've had plenty of time to think about the things I've done in life. I think it's ironic to say it's what happened after that is what taught me the most."

"I saw Serena put her sword to your neck. How did you remain so calm?"

"As much as she claims to hate me, she wouldn't kill me. There is something you must understand and it's this: Serena has a lot of mouth and the only action she does is in the form of paintings."

"She was an artist?"

"Yes, her paintings and portraits were her life. To be honest, her most treasured memento was her pendant given to her from her mother. Candice was always a strong source of inspiration. Serena had a way of being in tune with her mother's emotions, even from the time she was young."

"I had a connection similar to that. I never knew my parents, though my connection was to a woman who raised me as her own. She was the only family I had. Yet now, I'm here, in a world that makes no more sense to me than the one I came from."

"So you were a faceless ghost?"

"Exactly. Nothing really caught my attention in that world. Listen to me saying this! As if I am glad to be here!" Vega let out a small chuckle and shook his head.

"What's funny?"

"This world will do that to you," he said. "It draws you in, has a beautiful and ugly side. It makes you feel whole, yet lost. Complete, yet empty. Full of life, yet wishing for death. Such is the world created by my daughter."

"Serena created this world?" the boy asked.

"How about we discuss this at my dwelling?"

"You have a home here?"

"But of course."

"For a minute I thought you lived in the graveyard. Sorry about that."

"You wouldn't be wrong to think that. I have felt trapped for so long."

"Trapped?"

"Let us make haste, son."

"There you go again."

"What can I say? I can't help but feel like I know you."

"Whatever."

A small wooden hut, surrounded by tree stumps, was what Mitchell Vega now called home. He stooped before reaching the door. He turned to the boy. "It's funny. At one time I was staying in eight-hundred-dollars-a-night hotels, eating the finest cuisine. Now I only—"

"Save it for dinner. I am starving!" The inside of Vega's home was a simple abode. A bed, study chair, books, and small cooking area. The floor was wooden and nothing special.

Chapter 6

Finding Him

Serena's Creed
In blood I shed
In life and death
I gave birth to Jay
Only to watch his last breath
My child taken so young
By the lick of Death's slippery tongue
My world crumbled and hope faded
My head hangs low in a world so jaded
I could not be calmed, I would not be held
All I hear is the silence when his heart failed
My Perfect Portrait destroyed, my dreams shattered
Life from that point never mattered
So I went to the darkest corner of the earth
Where nightmares and terror are given birth
I made a deal that sealed my fate
For Jay there is hope
For me it's too late…

Cold skies and a grey scenery did not shake Serena's determination. Her eyes set on one mission…to rebuild what was lost and start anew. Her friend

Broun flew close behind. "A few of the others have found the location, my lady," he said.

"I already know," Serena said. "It was you who told me. Repetition is painful."

"Sorry, my lady."

"Never mind the apologies. Keep focused on our goal."

"Might I ask something?"

"Don't ask, just ask," Serena snapped. Broun knew Serena was all seriousness. In this world, this plane of existence she had created, her word was final. Once her mind was set on something, questions and answers were the last thing to partake in.

"Why did you spare him?"

"Now isn't the time for this, Broun," Serena said. "Yet seeing as how you're one of the few souls I trust, it wouldn't hurt to say. His time hasn't come yet. It would be a waste to kill my father now, despite how his sight disgusts me."

"You could have pressed further."

"Liars always reveal themselves in the end."

"I think deep inside you don't want to hurt him."

Serena stopped midflight and turned to face Broun. She came within inches of his face. "It is not up to you to decide how I handle my affairs. I have my reasons, no more or less. Know your place, Broun."

"Sorry, my lady." Serena smirked.

"Now, where is the location I seek?"

"Further up ahead."

"Good."

Broun remained silent as they approached the Solemn Sanctum. "I thought this castle was abandoned long ago," Serena said to Broun. "I have heard stories about this place; a place where sacrifices were made to a bullshit God."

"Yes, my lady. Our sources have reported seeing him here."

"Speaking of which, where are those sources?"

"Apparently, they left."

"No shit. They report information and then they leave? Figures."

"What?"

The Perfect Portrait

"Never mind. I am only here to find him."

"Do you need me to go with you?"

"No. I need to go in alone."

Serena inspected the façade. Weeds had grown between the meetings of the stones. The windows were cracked and missing in some areas. Flowers were withered and full of ant beds. She turned to Broun. "I heard about this place from an old woman. At one time, its seventy-five rooms, four kitchens, garden area all hosted many festivities of the king and his men. Merchants traveled to this area to trade and sell their goods."

"It's a fictitious story," Broun said.

"Nothing here is what it seems. Anyway, wait here for me. I will return shortly."

Serena walked to the front door. The double cemented doors were bound shut and the bolts were rusted. She took her sword and cut the bolts, causing them to fall down. She opened the doors and went inside. Immediately, she was hit with a smell of dank air and rotting wood. The floor, what looked to be marble, was cracked and missing in some areas. "Shit!" she said. She kept her hand to her nose and her sword in the other as she made her way down the corridor. The first floor consisted of the kitchen, six bedrooms, and a spacious living area. "Looks more like a guest area."

Serena went into the kitchen and was horrified by what she saw and smelled. Pots and food were strewn about, the pantry hosted what looked to be bread that molded and had flies eating and living in the withered loaves. On the counter was a rotted pig's head with the eyes eaten away and maggots making love to the pieces of flesh as they fell of the bone and into the stew, which resembled the color of a puss-filled sore with turpentine over it. "Okay, I have had enough," Serena said as she turned and walked out of the kitchen.

The hall that hosted the six bedrooms was sealed off at the end. Serena found this puzzling considering the size of the castle. Although the sun did allow light to come in, something about the hallway felt dark and foreboding. Serena went to the first door to her left. Above it hung a roman numeral one and an inscription was written on the wall beside it:

John Paul Shuman Jr.

On these doors in this place
Rest six tales of souls gone by
A story of adventure, hate, and unrest
The story of Lost Souls put to the test
To go further, listen to these words of a ghost
At the end will be what you desire most

"So now I am listening to stories?" Serena laughed. "This is bullshit!" She shook her head. "Shit, oh well! Let's listen to what the six rooms have to say." Serena opened the first door and the area inside was pitch black. There was no sound, and the air was quiet and lifeless. She went inside, sword drawn. The door shut behind her and locked. For someone who never felt fear in her life, Serena could feel her heart began to race.

"Heart racing, mind wondering," said a voice that echoed throughout the room. "This is what many feel inside, that creeping dread that holds them back. Tell me, Serena, do you hold fast to that sword to protect or is it something else?" Serena gripped her sword tighter.

"Who the hell are you and how do you know my name?"

"Is it hard to understand? I have been with you since the day of your existence. Since the days you first saw the world. Although you were innocent, you could still feel it. How could something so innocent feel this dread, the dread that caused you to bend the very rules of life itself? Is it to cover up the fact that you're afraid of what's meant to be? How you traded your existence so one young boy could live?"

"I live for my son, you bastard!" Serena yelled. "What do I have to fear?"

"You're better off posing that question to yourself. Yet, I feel that more truths lie in the other five rooms."

"I'll lay my sword in your chest!"

"See? Quick to rush blindly, not knowing which way I will strike. The main question I pose is this: How can you destroy something that has always been around?" Serena could feel her blood beginning to boil. "I have said enough. Off with you! The next one awaits."

The Perfect Portrait

Serena found herself back in the hallway. She had her sword in hand, yet she couldn't shake the words of the mysterious voice. "I am not afraid," she said. "I did this for my son." She walked to the second door. This one was red with rose petals at the foot of it. "Should I?" Serena said. "I should. The quicker I find him the better." She opened the door and was greeted by the sight of a large white room, with countless roses on the ground. The room was brightly lit, almost to the point of blinding. There were no windows. In the middle of the room was a table with two wine glasses. Serena couldn't help but smile.

"I see the visions of romance pleases you."

"It beats darkness," Serena said.

"Even in the midst of great turmoil, love still finds a way to blossom. Even the evilest demon on earth has someone or something that they love. Love takes many forms, but this sight is the most noticeable. Such it was the day you felt it, for the man you were destined to marry."

"It was," Serena said. "But why is it so quiet in here?"

"Why shouldn't it be? The dinner you and he shared that fateful night. Oh, how it seemed even time stood still. It was just the two of you, amidst a busy scene, a joyous time."

"That it was."

"But yet, more rooms are ahead."

"No, wait! Why can't I stay here just a bit longer? I hate that hallway of horror bullshit!"

"Oh, Serena, must I remind you that all good things must come to an end? As joyous as this feeling is, it did not last."

"What do you mean?"

"Surely you must know. The inner demons you hid from him, the man you said you loved. Little did he know about the hidden anger you felt towards your father."

"What the hell? You son of a bitch! How dare you ruin a grand moment with the mention of my father!"

"Temper, temper, little girl. Is it odd that your husband had to calm you down when your father would come near? You had the most bitter…"

"SHUT UP! I did not deserve to have my portrait ruined! I wanted to have my own life and my own family!"

"Serena, your very anger is twisting the world around you. I regret showing you this room. It seems you're not capable of comprehension of compassion. So go!"

"Fine! Maybe next time you'll show me some fucking respect, you pompous pig shit-eating bastard!"

Serena found herself back in the hallway a second time. "Okay, enough of this childish playground bullshit! I want to find my goddamn husband! Now!"

"Serena, Serena," said the voice from the second room. You are not proving yourself a good wife. But alas, four more doors await. If affairs with others won't shape you, maybe a look inside your own soul will."

"No! Enough! I…"

"Four more doors. Perhaps the next two will be to your taste."

"I said no more."

"I insist. Now, shut the fuck up and go to door number three. Now!" Serena stood there, shaking her head.

"Fine."

Door number three had a picture of a familiar face on it. It was a picture of a monk's withered face, yet smiling. The sign of his aged years showing in his wrinkled skin and gray beard. His robe, however, was still as clean and white as the day he adorned it, and by his side was the ferret that had guided him to the stream, the everlasting manifestation of truth. "I don't believe this," Serena said. "I haven't seen this painting in years."

"You should remember," said the voice from door number two. "It was the painting that you first showcased, a sketch that would become your most inspirational portrait, a portrait of happiness more beloved that the angels you worshipped. As you once said, 'I painted this portrait to show that even the blind have faith and truth can come from anywhere, even from the mouth of a lowly ferret.' Those words moved many, Serena. To be so young and have that much insight. But I must ask this: who was the inspiration for that painting?"

"That simply came from the corridors of my mind."

"Don't lie to me. Everything stems from something. You fail to realize that for someone who harbored so much hate for their father, you often talked much about him."

"There you go again. I am getting tired of your references to that cheating bastard!"

"Serena, the so-called act he committed was one of many men have done. He was the other two monks who set out like all do to find a higher path in life yet often get lost along the way."

"Now you're making excuses for him? You…"

"Silence!" Serena tried to speak further but her mouth was bound shut. "Allow me to speak, please. So it was the fact that Mitchell Vega turned and got burned, but over the years he learned. The riches of the world captivated his eyes and turned to lies, for countless nights did his wife cry. This wasn't a fight for you to partake in your father's sin. To his wife did he face in the familiar place where many called home, where a wife was left alone. So did you try to fight your mother's war, as Vega walked through the door. 'Yet, leave this to me, Serena,' your mother said, but these words simply went over your head."

Serena could feel her anger beginning to swell. She raised her sword and aimed for the door. "You would destroy that which gave you life?" the voice said.

"I…" she managed to say through a slight opening, "…am…going…"

"Your anger knows no bounds, does it, Serena?"

"I am going to kill you!" Serena yelled, breaking free of her verbal restraints. "I am the beginning and the end of this world! I am its light, its darkness! Its salvation and damnation! I am that which judges and you can take this door and this fucking piece of shit rat ass castle and go to hell!"

"Fine, you want to destroy me so bad? If it is bloodlust you seek to quench, then come…come to the very top of the castle by taking the stairs at the end of the hallway. Maybe then you will be satisfied." Serena looked and saw the staircase at the end of the hallway.

"Finally!" she said, sword still in hand. She walked up two flights and came to another hallway. "You have got to be kidding me."

"Did you think I would just give in, Serena?" said the now all-too-familiar voice. "Nothing is as ever what it seems. If you want it, earn it, as doors four and five will show you!"

"I will not be a part of this anymore!" Serena said.

"In the end, we have no choice what we are a part of. Now, go to door number four and stop wasting my time!"

Serena went to the fourth door and opened it. Inside was a hallway scattered with paint brushes on the floor. The walls were covered with unfinished paintings. Serena walked into the hallway and viewed each painting. "Why would you put up crappy unfinished work?" she asked.

"I guess your life could be summed up the same way," said a voice behind her. Serena turned around and saw…herself. She was dressed in her famous red sweater and blue jeans. Her burnished auburn hair was pulled back in a ponytail. Her eyes had life to them, the color of rich chocolate. "Don't look so surprised," her other half said. "Even the greatest artist has work left unfinished. You know it's not easy starting out by yourself. Not everyone embraces the ideas of angelic figures and monks seeing truth."

"What are you talking about?" Serena said. "You had it easy."

"Just because someone comes from money doesn't mean they will always have it easy. And good skill takes time, patience, and persistence. There was those that love my works, but I also had my critics. Some people never got the message, which was sad but understandable. You can't make people see the big picture."

"Trust me," Serena said, "One good sword to the throat makes them see."

"As usual, men pave the road of progress with blood. I actually did a portrait of that, if you want to see."

"No, I have matters to attend to."

"You know, I often wondered what justified my feelings of bitterness towards Mitch. It wasn't my fight, and to be honest, my anger was wasted."

"Oh, for fuck's sake!" Serena said. "This again?"

"Trust me, hon, you will like this."

"I don't see how."

The Perfect Portrait

"People make mistakes, deliberate and otherwise. Vega simply lost sight of what was in front of him. That day he walked through that door, I could tell he knew he was wrong. It's not often a man admits to the fact that he did wrong. But it makes me wonder at times that perhaps there could be some overreacting on my mother's part. Maybe she wouldn't learn to see a busy man, or maybe a portrait was being painted that wasn't real. You see, Mother never told you that she could be real possessive at times. Although Vega did screw around, Candice was very…how should I say, an imperfect portrait in her own right. In fact, you were often alone in that house for hours on end. Sure, you didn't get yourself into any trouble, but still. As angelic as Candice may have appeared in your eyes, she wasn't perfect."

"No, she wasn't," Serena admitted.

"But oh, this whole world, these unfinished portraits have nothing to do with Mitchell Vega. This is all to undo the death of your son."

"Excuse me?" Serena said. Her voice going from calm to insulted.

"Your son that died shortly after he was born. The boy that never made it into the portrait. Ah, yes. Little Jay. Jay, the boy, who died as a baby. You would have given anything to have him back. He was the light of your life. You and Julius, the man you loved so dear, wept at his death. You had to create a scapegoat, someone to vent the frustration out on. Who better than Mitchell Vega, the man who, in your eyes, had already stained his own portrait." Serena drew her sword.

"Julius and I did not deserve that shit!" she said. "We were looking forward to starting our family. I wanted to show my father that I could raise a family better than he could. My son Jay did not even have a chance to experience this life! I was hurt!"

"You're just like your mother," her other half said. "Self-righteous to the end. Maybe it was not meant for Jay to experience this life. You know, these things happen. Unexplainable? I think not. But in your sadness, at that very moment, you looked to Mitch for comfort, who ironically talked with Julius about how things were between you two."

"I told Julius not to speak with that filthy bastard," Serena said. "I loved my husband, but he always tried to build bridges with people who were impossible."

"Well, hey, the man was the owner of the second most prestigious art gallery in the country. I am sure he reached out to many others."

"Jay's death tore me up inside. I lost interest in things, mainly my work and marriage. I even pushed my husband away. He tried to comfort me, as well as that bastard of a father of mine. My mother was absent in all of this. I tried to reach out to her but to no avail. I withdrew from the world, withdrew from myself. I even told Julius if I could trade my soul for his I would. He told me not to talk like that. That what happened was how life goes sometimes. I did not want to hear that. Not then, not ever. To be honest, I hated everything and everyone after that. I stopped loving and started hating. I said that if there is a God and I ever met him, I would rip out his heart and make his so-called angels watch. I would kick his ass myself. I despised churches, the light, my own parents, especially my father even more. I went to a very dark place, dyed my hair black, and became a lost soul."

Serena's other half shook her head. "There was one final painting you did," she said. *"The Angel's Lament."*

"An angel saying goodbye to her child," Serena said. "It was the last time I would pick up a brush. My life was over, and death seemed to be the only way. That was until I found a way. A way to bring my son back, to get it all back. I must say the mind is a powerful thing but so is the soul. I gave it at the very cemetery Jay rested at. I wanted to give my very being so he could live. What did I have to lose?"

"So you switched places?"

"Yes. I saw the world he was in and how dull it was. I knew that if I could switch places with him, I would give him a second chance, nay, the chance he never had. I would paint a new portrait of the other world and show him the life he never knew. I would be the final word, the only word."

"Alas, it all backfired, Serena. Your son was lost in the echo, your mother is gone, your father is stuck in limbo, and you have nothing, not even a soul to shine light on. Was any of this worth it?"

The Perfect Portrait

"I wouldn't expect you to understand. I am too far gone to save, but I will take back what destiny and your so-called God took away. I will have what is due me."

"Are you sure of this?" Serena took her sword and put into her other half's chest. "You would kill the very inspiration that gave you life?"

"Let me see…fuck yes!" With a quick thrust, Serena plunged her blade into her other half's chest. "I told you and that fucking bastard, I AM GOD OF THIS WORLD AND I WILL HAVE WHAT I CAME FOR! FUCK THE COMMANDMENTS, FUCK MERCY, AND FUCK HUMANITY! I DON'T NEED ANY DISTRACTIONS! THAT INCLUDES YOU, MY FATHER, OR A GODDAMN FERRET LEADING SOME BLIND OLD BASTARD!" Serena's voice roared. As blood spurted from other half's mouth, Serena was delighted.

"W-w-why?" was the final word that was spoken. Serena knelt beside her and whispered…

"Because I can and say so." Serena withdrew her blade and stood. "Now you see what happens when you piss me off!"

"Serena, Serena," said the voice from before. "I must say, a lasting portrait of red on your sullen record is not very attractive. I am sure your friends were quite pleased to be displeased."

"Where are you, pig? You're next!"

"Oh, but we have yet one more door to see in your mental state of misery."

"No, enough! I have played along for a while, but now I'M DONE with it! You will show your face to me or I swear I will end you!"

"Empty threats get you nowhere, little girl. One more door to go, or are you scared?"

"What? Scared? NO WAY! Let's get on with it! Put me back in the hallway."

"Serena, there is no need for that."

"Why not?"

"At the end of the hall of painting is a door. You next room is beyond that door."

"Fine. Oh, by the way, there is a dead bitch on the floor. I don't want to get my precious Heavenly boots wet. I like red, but not one me. Clean it up!"

There was no reply from the voice. "Whatever." Serena stepped over the body towards the end of hallway of paintings. As she approached the door, she felt her blade, its dark edge that could cut even the sharpest steel. "Perfect," she exclaimed.

She opened the door and saw an empty field. The area was barren, no trees, color, animals, nor sea, nothing. "What the hell is this?" Serena said. There was no answer from her mysterious guide. She walked through the wasteland and saw nothing in any direction. "Okay, what's going on?" Still no answer. She continued walking yet saw no sign of life. Dark storm clouds hung above, and occasional sounds of thunder could be heard. "This is bullshit!" She turned around and saw a figure in the distance. "Hmmm."

She put her sword back in its sheath and started towards the figure. As she neared, a feeling came over her. "That feeling," she said. "Could it be?" She hastened forward and saw it was a small child standing there. Serena now stood within inches of the boy. He was small, horribly thin, his shirt tattered with holes in it. He wore no shoes or pants, his hair was messy. She was speechless as she beheld the sight of this pitiful looking child. She reached her hand and felt the child's pale skin, which was dry and had blisters in some spots. The boy looked at up at Serena and she was horrified to see his eyes were missing, showing only empty bloody sockets. She stepped back, not sure what to say.

"Where is Mommy?" the boy said, reaching his hands out to feel. "Where is Mommy?" the boy said again. For the first time Serena did not know how to respond. This wasn't just some hallucination or abstract manifestation. She could feel the anguish in the boy's voice and the sorrow in his heart. The boy continued asking the three-worded question, and started to walk towards Serena, arms outstretched. Serena put her hand on the butt of her sword, but could not pull out her blade. No, not on a child. The boy continued walking towards her.

"Get back!" she said, her hand tightening on her sword.

"Mommy?" the boy said inches from her. "Are you Mommy?" She could not believe this. She stood inches from this boy who had no eyes yet had found his way to her. "I am scared, Mommy. I don't want to be here."

The Perfect Portrait

Serena let loose of her sword and knelt down in front of him. In a way she couldn't help but pity the child. She turned her eyes away. He was too pitiful to look at. "Why won't you look at me, Mommy? I love you." Serena glanced back at the child.

"W-w-who are you?" she stuttered.

"It's me, Mommy, Jay!" The boy reached out and put his arms around Serena. Upon his touch, she felt a cold chill run through her body. This couldn't be her son. No! This had to be just an illusion. By now her mind and body were tired and her voice lacking from all the yelling she had done. She had exerted too much energy arguing with the voice that she viewed as a nuisance. Her mind was weary. This could not be real.

"W-w-why?" Serena asked weakly.

"Mommy, who are you talking to?" the boy asked.

"W-w…" She tried to speak but couldn't finish.

"I missed you, Mommy. I was so scared. I'm glad you came, Mommy…." Serena felt a bone-chilling sensation, worse than the first that came over her. The boy's hug grew tighter, and Serena found herself caught, too weak to break free. "Don't you miss me, Mother?"

The boy looked up and Serena saw the empty sockets had been filled with eyes. Blank, blackened, cold, soulless eyes. "What's wrong, Mother? Are you afraid?" Serena still could not move. This was true fear she felt. The boy then grabbed Serena by her hair, his embrace still tight. "Look at me!" the boy yelled, pulling her head back so that she gazed at the blackened sky. "I could have been happy! I wanted to go to Heaven! But you didn't want me to leave. You had to have me stuck in this shit world! Oh, what's that, Mommy? You can't breathe? Good! I hope you enjoy feeling the last drop of breath leave your body!"

Serena was frozen with the very fear she had instilled in others. This boy wasn't her son. No, this was something much worse. The boy tightened his grip, so much that Serena's armor began to crack. "Oh, you have a chink in your armor, your perfect armor, Mother? That's what being human is like, in case you forgot. You know, learning to live with chinks in your armor all the time."

"D-da...mn...you..."

"Trust me, Mother, you have damned my soul enough! I am just showing you the same love. You know, Mother, love fucking hurts, doesn't it? You know something else, Mother? They say if you breastfeed your baby, they grow closer to you. You get my drift, bitch?" The boy grabbed Serena's armor by the crack and tore it off. "You know, Mother, nudity inspired some art. Let's see what portrait yours truly can come up with." He threw Serena to the ground, her naked chest on display. The boy grabbed Serena's sword. "Where did you get this, Mother?" Serena gasped, trying to catch her breath. The boy took the sword and put the tip on her chest. "Eeny, meeny, miny, mo. Which nipple will be the first to go? So big they are and so dark. Cut them off and go for the heart. Left, right, which will stay? Right, left, my choice is made!" With a quick flick he drew the sword back and prepared to strike.

"Wait!" yelled a voice. The boy stopped mid-strike. Serena listened and noticed it was an all-too-familiar voice, one she thought she would never hear again. She looked and saw someone approaching. A man, clad in green-and-gold armor. His face was tanned, a beard hanging from his chin. His hair was the color of onyx and hung mid-way down his back. He had to be at least six feet tall, shortly taller than Serena. On his side was a golden blade, the handle in the shape of a cross. "Enough, boy!" the man commanded.

"What? Aww, come on! I was about to get a drink."

"I said enough!" The boy lowered Serena's blade and looked saddened. "Be gone!"

"But—"

"Go!" The boy took the blade and disappeared into the still air. Serena, finally catching her breath, looked up at the man. His eyes, as brown as the desert sands, met hers. "Glad to finally see you again, Serena Vega."

Chapter 7

Decisions

Serena looked into the man's eyes. Those eyes that were the color of the very dirt from whence life came now stared back at her. She lay there, naked, power drained, and mind wondering what the hell just happened. She reached for sword, but it was gone. Her wings, once one of the defining symbols of her perfection and ascension, were now gone. "You have no sword reach for now, Serena. It's over."

"You have some nerve showing your face, Julius," Serena mocked. "You always remained calm, even when I was a total bitch. I knew that voice sounded familiar. Is this how you want me? Nude and at your feet?"

"Woman, you speak foolishness. I never intended for you to be such an embarrassment to yourself and our family. I wanted you to learn some truth. I told you from the moment we met I wasn't going to baby you. You know what kind of man I am."

"Oh, yes, the kind of man who has some little bastard strip me of my fucking power! Oh, you make me so…so…"

"Ran out of insults? Oh, wait, 'pig-shit eating bastard.'"

"Don't tempt me."

"You're the one lying naked."

"What gave that away?" Julius reached out his hand. "Nope. No! I will not take your hand, not this time!"

"From the looks of it, you're in no position to be making demands or threats. We have much to discuss."

"Oh, really? Oh, the Knight Julius rescues the fallen helpless angel. Give me a break!"

"Serena, you don't even have wings anymore, and to be honest, you're just as mortal now as the day you were born. You can wallow in this filth or you can taste *my* blade, or you can come with me and allow me to help you regain some composure. Your call." Serena shook her head.

"Just who was that little bastard?"

"I will explain back home."

"Home?"

"Yes, home. Sanctuary, sanctum, abode. Food, water, shelter, for Christ's sake some clothes for you, woman!"

"Goddamnit!" Serena yelled, pounding her fist into the dirt. "And I can't fight you?"

"You can try, but you will lose, trust me. Now, for the last time, can we leave this hellhole?"

"Shit!" Serena screamed. She shook her head once again. "You owe me an explanation for this, Julius."

"Not nearly as much as you owe me. Come, let's go."

Serena and Julius emerged from the ruins of the castle. Serena could see Broun waiting outside, his fat, pudgy angelic face lighting up with a smile. "Oh, my lady!" Broun said, running over to them. "What happened?"

"I am not your lady," Serena said, holding her arms over her chest. "Just call me Serena."

"Yes, my lady!"

"Oh, Broun," Julius said cheerfully. "Still as cheerful and loyal as ever."

"Wait a second, you two know each other?"

"Know Julius? He's practically family to me, my lady."

"I thought I told you…"

"It's okay, Serena," Julius told her. "Broun has always had a cheerful, pleasing personality. Anyway, the missus and I will be heading back to Akoran. Will you please deliver the package to Mitchell?"

The Perfect Portrait

"Yes, sir!" Broun said, saluting. "Second-in-command to the Templar, Archangel Broun will deliver!" With those words, he flew off.

"That fat bastard is an archangel?" Serena said.

"Hey, loyalty comes in all forms, just as portraits do."

"Fuck you, Julius."

"We did that back at one time. I must say, you were a shy…" Before he could finish, Serena slapped his cheek. "You slap like a child, Serena. But let's move on."

"F-U-C-K Y-O-U !" Serena yelled.

"Yes, I know you're on your period."

"So what now?"

"We head for Akoran," Julius answered.

"I have never heard of that place."

"You have been in the dark too long. It's a place that, for one, has color, and there is more opportunity. Yet, I don't see how they will take to those blackened eyes of yours. How do you see like that?"

"You wouldn't understand, fool. Enough with the small talk. I am starting to get cold."

"The boy must have also made you mortal when he took your power."

"No shit! Not to mention the little bastard looked like he wanted to…"

"You need not say, Serena. The Felidar Forest is a little way from here. I will warn you it's not a short journey through these woods. I had to use Silverblade here more than once."

"You named your sword? Oh, my goodness! Men and their toys. Please tell me you have something for me to put on. I am cold!"

"I don't." Serena's black eyes looked as though they turned red.

"You mean I am going to be walking around in the woods butt naked?"

"I have a camp set up in the woods."

"That's then, Julius! I mean now!"

"Sorry."

"Julius, I swear on our son's grave, you were smart as hell but sometimes you could overlook some of the smallest details."

"I am not perfect, Serena. I did not intend for the last door to do that to you."
"Really? You sounded like it."
"I only wanted to instill some sense into you."
"By using our son to do it?"
"That wasn't our son. That was warped."
"Enough of this. Let's just go."
"Ahem."
"Lead the way, darling!" Serena said sarcastically.
"Still as smart mouth as ever," Julius said, shaking his head.

They walked towards the wood's edge. "Is it dense?" Serena asked.

"It's your world, Serena," Julius said. "Surely you can recall the details of a simple forest."

"When you're flying high, it's hard to look down. I had people scout out things for me."

"Now you're the scouter. It sucks that abomination had to take your, how did you say, 'heavenly boots' because there are stickers and critters in these woods."

"Can't you just carry me?"

"Nope. You will have to walk like everyone else. Now, let's move."

As they walked, Serena could feel the leaves crunching underneath her feet. Cold, wet leaves, small bugs, and sticks were met by feet that once never had to touch the ground. Serena looked at the trees and noticed how bare they looked. Maybe her own emotions did in fact influence the world around her. This was a portrait right from the fabric of her mind. "So, tell me about why you're here." she asked Julius, who was walking a few feet ahead. "Hey, don't walk so far ahead!" Julius stopped and turned to her.

"True success leaves failure behind," he said.

"Are you insulting me?"

"As you once said, Serena, I'll leave that for you to decide. To answer your question, I am here to seek out the truth, no more, no less. I have many questions but little answers."

"Questions such as?"

"Why does this plane exist? What reasons were you attacked, and what is the grand scheme of all this?"

"Don't you mourn Jay's death?"

"I miss our son dearly, yes; however, I will not allow the hand of death to sullen my determination nor sway my priorities."

"You have no idea, do you?"

"Of what?"

"He is not dead, Julius. I swear he lives!"

"Serena, I know you have been through a lot, especially considering what's happened recently, but our son, bless his soul, is gone. I hurt yes, but I must go on. We must go on."

"He lives, Julius." Julius shook his head.

"There is a blackberry bush up ahead. You should eat something until we reach the camp."

Julius partook in some sword practice as Serena ate of the berries. "Mmm," she said as each of the sweetened fruits burst in her mouth. "You want some?" she asked.

"I already ate," Julius said. "You need the energy."

"Need energy? I create it. Well, used to."

"Don't gorge too much on them."

"Why?"

"Need I dare say?" Julius smiled as he thrust his sword into a rock. "Now you see what a true blade can do."

"Showoff."

"Partake a few more, then we must continue. I want us to reach camp before light's end."

"All these damn bugs under my feet!" Serena said. "Damn slugs and worms! Shit!"

"I told you these woods had creatures. You can wash in the stream."

"Wash?" Serena asked.

"Yes. Being human, or mortal, period, means you have to take care of your body. When was the last time you cleaned?"

"How dare you ask me that! We angels are kept…"

"Serena, you're not an angel anymore."

"Whatever, Julius! Hey, is that a tent and fire up ahead?"

"Yes, camp is just up ahead."

"Race you to it!" Serena said, taking off.

"Just like a little girl," Julius said to himself. "She was always childish." Serena looked back and saw Julius wasn't running.

"Ah, come on! Even Broun's fat ass could put up something! You're no fun."

"Serena."

"Nope, not stopping!"

"Serena, wait!"

"I said…" Serena looked and stopped. Right in front of the canvas tent was a wolf. Her fur was a mixture of gray, black, and white. She looked at Serena with silvery blue eyes and stood, her fur standing on end. "Um, nice puppy," Serena said nervously. The wolf started to growl. Julius ran to the scene, laughing. "What's so funny?" Julius walked up to the wolf, and it calmed once she saw him.

"It's okay, Snow," Julius said, rubbing her fur.

"Kill it!" Serena screamed.

"Don't be silly. Snow's just guarding camp. She wouldn't hurt anyone who doesn't pose a threat. It's just she doesn't know you. Come pet her."

"No fucking way!"

"The key is not to show fear. I know that may be hard for you but, it's worth not to show it. Come on."

Serena tiptoed towards the wolf, who still had a stern look in her eyes. "No fear, Serena."

"Why should I pet her?"

"You don't trust me?"

"After what happened recently? No!"

"O' ye of little faith. Look, I have Snow calmed. She won't hurt you. Trust me." Serena eased up to Snow, slowly out stretching her shaking hand. "That's it, a little more." Serena rubbed Snow's head slowly and in turn Snow licked her hand. "See? It's easy." Snow walked closer to Serena, allowing her to rub her fur.

"It's so soft," Serena said.

"Been like that since she was a pup. Snow's become a second wife to me."

"Hey."

"Just kidding! Lighten up!"

"So this is your camp?"

"Yes. I have firewood, a stream a little ways back, and a nice sword to slay wild game."

"Ha, you kill living things too!"

"Only what is needed. Serena, I don't like killing anything."

"Wuss!"

"Call me what you want, but you are starting to smell."

"What?"

"I can smell you from here, and you don't smell like an angel."

"Fuck you, I am going to the stream!"

"All right. I will have something for you to wear and dinner will be started."

Serena waded in the stream by the edge of the bank. It was the first time she had felt water on her body after creating her new world. The water was warm, despite the area being cold. "I never paid much attention to my body," she said. "Shame, but I guess it's better than smelling like a wild animal. Julius seems to now know Jay is alive. I asked my father about his whereabouts and her bold-faced lied to me. I could sense my son. I knew he was there. I was so close to having him back before Broun's fat ass showed up. And how in the hell did that kid manage to overpower me? He was just a kid! A child! Yet, I couldn't bring myself to kill him. Maybe my time in that place did dampen my abilities. My sword is gone, my armor is decimated, and although I found my husband, I feel I need to guard. Why? He's my husband! Yet maybe I never knew what love really was. He could have killed me right there, but he didn't. I am less than an angel. Damn! Damn it all to hell! Maybe if I had allowed pudge cake to go with me, I would still have my abilities. I guess that's what I get for trying to be something I am not. Look at me! Doubting myself! The old Serena would have fought, shown some brevity! But in that moment, when the kid held me, I felt afraid. I actually felt afraid and alone. If I knew this would happen I would never… no, now is the time for regrets. I hate working with people, but to get back on top I guess I could make this one exception."

Serena felt odd wearing clothes normally worn by commoners. "I can't believe this!" she said. "This is it? A pelt brown shirt and green pants. Really, Julius?"

"It's the main wear in Akoran," he said, roasting a rabbit over the fire. Snow sat close by, mouth watering at the sight of the roasting meat. "It looks good on you."

"Bullshit! I look like a common peasant from a backwards village."

"Whatever, Serena."

"What is for dinner?"

"Rabbit with some seasoned blackberry jam and bread."

"Eh, shit!"

"Aww, come on! It's good. Snow likes it. Besides, what did you eat as an angel?"

"I knew no hunger. My fill was simply being large and in charge."

"Well, now you're small and famished."

"Whatever you say, darling! I guess I could try some of that. Wait a minute! Why haven't you taken your armor off?"

"I must stay prepared for anything."

"When was the last time you bathed?"

"I always stay clean."

"Uh huh. I think you're afraid someone will see you."

"No! I just—"

"Admit it, Julius. You're self-conscious of your own body. Come on, get comfortable and let me see that beautiful body that won me over that first night."

"Rabbit's done."

As the three of them ate, Serena delighted in the taste of the succulent morsel, the sweetness of the jam, and the thought of…supremacy. "Oh my, this is good!"

"Told you it was."

"So tell me, Julius, do you still love me?"

"Pardon?"

"You heard. Do you still love me?" Julius finished his piece of rabbit leg and set it aside. He wiped his mouth and took a sip of water.

"I care for you, a lot, Serena. I don't care for the decisions you made and how you squandered such a beautiful gift. I don't blame you for being upset over Jay's death. Even now, I sometimes see his face, the face that shone life for those few seconds before the cold hand of death snatched him away. What I can't forgive is how you allowed it corrupt you and push the ones you loved, or say you loved, away. Even though your eyes are dark, I still envision the day I saw those beautiful dark brown eyes whose color was that of autumn leaves. I miss that Serena."

"You're making me blush, Julius."

"Ha ha! Just like a schoolgirl."

"I sometimes do dream, during the few moments I slept. I dream of the three of us, living as a family, our son running around, playing with toys. You and I kissing in the sunset among a cool autumn night. I see my life as a portrait of success, completed with the intoxicating aroma of romance. To be honest… I miss it."

"Then why don't you strive for it?"

"I can't. I have a mission."

"Really?"

"Yes. Angel or not, I have to find our son. All I want is for our family to be as one again. I don't care if you say I am delusional. Maybe I am. However, I won't stop until I see him again, Julius. I want that one thing, are you with me?"

Julius sipped his water again.

"I don't chase empty dreams, Serena."

"This isn't empty. I know he lives, and if you give me a chance, give us a chance, I will show you. Please…" Julius sighed.

"Fine, but on one condition."

"Yes?"

"You come with me allow me take you to Akoran. There are some personal matters I need to handle, and I could use some help."

"Anything, darling!" Serena said.

"Good, we set out at first light. I will clean up here. You can rest if you want."

"Okay," Serena said cheerfully. She got up and went into the tent. She lay there on the wool pillow, a big grin on her face.

"Step One: Gain the trust.

"Step Two: Move in.

"Step Three: Conquer and destroy.

"Easy as taking candy from a baby!" Serena said, a glint of deceit shimmering in her cold, lifeless eyes.

Chapter 8

Voyage

I must say, I have grown fond of the old man, or Mitchell Vega, as is his name. I help him do the daily works, from digging a few graves, to getting wood and food. I have learned to like that once-disgusting tasting soup he made when I first arrived. At night, when he sleeps, I read some of his journals. Who knew he kept all those thoughts inside. Also, I keep seeing a mention about a man named Julius, and a boy named Jay. They must have been close to him, but that's as much as I can gather.

As for my dreams, I haven't had any lately, and to be honest, I have had some of the best sleep lately. My pendant hasn't been acting funny and I haven't seen any sign of Serena at all. I am still getting used to some things in this world, but so far so good.

The Wandering Boy

Chopping wood had become a typical way to start the day for Mitch and I. I had grown to, in a way, call this place my new home. For someone that had done wrong back in the day, Vega seemed to have learned from his mistakes. Even I had to nod to that. Today was surprisingly warmer compared to the usual freezing days, and some color had returned. Instead of gray, the sky was a pale semi-lifeless blue, but I had grown to love even that much. Mitchell was smiling, even laughing as he dug graves, which was rare.

As I chopped the last of the wood, I saw something approaching from above. As it came closer, I could see it was an angel, but not Serena. This one was fat, his wings pure white, and had baby blue eyes. He landed in front of Vega. I felt nothing bad from him and no need to hide. He hugged Vega and smiled, even laughed with him. He spoke a few words with him and just as quickly parted. Curious, I went over to see what transpired. "Who was that?" I asked.

"Broun, the archangel. He has told me that Julius the Knight has found Serena and that her powers are gone. She is no longer a threat."

"So that explains the increase in temperature. I even broke a sweat yesterday. Is this the same Julius I have read about in your journal?"

"You've been reading them?"

"Ooops! Sorry!"

"No, it's good that you did. With Serena's powers dampened, there may be hope for this world after all."

"Finally, some color! I grew tired of dull gray. Ha ha!"

"Alas, that also means something else for you that is."

"What's that?" Vega turned his head away. "I am going to die, huh?"

"No, son. Yet it will feel like it."

"Come on, Vega. Spit it out."

"The time has come for you. I have taught you much and I must say, it's been the happiest moment in my existence. Yet, I can only teach you so much, and with vigor returning, there is much for you to see."

"Ah, come on! I like it here. Hell, you and me become like family." Vega smiled.

"Yes, that's true, but there is still a world for you to see. Remember when I said to you to explore as much as you can? Now that time has come." I was speechless. Was Vega pushing me off? "And no, I am not pushing you off. You knew this moment would come."

"I was afraid it would. I don't know how I will survive out there though. I have grown used to this place."

"Complacency leads to nothing but disappointment. Never settle. You are young yet and there is a vast world for you to explore, people for you to meet, and things to see. This was only a foundation, which you never had. I must say you've grown much and that has made me the happiest of all. Ha ha!" The smile was real, but so was that feeling of parting ways. "Come, child, there is something I want to give you." We went back to his home, and inside the living area, Vega retrieved the closed chest from the corner.

"What's in there?" I asked. Vega put the chest on the table and opened it. Inside was a sword, a map, three bottles of water, six loaves of bread, wrapped twine, three aloe vera plants, three notebooks, leather clogs, a shirt made of deer hide, pants, a compass, and one lone angel pendant.

"This," he said, "will start you out. I have kept this here, locked away for years. Now, that you've grown to be more of a responsible person, you must take these tools and go forth."

"Must I leave now?"

"No, my lad! One last meal as I discuss the details with you. Besides, you have to see a colorful sunrise."

"At least I get to spend one more night here."

For dinner that night, Vega fixed a special meal: stewed fish soup with potatoes. It was actually the finest meal I had in a while. We ate outside, the day gone. I looked up and saw the stars for the first time. "It's beautiful!" I said. "May I ask something?"

"Sure. You can asks anything."

"The angel pendant you've been fondling. Is that…?"

"Yes, it's Serena's. Well, was Serena's. I got it for her on her twenty-seventh birthday. I knew she didn't want to see me again, but I felt at least she would know, or at least try to see, that deep inside, I did love her and Candice. Maybe through her, some reason would still remain."

"Why don't you just give it to her?"

"No, I can't. You could, seeing as how you…"

"I what? Come on, spit it out."

"As how maybe you would be a light she threw away long ago."

"You make little sense."

"It's not that hard to see. Trust me when I say your travels will show you some things and you will know why I say you must be the one. Here." He handed the pendant over to me. "Take it."

I took the pendant and looked at it. It was of an angel with her hands crossed and her eyes lifted up, a tear coming from her left eye. "When the time comes, and you will see her again, give that to her. Tell her I am sorry."

"I will, I promise."

"Now, let's enjoy the rest of tonight. I even made us my special blackberry rum."

"Really? I never drunk a day in my life."

"Not to get drunk. Just a drink as family in arms." Vega poured us both a cup. The smell was quite strong, and I felt a little dizzy. "It's strong. Take sips if you have to."

"It's fine."

"A toast," he said, raising his cup. "To a starry night and a brighter tomorrow."

"Indeed," I said, raising my cup to meet his.

For the first time in twenty-two years I was glad to see the sunrise. The melting of the darkness of the night, the deep dark blue mixing with the heavenly, orange bliss of the golden sphere. I was alive. I was awake to see that moment. Vega had packed me some of the fish in my pouch, my "Life Pouch" as he called it. "The journey won't be easy. The next village is twenty miles northeast of here. The village of Sumurka. The woods are teeming with poisonous plants and animals, but with this sword you should have no problems."

"What will you do?" I asked, now dressed in the clothes from the chest, which fit me nicely. Vega smiled.

"I will do what I never truly did… Live."

"Thank you for everything, Vega. I owe you for this. You helped me grow."

"Your repayment to me will be to learn from what I taught you."

"I can do that."

"Remember to keep that pendant close. Yours and Serena's."

"Gotcha!" Vega and I stood, not as a gravedigger and a boy, but as equals.

"Take care, young one."

"You too, Vega. Thank you, and I will be sure to deliver this pendant to your daughter."

"Thank you, young one. You have given me reason now. Reason to smile. You have my deepest blessing."

I took my items and sword. As I stood at the edge of a new world, I remembered what the gray, dreary world had taught me, and in all that bleakness, there was still a spark of light. A spark Vega and I would use to light the world.

PART THREE

Visions of Old and New

It seemed odd that I now see the actual colors of the new world around me. The sky is crisp, clear blue. The grass is a lively green. Even the birds have returned, flowers have started to bloom, and for once, I love life. I am curious as to where my journey will take me, and who this Serena woman is. Hell, I only saw her from far away, but I can say the voice she has is the same one from the dreams I used to have. As for who I am, I still have no clue. I've been called "son," "The Wandering Boy." Yet I view myself as a person who is starting a new journey. I think that speaks volumes enough.

The Wondering Boy

Chapter 9

The Journey

From what Vega told me, my destination was the village of Sumurka, twenty miles past a dense forest. My pack weighed heavily on my shoulders. "All that chopping wood and I am still skinny." My worry with physical appearance, or lack of one thereof, was eased by the vibrant sight of a world filled with color. Even the graveyard's grass was green, despite the tombstones still appearing to be a dull gray. "This is the first time I have ever had to do something by myself. I guess Vega figured it was time I made the journey alone. It's just twenty miles in a dense forest. What could go wrong?"

I made my way into the forest and immediately smelled the flowers that had begun to take hold. The smell was heavenly, almost intoxicating. A few steps in and already I needed to rest. "Damn, I am weak. Just at the edge and already tired." I sat my bag down and sat against the edge of a tree. I ran my fingers against the bark and saw it oozing tree sap. "Just like home." I gathered some of the golden flow, and putting it in my mouth, my lips twisted, and I spit. "Not for consumption, though."

A few squirrels were playing nearby, near a bush, not paying me any mind. Birds were chirping in a tree brand above me, and I got a bird's welcome on my shoulder. "Shit!" I took some of the leaves on the ground and wiped the crap off. "Okay, enough sitting around. I need to get going." I ignored the pain as I walked. It felt as if Vega had packed weights in my bag, or maybe the feeling was that heavy sensation one gets when doing something solo for the first time. I sat my bag down again and checked inside. "No compass," I said. "Vega said twenty miles to the northeast. Wait a minute! How could I forget? I have a map." I took the map out and opened it on the forest floor. "So the village is this way and I am in the Hallougen Woods. Wait, what?" I checked the map again and saw the sheer size of the area, marked by a deep green. It took up a good amount of space and had the weirdest name. "Hallougen Woods. Sounds like some fairy shit." I kept the map out and continued on, keeping the map as a guide.

As I continued, the sweet smell lingered, yet it was starting to act on my nose. It was worse than a man or woman who put on too much fragrance. I set my bag down and noticed my vision was starting to double. "What the hell?" I said. I reached for a rag and some of the water to wash my face and cover it. The scent was too much. "Better!" I said, muffled under the rag that covered my nose and mouth. I noticed there were more flowers in this area. They were red, yellow, green, pink, blue, and even black. "A black flower?" I said. I knelt down and picked a few. Their petals were as black as night, but the center was half white, half pink. "Weird." I opened the bag and tucked it inside. "Might as well take a souvenir, huh?"

After two more miles of trekking, my feet were exhausted, and my stomach had started to growl. I decided to settle in a small clearing for a while. I opened my bag and took out a bottle of water, a piece of fish, and a slice of bread. As I bit into my makeshift fish sandwich, I noticed a raccoon walking nearby. He was small, yet still had that bandit-looking face. His tail was gray mixed with black. He saw me and paused. He looked at me, his tail moving back and forth, his tongue licking over his chops. "You're hungry, huh?"

"Yes," he said. My eyes widened and my mouth stopped as I ceased chewing. I must have been seeing things, but I swore I had heard the raccoon say "Yes." He circled over to me, and I dropped my sandwich, scooting back. "No need to fear me," he said.

"You can talk?" I asked.

"Why, yes. I suppose in these woods, a bird could sing, so why not. Anyway, I do not mean to frighten you, young lad. I could not help but notice you partaking in such a delicate mackerel." I was still stunned that this raccoon was talking to me. "Well, I guess my speech has left you speechless."

"No, it hasn't. I have never seen an animal talk."

"In this world, it's possible. Now, mind you, young man. I do care for a piece of your mackerel."

"This is salmon."

"Ha, even better!"

I tore off a piece and handed it to him. In one quick motion he reached out his paws and grabbed it, eating it quickly. "Hmmm…oh my! This is splendid I must say! Do you have another piece?"

"Here," I said, giving him my sandwich, which I hadn't even really gotten to enjoy. The raccoon savored every bite as he seemed to smile as he ate. As he finished, he licked his chops more.

"Splendid! I must say for such a primitive creature, you humans do stir up an appetizing palate!"

"Thank you for insulting me," I said.

"I insult every human, mind you."

"We are done here."

"Wait! I believe you and I have struck a glorious friendship."

"Really? Fish and insults. Yes, that's just lovely."

"I am serious. Besides, you will need some help in these woods."

"Why is that?"

"Have you noticed? This isn't called the Hallougen Woods for nothing. Some of the flowers here emit a strong scent that causes one to hallucinate and become lost."

"I have a rag to cover my nose."

"That won't suffice. Trust me, there are pit traps here you wouldn't be able to see on your own. Don't get me started on those pesky pig fairies."

"Pig fairies?"

"Yes. Little Tinkerbell knockoffs with the body of a pig, wings, and naked."

"Naked pig fairies…hmm."

"You naughty child! I am serious here."

"Well, I need a girl anyway. Where are they at?"

The raccoon jumped up on his hind legs and swiped my face. "I am serious!"

"All right, all right! You can come. Just watch the paws."

As we walked, the raccoon would not shut up. Even though he claimed to know the way better than me, which he probably did, I still put my bet on Vega's map. "Why, are you not listening to me?"

"No, I am not," I said.

"Snowden Sootshire does not like to be ignored young man!" I stopped and turned to look down at the raccoon.

"Well, I have you know that there's a hot fire and a pot with your name on it."

"You lowly stupid bastard!"

"Look, I could easily kill you, but I am not. I have more important matters to attend to."

"Trust me, young man, I am equally as important. You'd be lost in hallucinations by now if it weren't for me."

"Sure. Come on, let's go."

"I am not the one stalling."

Although I didn't have a watch or anything to keep track of time, it felt like hours had passed. Ironically, Mr. Sootshire was leading us pretty well, avoiding the most "beautiful and dangerous flowers on earth," as he said.

"Just need to rest my muscles a bit," I said. "According to my map, we've been going for at least six miles. Damn! Still got fourteen more to go, and it's already midafternoon."

"This forest is quite a journey. I might say. Well, we could continue for a little ways more, then set up camp for tonight."

"I actually agree with you there. I feel like I have got a hundred blisters on my feet." I sat down and stretched out my legs. "So, what did you ask me?"

"Your name."

"Hell if I know. I have been called 'son,' 'young man,' 'kid.' I wouldn't know my name to save my life."

"Hmmm…interesting."

The Perfect Portrait

"Why do you say that?"

"Usually, most people can recall, but you can't. It's like being born but never truly being born."

"You are not making any sense right not."

"How did you not get a name? How did you go to school?"

"I didn't. Life itself and a woman named Glenda were my only teachers. She told me that the kids and teachers would not be able to truly see me, whatever that means. So, I learned from her. She was highly religious, often telling me about the existence of God, angels, and that evil existed. The latter I could understand because that's all the world had to offer. I couldn't attest to the former two. Hell, I didn't even know my own self. But why do you care?"

"Getting to know oneself is important. Besides, I believe in setting a foundation for a meeting between two souls."

"Souls? Hmm…"

"Scoff if you want but I believe you're on a quest to find something. Something that was missing in your life."

"I am on a quest to find someone, no more, no less. After that, I don't care what happens."

"You know, I hate 'leaf in the wind' mentalities."

"What?"

"Everybody knows about that. It's—"

"I know what the mentality is, but why are you telling me?"

"Think about this: there are four types of people in this world."

"I don't want to hear this." I started to get up, but Sootshire swiped my legs.

"You will listen! For grace's sake for once in your life, you will listen!" I was shocked to hear those words coming from his mouth. It was those very words from Vega that had started me on a straighter path. I sat back down. "There are four types of people in this world: people who are born with their paths already chosen. Then you have people with no direction. Then there are those with some direction, and finally people with their own direction."

"So let me guess, you're equating this to the ground, tree, leaf, and wind, right?"

"Yes. The former is shaped by the latter, but the wind has its own direction."

"Come on, Sooty!"

"Sootshire!"

"Whatever. Even I know everything is influenced by something."

"Then I ask again, young man, why are you on this journey?"

"To…"

"To what? Be like a leaf in the wind?"

"What are you saying?"

"You're an interesting character, I will give you that. Last time, why are *you* on this journey? What do you hope to find?"

"I could ask the same of you."

"I am not the one waiting for a gust of wind to whisper in my ear. You can't answer my question, can you?"

"Why should I?"

"With that kind of attitude, you'll be toppled like a weakened tree in broken earth during a storm."

"Uh huh."

"Tell you what. I will ask the question again, Wayward Leaf. Yes, your name is Wayward Leaf. I will ask again but as to when will be my choosing. By that time, hopefully, you will be as the wind, having your own direction and not easily being swayed. If you can answer it, I will tell you something very interesting. Sound fair?"

"What sounds fair is something to eat. I am starving." Sooty shook his head.

"If I wasn't solid earth, you'd be lost in hallucination. Heaven help him. Let's just set up camp here. A baby could comprehend its own needs, but you haven't the clue to a complete yet simple question. Heaven help you."

"What?"

"Enough. I swear this world now has color but your mind is pale right now."

"Whatever you say, Sooty."

"Oh, my…" Sooty just shook his head.

"For now, you are Wayward Leaf. Plain and simple."

Chapter 10

Detour

The stars were shining brightly that night. It was the first time I ever truly appreciated the heavens. Sooty was resting after I shared more of my fish with him. Even though he was able to talk, he still abided by the nature of raccoons, eat and sleep. A fire was burning brightly in our camp, and I sat close, although not out of being cold. "What do you want?" was the question that kept running through my mind. In my twenty-two years of life, I never really thought much about what I wanted. It was mainly day-to-day life in my small hometown. Although I feel more alive, I still feel "ghostly" in a sense. Maybe it is because I am just like a leaf in the wind.

    I also wanted to know Serena's role in all this. I only saw her once that fateful day at the lake. Those cold, lifeless eyes. The sword, with a blade as dark as the abyss and as sharp as a winter morning chill. She told me it was time, but for what? Why did I hear her voice in my dreams? Why did I envision her wedding day in the church? Vega told me once that we are all a part of something. That each person was connected. What did he mean? I had so many questions that hopefully this angel bitch could answer. I miss home, well, what came to be home. I miss Glenda's voice waking me up in the morning. I even miss the forest, my forest. Even in a world so colorful, I feel empty.

    I decided to walk around to clear my head. The moon was out, and the fire emitted more than enough light for me. Sooty would be all right until I got back. I walked to a stream we had passed earlier. The sound of the water was calming to me and maybe it would help me sleep. I walked towards the sound of the water, my legs rubbing up against a few flowers. I sat on the edge of the bank and listened to nature. Crickets were also chirping, and a few were wondering around. "This is so peaceful," I said, taking a sniff of the sweet fragrance in the air.

Even at night the woods felt and smelled peaceful. I lay back in the leaves and looked up at the sky. The hypnotic gaze of the moonlight, the stars sparkling above. It was all peaceful to me. I began to feel my vision starting to blur from the overwhelming smell of the flowers nearby. I wanted to head back to the camp, but something in me just wanted to stay right there, in the bliss. I turned my head and saw little pink lights in the darkness. "Pretty…" I said. Several more of the lights appeared and were near my face. I stared at the sight of those pretty mixes of pink around my head. One floated right in front of my face and I saw it was a small creature. The face was chubby, with small blue eyes. The snout was pointed up and the body was naked with a resemblance of a pig. The breast was not pig breast but looked more human. The creature had the hands and feet of a human as well and shiny yellow wings. "What are you?" I asked, my voice slurring from the overwhelming scent of the flowers. The flying pig bitch simply smiled and motioned the others.

"We are about to have fun, little boy," she said, her eyes turning darker.

Sootshire awoke, his ears beginning to twitch. He rubbed them while looking around. "Wayward Leaf?" He saw the fire burning, but the boy was not there. He called out again, still receiving no answer. "I know he is lost in the head, but I know he couldn't have gone far." Sootshire sighed and shook his head. "Heaven help him." He reached into the bag for a piece of fish. Eating it quickly, he set out to find the boy. "This is not funny!" Sootshire yelled as followed the boy's scent. "So much for creating them to rule over animals. Good man, where are…" He stopped when he saw the boy dancing around without his clothes and little pink lights flying around him. "Good God!" Sootshire yelled. The boy was lost in the motions and talking to the lights. "What are you doing?" he yelled at the boy.

The Perfect Portrait

"It's so pretty!" the boy said, giggling like a school kid who just farted in a quiet classroom. "Sooo much light!"

"Damn it all to hell!" Sootshire screamed. He scurried up to the boy but was stopped by a few of the fairies.

"And what are you doing?" they asked.

"Get out of my way, you pork flies with sugar!" The fairies grew closer.

"You're mean! We are going to have to deal with you!"

"Aww, come on, Sooty," the boy said, dancing and giggling.

"Shut it, Wandering Leaf!" Sootshire yelled.

"What dish should we cook with him?" the fairy in front of him asked the others.

"Raccoon casserole!" the others said.

"Good by me. Get him, ladies!"

The flock of sparkling piglets flew towards Sootshire. They tried blowing the hallucinogenic mist in his face to knock him out, but it had no effect. "What the?" the lead fairy said.

"Hah!" Sootshire said. "It will take more than mist to down me!"

"What a smartass!" the fairy said. "You know what, forget him. We have what we want."

"You're not taking Wandering Leaf!"

"The boy? Oh, please! We just wanted to toy with him. We really wanted these." Sootshire looked and saw in the hand of the lead fairy were two pendants. One was in the shape of an angel, while the other was silver.

"Give those back!" he yelled. The fairies giggled.

"Oooh! A little forest rat is going to challenge us. This could be fun. How about we play hide and seek?"

"How about you give us back those pendants?"

"Us?"

"Those belong to Leaf and I."

"You're lying. Now we don't want to play with you. Come, ladies! Let's leave!" Sootshire started to reach for the pendants, but they were already gone.

"Shit! I should've known not to try to lie to a liar. Leaf, we should go after them. Leaf?"

The boy was still dancing and giggling. Sootshire tried to scratch and bite, but it had no effect. "Great! Just great!" Sootshire looked for a trail to follow, but there wasn't one. "Heaven help us! This isn't good."

"Let's sparkle!" the boy giggled.

"Shut it!" Sootshire yelled. "We've got to figure out a way to get those pendants back!"

"I just want to dance and let the sparkles fly over me!"

"We're fucked!" Sootshire said, shaking his head.

Trapped in the night
Hope is weary
Outsmarted and tricked
By a damn pig fairy!

Chapter 11

Reprieve

The group of fairies stopped at the edge of the covet of flowers, a large group of black flowers Sootshire had warned the boy about. "I can't believe how easy that was," said Pixana. She was the leader of the sparkles of swine. She was adorned in a golden dress, a symbol of her leadership. Her eyes were a mixture of red, blue, and black. On her ears were earrings in the shape of stars. Her face was like a pig's, but her cheeks were slightly smaller, and her nose wasn't as stuck-up. She deemed herself "the one pig that could always fool a person." She held the pendants for her fellow fairies to see. They were awestruck at the way the moonlight shone off of them. "A token of our majestic reign," she said. The other fairies cheered.

"So, what is it?" one of the others asked.

"What do you mean what is it?" Pixana snapped. "It's obviously an angel on the first and some scribble on silver on the second one. Humans and their meaningless attempts to find inner peace. Ha ha! Hee hee! That's why we are better than they are! Ha!"

"What should we do with them?"

"We? I took them off the fool's neck. All I did was whisper sweet nothings in his ear and he was mine. I will wear them to declare myself…"

Her speech was stopped by the sound of something hitting a tree. She looked and saw one of her fellow sisters pinned against a tree, an arrow straight through her chest. Before Pixana could say anything, another arrow found another swine. "What the hell?" She looked and saw a masked figure crouched in position with a bow drawn. "You! That does it! Get him!" The other fairies charged towards the position of the masked intruder. As they neared, the figure shot one arrow, hitting three fairies. The figure was ready for more and delivered arrow after arrow, finding wings and pig skin. Pixana was stunned. The figure came from its hiding spot and stood before Pixana.

The figure was hard to see, even with the ample moonlight and the light coming from her wings. "Excuse me!" she yelled, facing the figure. "Who the hell are you?"

"I believe you have something that is not yours," the figure said.

"I have no idea what you mean," Pixana said. The figure reached out its hand and pointed to the pendants. "Oh, these? I found them."

"You're lying," the figure snarled. "You stole those."

"Why, how dare you accuse me, Pixana, of stealing!"

"Hard to lie when you have been caught red-handed. Hand them over."

"Over my dead body I will!"

"I can arrange that," the figure said, preparing another arrow and taking aim.

"You wouldn't do it," Pixana said. "You couldn't hurt the most beautiful fairy this world has ever seen!"

"Looks are just looks. Last chance to hand over the pendants."

"You bastard!" Pixana said. The figure inched the arrow back a little more. "Fine! Here!" Pixana threw the pendants into the figure's hand.

"Thank you, miss," said the figure.

"You will see me again! All of you will!" The figure said nothing as it walked back into the woods.

Sootshire was wondering what to do with the boy, who was still dancing. Repeated bites and scratching proved to be unsuccessful. Nothing was working. "This is crazy. Usually this wears off by now, but for some reason it hasn't." Sootshire heard footsteps approaching and leaves crunching. "Shit!"

Sootshire hid behind a tree, leaving the Leaf to the wind of what was coming. He peered from behind the tree and saw a figure approach Leaf. The figure seemed to be a little shorter than him and simply stood in front of the boy.

The Perfect Portrait

The figure raised its hand and Sootshire could see the pendants were back. The figure put its free hand on the boy to hold him while the other hand slipped the pendants back on. The boy stopped dancing and passed out. Sootshire ran from his cover and went to the boy.

"He is fine," the figure said. "Just exhausted." Sootshire looked up at the figure, whose face he could not see.

"Thank you," he said. The figure picked up the boy and his clothing. "Hmmm, light as a ghost. Lead the way to the camp."

"Um, yes. Follow me."

The fire was still burning brightly as the boy, now clothed, rested. Sootshire and the figure sat by the fire and talked. He could see the figure was dressed in a brown overcoat with what looked like snakeskin pants. On its feet were boots and it had a bow and quiver of arrows on its back. Its face was covered with a mask and on its head was a straw hat. "Thank you, again."

"No need. I hate liars and deceivers. Those fairies are up to no good."

"That's what I tried to tell Wandering Leaf here, but…"

"No need to scold, forest dweller. The boy is young yet, and young minds tend to explore. I raised one."

"Really?"

"Yes. Watching someone go from crying to talking is quite the experience, especially since you carried it for nine months."

"Good thing I am a male, huh?"

"Sperm donor is more like it."

"Why I never!"

"Calm yourself, forest dweller. I have no intentions of quarreling with you."

"I the same! Anyway, what brings you here?"

"I am seeking someone. I am looking for answers to questions long ago forgotten."

"Oh, really? What might those be?"

"That is really no concern of yours." Sootshire was shocked by the smart remark.

"Can you take off your mask?"

"I will not to you. I will when the time is right." The figure stood up and reached into its pocket and retrieved a red-and-white envelope. "Give this to my beloved child when the time comes. After this is all over, maybe she will be willing to forgive more than just one soul."

"Wait, who is your child?"

The figure simply walked off, without saying another word. Sootshire held the letter, tempted to open it. The figure stopped and turned to face him. "Open that letter and I will hunt you down. It is for her eyes only!"

"Yes, ma'am!" Sootshire said as the figure walked off. "What a bitch!" He looked to the boy, who was sleeping soundly. "Sleep well, Wandering Leaf. A new world awaits."

Chapter 12

A Meeting of Minds

I have crossed into this world, this colorful plane of existence. How the years have turned my hair into a shadow of what it once was. I have left behind all those material possessions for the truth. I want to finally hear from his mouth the answers I have wanted to hear for so long. I came across a field full of flowers. Dandelions, roses, and in the distance, graves, a small wooden hut, and a broken church farther away. I wear a mask I fashioned from porcelain, a theatrical cover to hide my true face. My eyes glazed, barely able to function as they once had, but still able to see through lies and deception.

I examined the graves as I walked, nameless headstones, homage to no one. I sense my daughter has been here. A mother never loses track of her child. Her energy has changed. It is not the same as the last time I saw her that fateful day, when we waited for Mitchell to walk through the door. That day, when I told her this was my fight, not hers. That day, she swore to make Mitchell pay for the pain he put me through. I love Serena, but she is a fool at times. My daughter, who refuses to see past the things I have. My daughter is a fool.

The façade of Mitchell's home is quite humble compared to what he's used to; the wooden façade, the stone steps. I can tell he built this himself. The graves tasked to him by Serena. I opened the door and stepped inside. A humble abode for such an extravagant liar. On the table is a flower, its petals a radiant pink. In the corner of the living area was a chest of journals detailing days gone by. A desk to record daily events. In the kitchen area is a small wood burner for cooking. He is living simple life now. I saw a small washroom for his body, a straw cot to rest on, and dirty clothes. It was no wonder I did all the laundry. Our home was only an occasional pit stop for him.

I go into the restroom and see a wash tub and a toilet that looks like a child put it together. My goodness, Mitchell! How have you fallen so hard? I looked and saw a broken medium-sized shard of a mirror. I looked into it and saw a masked face stare back at me. The time for hiding was over. I removed my hat, which revealed the aged hair that flows to my shoulders. I take off the mask, which shows wrinkles, sagging jowls, and glazed eyes. I have no need to hide anymore. Mitchell hid behind his insatiable appetite for more. My grandson hides behind a casket. My son-in-law hides behind his stern beliefs, and I hide behind nothing…at least not anymore.

I sat in the living room and looked through Mitchell's journals. The cover is worn, parts peeling off, yet the title is still visible. "My Deepest Regrets," by Mitchell S. Vega.

"Really?" I said sarcastically. I open the cover and see that it is indeed his handwriting. I see the entry…

> *The weather is hot, yet inside I feel cold. I sit here in a hotel room overlooking a beach. People are outside in the sand, bathing in the light. Children are playing with toys and in the waves that are the very hands of nature itself. I have a hard time resting my weary eyes after what has happened. Candice and I divorced, the proceedings happening just last week. I was not able to lie my way out of what I had done, which I admit to now. I don't blame her or Serena for being angry. I am angry at myself for not seeing what was right in front of me. I constantly dream about the promise Serena made to get back at me will come. The look she gave me wasn't her own. I don't blame her, but I know what I saw at that moment wasn't my daughter. What exactly did she find out in this world? I may never know.*
>
> *M.S.V.*

The Perfect Portrait

I honestly was disgusted by the sight of what I had just read. To think that, after the fact, Mitchell would begin to show remorse only after he got caught. I wasn't moved at all by his worries. Honestly, Serena would be the last of his worries. I could not stress how much I warned her to leave it all alone, yet she wouldn't. I didn't keep a close enough eye on her and I wasn't there to comfort her when she lost Jay. Her anger, not matter how it is put, is misplaced. I know this is her world for it has all the markings of her on it, including that fat bastard Broun, whom I saw flying overhead when I got here. Only Serena would take a vengeful stance like an angry angel. I will show her true anger after I am done with Mitchell.

Mitchell still hadn't returned home after an hour. I wasn't worried as, just like before, he would return sooner or later. The next journal I read detailed how he claimed to have finally met Jay, Serena's child who died shortly after being born. I know Vega was a lying bastard, but crazy? No, at least I didn't think he was. How could Jay be alive after what happened? The journal entries Mitchell wrote clearly said he had met and spoken with Jay and that he even spent time with him. Wait a minute! That boy from the Hallougen Woods, with the raccoon. That couldn't have been Jay! He is dead. That kid must have been someone else! My thoughts were interrupted by the sound of footsteps approaching the front door. I knew who it was. I readied my bow. It was time to tell the truth.

As the door opened, I readied myself. He looked and saw me, bow in hand, at the ready. He had changed to such a pitiful sight over the years. A gray beard hanging from aged skin. Gray, thinning hair. A dirty overcoat, and ragged pants, resting upon worn shoes. He stood there, a rose in his hand, his aged eyes locking with mine. "Please, Mitchell Samuel Vega, step inside," I said, motioning with my bow, which could end him at any time. He slowly stepped inside, closing the door behind him. "Sit down here at the table." He obliged. "Do you remember me?" He laid the rose on the table, took out a pipe, and lit it. He took two hits before he turned to me.

"How can I forget those eyes, Candice? I see them every night in my dreams."

"Do you know why I am here?"

"Actually, I don't. I don't see why you're wasting my time on a delightful day."

"What did you say?"

"You can hear. I've already faced death itself. I am not scared of you or your bow and arrow."

"I must say for an old man, you have got nerve. You always had a sly way of insulting people."

"It must have worked for you to say yes to me. I hope you visited your daughter before you trespassed on my property."

"Serena wouldn't be ready to meet me yet. This is between you and me. You have some explaining to do."

"Let's see. The proceedings ended with you getting over half my assets. I lost over seventy percent of my clientele. I lived in three different motels with roaches crawling from cracks in the bathroom. I couldn't sleep for weeks on end at times, and I had a sword put to my throat by my own daughter. Candice, I don't owe you a damn thing."

"You just won't let go of the pride, will you?"

"I already did. Why don't you? Serena was going around hating me for not being there, blaming me for Jay's death, yet you were just as absent. You spent countless hours away yourself, and need I remind you that they were not at the office. Does Serena know this?"

"She wouldn't understand."

"No, you didn't want her to understand."

"What is this about Jay being alive?"

"The boy lives. I saw him when he first arrived, back when the world stood still. He doesn't understand himself, who he is, or even who I really am. I know I was looking at a body that had faded but a spirit that still lived on. A soul that just wanted to be real. He lived here in this house with me. We laughed, talked, ate together. He told me at the end that he was glad to meet me, and I will tell you something else and you listen to me: it won't be up to you or me to speak sense into Serena. It will be upon him."

"I am not buying this, Mitchell."

The Perfect Portrait

"I wouldn't expect you to, Candice. I tell you something is residing within our daughter and grandson. They're very special, but it's Serena I fear for. I pity not my own soul, but hers. Jay will be successful. I have repented and Julius will see what I have seen, and you can get the hell out."

"You SON OF A BITCH! You're just making excuses."

"At one time I did, but not anymore. When you stare death in the face, it does something to you. Yet, the Angel of Death herself is but a pawn to something that existed long before. If you came here to kill me, go ahead. I have repented and see things in a new light. All I have left is for one wish, to finally see Jay's soul find what it is looking for. If you plan to rob me of that privilege, then God help you."

"You really mean this about my daughter?"

"Our daughter, Candice. She sold her soul to replace Jay's! You don't mess with fate! I love Serena but the girl needs help! Stop thinking about the past and work with me so we can all be a damn family again, woman!"

"She's not sick, Mitchell. She just has been alone too much."

"Oh, now look who's making excuses? You never really saw Serena's last portrait? I mean the one I found in her old apartment that she left behind. You never saw that, did you?"

"You're lying, Mitchell."

Mitchell got up and went to the chest in the corner and pulled out a painting covered by a red cloth. "Do you want to finally see the truth?"

"Whatever." He pulled the cloth off and what was revealed was a portrait of our daughter, eyes gouged out with blood rushing from her mouth. I turned my head away.

"This is what she felt inside all these years, Candice. Our daughter! She started to heal when she met Julius, but Jay's death was it for her. She went into a deep and dark depression after that. I tried to reach out, but nothing. She was lost, and we didn't help her. We were careless. This isn't about a cheating husband. This is about parents that neglected their child. Point that arrow at me but there equally should be one pointing at you. I have no idea where she is or what she's doing but this stunt you're pulling is no better."

"And do what, Mitchell? Live this sham life you're living?"

"Right now, this is Heaven. All I miss is my family. I don't want money. I don't miss the women. I just want my wife and daughter back."

"I am tempted to believe you. A man that could sell a dog back his own shit."

"All I have is this and hope."

"I don't believe I am hearing this from your mouth. I mean humble home, yes, but this? This? Mitchell Vega, you're an ass, but even donkeys live better than this."

"I would rather be a working filthy donkey than a suited-up snake."

"That's a first out of your mouth, Mitchell. Well, I must say I wasn't expecting this from you."

"I want to see my family as one, even if it's for the last time. That is why I still stand. We left the portrait unfinished once, Candice. Let's not do it again."

"You need my help, huh?"

"Yes, I do. I wasn't a husband back then. At least give me that chance now."

"I don't want those graves to be literal, Mitch."

"Death is inevitable, Candice. I just don't want that last mile to be so long. We have aged now. So drop the bow and act like a real mother. A real wife. A real human being."

"You just sold a bitch back her own shit," I said, lowering my bow.

"No, I just told my wife the truth."

PART 4

Discovery

As Wayward Leaf has finally come back to his senses, I can't help but wonder if he truly is prepared for this journey. He is still young and learning. I could easily leave him behind, but I won't. I can tell he will need a guide, a shoulder to lean on. I should know, for I have walked among others before.

S. Sootshire

Chapter 13

The Purrfect Village

The sun's rays burned my eyes like fire as I woke. My head felt as if it had been twisted and warped. "Now you awaken?" Sooty said, standing over me on his hind legs. I slowly sat up, my hand rubbing my head.

"What happened?" I asked. Sooty shook his head and scratched my face.

"You don't remember anything at all?"

"No, I don't."

"Heaven help you. How do I begin? Oh, that's right! You went off by your bloody self! I got chased and taunted by pig swines, and you were naked! How is that for what happened?"

"Cool," I said. Sootshire just shook his head.

"Heaven help you."

"Where are we?"

"Christ! We are back at camp. Luckily, some mysterious figure bailed us out. I also received a letter from this person."

"Really?"

"Yes, a letter to be delivered to Serena when the time is right."

"Sweet!"

"Anyway, I prepared some fish for us. We need to make a move on our journey."

"How far are we?"

"Seven miles in. Thirteen more to go."

"Shit! I don't feel like that long trek. I mean seven left blisters on my feet, man."

"Well, I don't see any other option unless you have a carriage in that bag."

"I don't."

"There is your answer. Sometimes in life you have to tough it out."

"Shit!"

"Stop whining and let's eat."

While I ate, I could still smell the roses, not the fish. Last night seemed to be a blur in my mind. Maybe I was a little hasty to want to explore an area I knew nothing about. At least Sooty was here to help me, but I had to be careful. The time may come when help may not be available.

Three more miles had been traversed by my feet, which still had blisters, and by the four paws of a raccoon, who seemed to take the path in stride. I stopped at a tree to rest. "We are halfway," Sooty said happily.

"You seem happy," I said.

"It's progress. Ten more miles, Wondering Leaf."

"Do you know anything about the village we are going to?"

"Sumurka?"

"You know about it?"

"Only heard of it."

"Really? I have a feeling you know more about it than you're letting on."

"You think so?"

"Look, I may be only twenty-two, young, and impulsive, but at times I can see when someone is hiding something. I don't know how I can do it, but I can."

"You have insight. Interesting."

"So spill it, Vega!"

"What did you just call me?"

"You remind me of Vega, the man I was staying with before I began this journey."

"You wouldn't believe me if I told you."

"Try me."

The Perfect Portrait

"The village of Sumurka is also known as the village of cats."

"What?"

"I knew you wouldn't believe me."

"It's not that. I was just not expecting that. Anything can be possible. So Sumurka is the village of cats."

"Yes. The people there look like cats, but they talk just like you and I and they walk on two feet."

"Interesting."

"That doesn't sound too interesting to me. I do not get along with cats too well."

"As you once asked me, how do you know this?"

"I never asked that. That's a question best posed to yourself. I have seen things and helped people."

"Oh, Sooty! Always being extraordinary."

"Better than a Leaf in the wind."

"Anyway, this village is beyond these woods?"

"Yes, so what's keeping us?"

"Blisters on top of blisters."

"Excuses, excuses!" I sighed and stood up. "Trust me, Wandering Leaf, this will all make sense when all is said and done."

"That's what I am afraid of, Sooty."

"Why be afraid of the truth?"

"It's what the truth is. Am I truly ready to be truly awakened?"

"That is up to you."

"That is what I am horrified of."

The Village of Sumurka

We are an independent people, a race of half-feline, half-human. Stripes and spots cover our bodies from head to toe. Our tails wave swiftly in the air. Our claws dig into our prey's flesh as we sink our teeth into the delicate morsel. Our eyes range in colors of the rainbow and glow in the quiet moonlight. Legs that are quick, our bodies moving gracefully and swiftly. Clothes, you may ask?

John Paul Shuman Jr.

Why should a cat cover its natural beauty? We believe in the natural as we are a part of nature itself. Milk, fertile ground, meat, and honey. These are the necessities we hold dear. Who could forget how close knit we cats are. Yes, we identify with our feline nature, despite having such human bodies.

Our people are led by our tribal leader, Elder Mikel. Older than the lives most cats have, he has seen countless generations come and go. Many in the village would say he has one hundred lives. To me, it would seem more. As for me, I am especially, how would I say, frisky when I want to be. Many of the males know I am keen to the nature of men and that I am not an easy catch. I have dedicated the last six years of my life to the nature of the animal so often overlooked by humans. To me, cats are the superior species. My dedication has our leader, who sometimes tells me I could be a bit too serious. I wouldn't have it any other way. I am who I am. My name is Catalina.

On this day, it began as any other for me. The village was gathering its daily supply of milk and meat. I prefer to gather alone, and I need no distractions. I am stuck up in a way, often stroking my fur under the brightest of days and the darkest of nights. The elder calls me his most trusted child for someone who never knew of her past. Yet, unlike humans, we cats naturally can adapt to anything. We existed long before humanity and will thrive even after everything is gone.

Forgive me, for my extensive explanation of self. If you don't know a cat by now, that's your loss. On this day, as I said, I was on a hunt in the woods. I have heard many stories about pig fairies that lurk in them and the hallucinogenic flowers abroad. I have learned how to avoid and deal with such threats, if one can consider them that. I view the fairies as a lowly creature that could have only been manifested from a deranged mind. They have been more active as of late, which puzzles even a creature that was once worshipped. Could it be due to the more fruitful days that have come? Or are they simply ready to play? To me, I couldn't care less, for I can defend myself against them. As I move among the trees and bushes, I get the scent of something. It's not a deer, or pig, but that of a human and something else. I patiently wait and blend in.

The Perfect Portrait

. . .

"If you would stop eating so much of my fish, we would have more," Wandering Leaf said.

"Hunger is hunger, you indecisive baboon!" said Sootshire.

"Well, I can see past this last little bit of bullshit is the village, and I think I see people with tails."

"Cat people, you ox!"

"Why are you so snappy? You know what, don't answer. Let's just go. My feet are killing me."

. . .

I can tell it's a person, but that other scent is something else. I see them approaching and I get my paws, mind, and teeth ready. As soon as I see his head, I pounce on him, my body knocking his to the ground. The boy looks young as I take a quick look before I sink my teeth and claws in. He is dressed plainly and smells of the flowers. "Good Scott!" yells his friend, which turns out to be a raccoon. Forest rat is more like it. He stands there, amazed at my sight yet terrified. Ironically, he doesn't run, but just looks. I turn my attention back to the boy and notice a smell coming from a bag he's wearing. The smell is fresh and heavenly to my nose. I look at the boy, who looks like a deer in the headlights, and resist the urge to kill him. If I were my more ferocious cousin, that would be a different story. I get off and stand before the terrified duo.

"Look what the cat found," I said, licking my lips, my tail waving back and forth. They still said nothing. "Talk! What are you doing here?" The raccoon still looked terrified at me. The boy, however, looked up at me. He sat up simply and gazed at me. "Last chance," I said, showing my claws.

"Wow!" the boy said. "Kitty bitch."

"What did you say?" my eyes narrowing. The raccoon came between us.

"Sorry, ma'am," he said.

"I am not your mother or babysitter. I am far above both of you and you're in my territory. Now, for the last time, what are you doing here?" The boy stood up.

"Let's see. A bitch told me to deliver something to another bitch and now I am looking for that bitch, so can you let us by, you spotted bitch!"

I lunged at him again and sat on top of him. There was something unique about this boy. He didn't fear me as one previous person did. No, this boy emitted an unusual aura from his body. It made my skin itch to be honest. I got off the boy and stood before him and his rodent companion. "What is in the bag?" I asked.

"What is it to you?" the forest rat said.

"Quiet!"

"A few clothes," said the boy. "Water, fish." My eyes lit up.

"Hmm. Interesting. Come with me."

"We will most certainly not!" said the rat. I quickly grabbed him and held him in one paw. He struggled, trying to scratch and bite. "Let me go! Let loose of me you flea-bitten two-legged pointy-eared whore!"

"Listen to the rat squirm. Don't you know to take it easy when in a cat's mouth?"

"That's lion's mouth, you bitch," the boy said. I quickly swiped my paw and got his cheek.

"Know your place and shut your mouth! Let's go."

My people were shocked to see what the cat dragged in. A few of them looked at the boy as if he were the most offensive sight and others eyes the raccoon for obvious reasons. No Tail, the only cat in our village without a tail, ran over to me. I must say if there was any cat that rivaled me in vanity, it was him. His whiskers came to his chest. His eyes were red, supposedly from his easy-to-get-mad temper. He had markings from his various hunts and did he ever smell like it, no matter how much he bathed. The male cats feared him in a way, but the females…need I say? "Catalina!" he said, coming over to me, a few of the other's joining him, claws and bows at the ready. "What is this?"

"Oh this? It's lunch."

The Perfect Portrait

"Why I say!" said the rat. I dug my claws into him to keep him quiet.

"That's not what I mean. I mean what are you doing with this filthy human?"

"Hey, asshole…I am not—" The boy was silenced by the threatening impalement of claws and spear tips.

"Oh, him? He's just lost that's all. Don't worry. The rat's for lunch and I will deal with him."

"You know we don't take to humans, Catalina."

"You know you should try some pants, man. I heard there's…" I gave him a shut the hell up look with my eyes.

"I will deal with him. He has no weapons on him, and if his tongue persists, I will rip it out."

"Give me the rat," No Tail said, his paw outstretched.

"Put your paws on me and I will—" Another claw shut him up.

"No Tail, you know me. This is me catch, not yours."

"Don't make me take it, Catalina."

"Try, fool, and the rat's hide won't be the only one hanging up." No Tail and his crew backed off.

"This isn't over, Catalina," he said.

"It is if I say it is. Now get out of my face." No Tail walked off, glowering back to give me the evil eye. The others that had crowded around went back to their business.

"Hey, that was cool!" the boy said. I slapped him.

"Idiot, I didn't do that for either of you. I am just the one who doesn't let others push me around."

"Smh!" said the rat.

"Let's go see the Elder. You two look like an interesting meal."

I took the boy and his rat to the house above all others. A humble sanctuary fashioned from wood and deer hides, with a small stream nearby. "This is it?" asked the boy.

"Quiet." I said. I knocked on the door and heard the sound of lapping. The Elder's afternoon milk feast. Oh, how he loves his milk. The lapping stopped and footsteps approached. The door opened, and there stood Elder

Mikel. In human years, he was fifteen, but for that age, he still kept a grace about himself that could only be respected. He was covered in a mixture of orange-and-black fur, with whiskers that curled up at the end. His eyes were as the golden sun and his ears were spotted. His skin had aged but not too much surprisingly. He was not stunned to see what was with me.

"Catalina!" he said.

"Elder Mikel, forgive me for disturbing you."

"No, child, it's okay. Who do we have here?"

"A smartass and a rat, sir."

"Hey!" said the boy and the rat in unison.

"Ha ha! Caty, how many times have I warned you about your mouth?"

"Sorry, sir."

"It has been at least a decade since a human has graced our land. I must say it's good to see…" He stopped and a puzzled look came across his face.

"Something wrong, sir?"

He came up to the boy and looked at him. His whiskers shook as he looked in his eyes and down towards his neck. Once he saw what looked to be necklaces around his neck, his eyes widened. "Sir?"

"Hmm, hmm," said the Elder. "Please, come inside."

The inside of the Elder's abode was simple, with his countless containers of milk and his table in the middle of the room. The floor was covered by a rug made from wool and duck feathers. On the wall were paintings of the Elder, our village, me, and a person, a human. I asked him about the man in the painting, but he told me I would know when the time came. "Please sit." The boy sat at the left and I sat in front of the Elder, the rat in my paw. "Caty, there's no need to hold the creature. He is good with me."

"Finally, some manners," said the boy.

"Watch your mouth," I said to him.

"Now, now, children. Some milk for anyone?"

"Sure, why not?" the boy said. I slapped him again.

"Now, now." The Elder poured three glasses and sat them in front of us. "So, Catalina, you found these two?"

The Perfect Portrait

"Yes, sir. Trespassing I might add."

"Hey, hold on!" said the boy.

"Shut it!" I said.

"Please, child. Let the boy speak."

"With all respect, sir, I and my companion here were simply on a mission."

"Mission?"

"Yes," said the rat. "We have someone we are supposed to meet."

"Someone of great power?"

"Yes, sir. The woman is named Serena."

"Hmm. Serena Vega, the Angel of Vengeance?"

"Wait, what?" I said. "Angel?"

"Yes," said the Elder. "That probably explains what happened recently."

"Wait, hold on!" the boy said. "Back up and explain all this!"

"It was ten years ago. I was five at the time, quite young in human time. I was training to be the Elder of this tribe, for my skills were quite proficient. One day, while myself and a few others were out tending to the crops, we happened upon the sight of something in the sky. It was larger than any bird we had seen, and it looked like a person. As the figure landed, we saw it was a woman. She had long flowing dark hair, a blade in hand, and was clad in a golden armor. Her eyes were black, as well as her wings. Myself and others were puzzled by the sight of this woman. Naturally, a few of the males went to get out tribal leader, Akobe.

"Akobe was a well-respected cat, both in our ways and human. He was diligent, resourceful, and always believed a hundred words are nothing if there isn't at least one action to support it. He approached the woman along with a few of our warriors, myself included. "What brings you here, Dark One?" he said. The woman smiled, as if complimented.

"You have led a village, Akobe," the woman said. "Yet, I will lead the world. Tend to the last of these crops for the color will fade and life will cease. Depend not on the ways of man. Abide only by your feline instincts. Stock up on meat, milk, and each other. Dark days I will bring to this land, but even I respect a man, not necessarily a human man, but any figure in power that can provide.

For this, will deplete your crops but leave you with fleshy sustenance and a stream of milk and honey. You need not toil for nothing as man does. My father abandoned me, but I will not leave you. So it is said by I, Serena, and so shall it be done."

With those words, she left. Myself and others were watchful of this strange woman. Something about her seemed off, but Akobe decided to take heed. Several of us questioned his decision, but he assured us it was for the betterment of all of us. In time, the days grew still and colder as opposed to the temperate days we were used to. The crops refused to grow, as we are part human, and depended on wheat, corn, and greens. Instead, we received our fish, pork, and vermin diet as well as a flow of milk and honey form the bees that remained in check.

One year passed. While hunting for a feral swine, I came across a man who was traversing the woods near our village. It was hard to say who was more puzzled of the two of us. He, however, was not afraid, and neither was I. The man said that he was hungry, as the area he was in was lifeless. I saw in his eyes that he spoke the truth. At the time I was, and even now, a forgiving person. I took the man, who was dressed as strangely as the woman back to our village. As expected, he wasn't met with kind eyes. We spoke with Akobe and learned the man was from another life and had trouble adjusting to this new world. Needless to say, Akobe made sure the man was fed, as well as commissioning myself and two others to help the man build a more stable dwelling, for he had been staying in an abandoned church.

"So that's who the man is in the painting," the boy said. "That's Vega!"

"Yes," said the Elder. "Vega told me he was in the midst of atoning for something, but he would not say. The painting he did was his repayment to me and Akobe for helping him. Of course, by this time, that woman whom we came to learn was his daughter had taken a darker path by the time. Yet, it seems that path has changed. Colorful again are the fields."

"Hmmm," said the rat.

"So birds can fly," I said. "This seems too fictitious."

"For all your will, you doubt, Catalina," the Elder said. "That was an angel no doubt."

The Perfect Portrait

"Oh, boy," I said.

"Trust me, I know the feeling," the boy said.

"Neither of two should be doubting," said the rat. "Serena could have easily decimated this village, but she spared it."

"He's right," said the Elder. "She spared us a fate worse than death. So, to some end, myself, others in our clan, and you, Catalina, owe her thanks."

"Sir, if you don't mind, may I ask something?" said the boy.

"Go ahead, young man."

"Vega and a person gave me some items to give Serena. The map he gave me shows that this village and the area he resides in are but a few places on this land. From here, I don't know where to go."

"Hmmm, you seek to find the Angel? This area is simple, but broader areas are across the waters. Across the waters is the continent of Shrineham and its capital Rhodam. To get there you will need to get to the sea and board a vessel."

"Is there one there?" asked the rat.

"Why, yes. It is owned by a man called 'The Logger.'"

"More like tough ass," I said. "That stubborn fool wouldn't take a gold nugget to cross."

"You forget, Catalina. The Logger is stubborn, yes, but does have some reason in him. I could speak with him and see what he can do."

"That would be great, sir! I really would appreciate it," said the boy.

"But please, spend the night here with us. We would be pleased to have you and your companion. What is your name, good man?"

"Wandering Leaf, and my friend is—"

"Snowden Sootshire," said the rat.

"Interesting. Our people would love your acquaintance."

"Hold on!" I said. "Elder, there is no way I am letting smart-mouth and rat man stay here with you!"

"Which is why they will rest in your dwelling, Catalina."

"What?"

"You were brave enough and trusted them enough to bring them to me, be nice and kind enough to let them lay their heads in your home."

"Yes, sir," I said. "I'll be watching you two."

"I don't steal," said the boy.

"I will make sure of that, don't worry," said the rat.

"Ho, ho! Good, good! Please, you two, enjoy yourselves in our village."

"Come on, you two," I said, "Someone has to watch you."

We thanked the Elder and I carried these two, my eyes on them both. That night I sat with the boy and his rodent friend for dinner. "Yes, yes!" said the rat. "Fish!" I noticed the boy had been quiet since we left the Elder's home. For some reason, that smart mouth of his had been quiet.

"Why so quiet?" I said, eyeing him and taking a bite of fish.

"I am curious about where this journey ends," he said. "I know I have to deliver these pieces to Serena, but I feel there is more to all this. The Elder didn't say much about my pendants, but he did look at them oddly."

"How did you get them?"

"The silver one I actually found. This might sound weird, but I am actually not from this world."

"Oh, boy! Is everyone on the supernatural train today?"

"Call it what you want but where I am from, there are no cat people. No angels, or even fairies. There's only dirt roads and cemented hearts. The only connection I had was a loving woman who treated me like a son."

"Whatever," I said.

"Yeah, whatever. I am not hungry. I am going to bed."

"Hey, can I have your fish?" asked the rat.

"Sure, take it." The rat eagerly grabbed the fish and wasted no time.

. . .

What could be the ultimate meaning of all this? As I lay here, eyes wide open, I can't help but wonder. Am I really a ghost or something more? This feeling, these pendants around my neck. One for me and one for Serena, a woman whom I know nothing about. Why have certain people, even in this world, given me the look as if I am from another world? Is my pseudo-bravado an attempt to escape form a truth that has been staring me in the face this whole time? With a new continent and challenges awaiting, maybe it's time to take things more seriously. Something does not feel right. One thing Glenda told me is this: the fiercest storms always come behind a quiet seemingly calm day.

"The Logger"

I stand watch by my treasured vessel, whom I named Estella. I have traversed the seas with her by my side and guiding me. For years, we have seen the shores of countless cities, towns, and landscapes. I have grown a love for the sea and vice versa. For now, I have settled on the edge of this land, the land of a strange people. I have not set foot deeper, as I am a busy man. This is only a rest stop, nothing more, nothing less. I hear footsteps approaching and ready my sword. From the inland I see three of the mysterious inhabitants. They are as strange as I envisioned the word to be, Cat People. The one in the middle must be their leader. He has come with two others, and they are armed. Do they want to wage war? The leader motions for him men to lower their weapons. Good job, sir! He walks up to me, a staff in his paws. "You need something?" I ask.

"You're the Logger, right?" he asks.

"Yes, who wants to know?"

"There is something I must ask of you. Yet, please forgive me for not introducing myself. I am Elder Mikel, leader of the village of Sumurka. I have heard of you."

"Really now?"

"Yes. Even in this world, water carries information as well as goods."

"You're very perceptive, old cat. I can respect that. If you were a bullshitter, then you wouldn't be standing before me."

"I am keen to liars as well," said the old cat.

"Anyway, what is the favor you ask of me?"

"A while ago, a young man came to me with a dilemma he was facing. He needs to deliver a special package to a person close to him. He needs to get to the city of Rhodam and…"

"You want to know if I can take him? You don't need to hesitate the question, old cat."

"He will not be traveling by himself, though."

"No problem. *Estella* could hold a hundred people. Ha ha! Just a figure of speech."

"I know, Logger. I may be old, but I still can catch a hint of humor. I would like to thank you, and you will be compensated for this."

"The ability to traverse the world is enough for me, old cat."

"Are you sure? We have a good bit of fresh delicacies in stock. Sharing, especially in this circumstance, is not a problem."

"Hmmm, I have a sweet tooth."

"Ah, I know just the thing for you, then. I will have it sent with the boy and his companions in the morning."

"All right, old cat."

"Thank you again, Logger. You have really been generous."

The old cat smiled as he and his men left. I really didn't want anything, but knowing some people, even cat people, get pissy when you actually refuse an offer, I couldn't say no. "Well, *Estella*," I said, putting my hand on her aged yet sturdy façade. "It's time to see the world one more time!"

The sun's rays awakened the world. Sooty was already up. He came into the room with me, very excited. "Good morning!" he said happily. I smiled and rubbed my eyes. "What was wrong with you last night? It isn't like you to skip out on a meal, especially fish."

"I just had something on my mind, that's all. I am fine now."

"Catalina is eating now. I must say she was concerned with your behavior last night."

"Really?"

"Why, yes actually. She asked me what was wrong, and I told her that you were pondering the journey ahead. Of course, she just her tail, but I know what was on your mind. It's not easy going on long voyages, I must say. This is the last useful place in this area. The rest is mostly forest, a few rivers and streams, and that's it."

"A new world awaits."

"It certainly does. Oh, yes! Before I forget, Catalina said the Elder wants to meet with us after breakfast."

"It must concern the boat."

"Yes, yes! So, get up, you lump!"

I got myself together and went into the room where Catalina and Sooty were eating. "There you are," she said.

"Good morning," I said.

"No smart remarks this morning?"

"There's no need for it. We have a mission to uphold."

"That is true and consider adding one more."

"Hold on!" Sooty said. "You are coming with us?"

"Yes, I am. Someone needs to watch you two, and also, you need a girl who's swift and to the point. If a couple of pig fairies outsmart an educated rat and a fairly stable boy, imagine what other places can bring."

"The more the merrier," Sooty said.

"Myself and the rat here actually came to an agreement on one thing: you two can't handle this alone. Besides, I am stronger than I look, which could come in handy. I will tell you this: no matter what world you come from, real or fiction, only the swift and strong survive."

"The three of us it will be, then," I said.

"Please tell me you are hungry. I actually felt bad watching the rat nibble and slurp your fish."

"Yes. Let's eat and get this show on the road."

We ate and went to see the Elder.

"Good to see you three!" he said. "I am pleased to say the Logger has agreed to take you across the waters."

"That's great," I said. "I hope he knows how grateful we are."

"He didn't mind, and before I forget." The Elder retrieved a jar of milk and a wrapped whole fish. "Be sure to give this to him. It's a token of our appreciation."

"I will," I said, taking the items. The Elder walked over to Catalina.

"Be safe, Catalina," he said.

"I will, sir. I am mainly concerned about these two."

"Don't count them out, Catalina. What awaits you three will require you to work together."

"A lot awaits us," I said.

"Look at you, Mr. Leader," Catalina said.

"I am not the leader. We all lead in this group. I can see now that I wouldn't be able to do this journey alone. Both of you have something to bring to the table. Sootshire with his intellect and deep insight, and you with your agility, strength, and boldness. For me to, no, for us to be successful, we will have to utilize all three."

"Ho, ho! Wondering Leaf, I see you have put some thought into this."

"The time in the woods taught me that."

"I love seeing young minds grow. You three will do well. I am sure of it."

"We will return, Elder," Catalina said. "I am sure we will have much to tell."

"I know you will. Be safe, you three."

"Keep plenty of fish waiting," Sootshire said.

"Oh, there will be a feast awaiting, I assure you."

The Logger awaited us as we reached the shore.

"So you three are the ones I am transporting?" he asked.

"Yes, sir," I said. "The Elder also wanted me to give this to you." I retrieved the milk and fish and handed it to him.

"Damn! This is what seafarer's love! All fresh!"

"Any last things, Wandering Leaf?" Sootshire asked.

"No. From here we move forward. A new world awaits."

"And some asses that may need to get kicked," Catalina said.

"And puzzles to be solved," Sootshire said.

"It seems you kids are set," said the Logger. "Ready?"

"Yes," I said. "Okay, guys, let's do this!"

Chapter 14

The City of Akoran

For a civilization to survive, its people need three things: a strong leader, stable work ethic, and access to the basic necessities. Survival of not only the individual but the entire people is top priority. We will, however, use any means necessary for the survival of our people. We are not beyond the use of force and/or violence to achieve our survival. We believe in our own abilities to survive and not the blind faith as the people of Rhodam do. Faith is blind; blood, sweat, and tears are our fruit. For those who come into our city, tread lightly and watch your tongue.

Akoran Creed

The City of Akoran

"A world I created and still I get bitten by mosquitoes and ants," Serena grumbled.

"The laws of nature always win," said Julius.

"You have been quiet since we left the mainland. That fisherman or whoever the hell he was did not like me."

"Serena, you kept trying to hit on him."

"What? Oh, come on. You can't say if it was the other way around, and it was a woman, you wouldn't try."

"Don't be silly. You may be mortal, but don't be foolish. Act with some decency."

"You need to lighten up, Julius. You act like someone with a stick up their ass."

"Trust me, if you knew where we were going, you would straighten up."

"Akoran, huh? This area looks like dirt with patches of shit on it. Oh, those are trees."

"The Akronian people have adapted to living in such harsh conditions like this. I am sure you can tell it's hot with very little rain. The will to survive is the key to making it here."

"In this hell hole? A fly couldn't survive here."

"I learned most of my abilities in battle here. Yet before we take another step, I must tell you this. These people don't like you or the city that worships you. Stay close to me and don't give anyone weird looks."

"All right, darling."

"And stop calling me that."

"Okay, darling."

Julius and Serena approached the gates of Akoran, a city fashioned out of seemingly nothing. The buildings were made of a mixture of sandstone and brick. The men wore robes and the women covered themselves, save for the head area. As they walked into the city, they were instantly met, especially Serena, with cold eyes. There were merchants lined along the streets, selling items from jewels to food and clothing. "Halt!" said a man approaching them. He was bald, with a sword on his side. He was shirtless, with only a loin cloth covering his groin area and coming midway down his legs. His skin was a shade darker that the desert sands and he had a scar across his chest.

"Obed," said Julius. The man shook his hand and withdrew his sword; a few more men walked up, swords drawn.

"What is this whore doing here in sacred land on sacred ground?"

"She is no longer a threat," said Julius.

"That's crap!" said one of the men. "This woman takes her monthly period out on people trying to survive. She turns lands barren and tries to take away our customs. As long as she lives, she is a threat."

The Perfect Portrait

"Trust me, Obed. You know I would never lie to you. In fact, I will show you." Julius withdrew his blade and held Serena's arm.

"Hey, wait a minute, you ass!" Serena yelled. Julius held her, despite her trying to get away. He took her arm and made a small cut. "Ouch, you bastard!" A small cut was made and out trickled blood. He then turned her around.

"See? She bleeds, she hurts, and she is wingless."

"Her eyes are still black," Obed said.

"Want one to go with them?" Serena said. Julius pulled her back. Obed walked up to her, his eyes meeting hers.

"Listen, bitch! I don't care if you bleed gold or shit diamonds. I will cut your head off here in front of Julius and feed your body to the buzzards. You are in our world now and you will know your place!"

"And you will know some mouthwash, man," Serena said. "Phew!"

Obed went to grab Serena, but Julius held him back with his free hand. "Save it, Obed," he said.

"What should we do with her?" Obed asked.

"Put the bitch to work," said one man.

"Don't worry. I know what to do. To your post, men," Julius said. The men and Obed held back.

"We are watching you," Obed said.

"Hey, if you guys want a show…" Julius silenced Serena before she made even more enemies.

"That's enough, woman," he said.

Julius walked Serena through the city, the eyes watching. "Where are we going?" she asked.

"The king resides in the Hall of Brevity up there. Show respect as you walk in."

"Fine, but tell the guards I want my feet rubbed when we get in." Julius ignored the request as they approached the Hall.

The place was quite grand in such a harsh environment. Its walls were made of smelted gold from the Isha Mountains three hundred miles to the north. The people of Akoran believed precious metals were one of the few everlasting things in the world. To build a civilization that relied on the earth would result in stability. As long as the earth lives, so will the village. Their leader, King Shikam, was nearly in the middle of his waning years. He was a fit man for most of his life and came to lead the people of Akoran quite well. Under his reign, the people came to amass wealth not known to many kingdoms of its era. It was an epicenter of commerce, trade, and manufacturing. The king saw to it that only the mightiest kingdoms survived. In time, he led conquests to the former regions of Dulban, Simara, and Ekish, now all owned by the capital of Akoran. King Shikam's most fabulous quote set the stage for Akoran's foundation and its people's survival:

> *Let your fates be left to the whim of God's and your toils unnoticed. Lead yourself blindly, hoping an angel will give you back your sight. Hold true to your blind faith and fail. As for my people, we will forge our own destiny. We are the true rulers. This world was created by the whim of one man but will be ran by the fires of many!*

It was a philosophy that King Shikam lived by. He also believed that people were to first show respect to themselves. "One who cannot serve himself cannot serve all," he said. Men were to provide and set examples of leadership. Women were to nurture and respect their bodies, which is why they were mostly covered.

It was in this that Julius received the foundation of his nature, and it was in this place where he would gain respect. The entrance to the opulent palace was guarded by a group of guards. Upon seeing Julius and the "Dark One," as they called Serena, they instantly halted the duo. "What is the Evil One doing here?" the head guard demanded.

"I seek King Shikam," Julius said. "As for Serena, she poses no threat."

"The snake said the same to the rat as well. She will not soil hallowed ground."

"And you won't see the light of day again, asshole!" Serena said.

"She is coming with us, now!"

The Perfect Portrait

Julius retrieved his sword and pointed it. "I told you she has no power! Now let us pass!" The guards withdrew.

"That woman is as foul as the serpent and vile as the waste from a pig! She will be your undoing!"

"This woman will not harm anyone," Julius said. "Step aside." As they proceeded, Serena hugged Julius.

"My hero," she said.

"Don't get too far ahead, Serena. We are her to meet King Shikam. No more, no less."

"As you say."

They entered the front hall, Julius having his sword drawn for anymore guards. "This place is still as beautiful and majestic as I remembered it. The grand hall, the rooms abroad. It truly is a king's seat of power."

"You would be suited for the role. Imagine being king of all this," Serena said.

"Don't be foolish, Serena. King Shikam may be aging, but he is still a respectable man a powerful one at that."

"Trust me, Julius. We could send this world into a new era. I mean, honestly, these people look like barbarians. Give me a chance and I will show you true leadership and a new plane of existence."

"Serena, you threatened to wipe this place before. The Akronian people would not take to you being over them too easily. Now enough of this. King Shikam awaits."

"Lead the way."

The hall leading to the throne room was decorated with paintings of the kingdom, it's people and King Shikam. He viewed the portraits not as bragging rights, but as a sign of an empire that was self-sufficient and reliant. As they approached the massive double doors, a few guards approached. The lead one, named Mulhan, came towards Julius. Mulhan was only twenty years old, quite young for someone wanting to be in the guard. Yet, from a young age, he wanted to serve a purpose. He admired King Shikam and his teachings of self-reliance, communitive right, and seizure of opportunity. He wanted to be in that presence. Even at a young age, he showed dedication to the Akroanian role of a man to provide, serve, and protect. As Shikam stated, these three things made a true man.

Mulhan was not as built as most men, but he made up for that in speed and loyalty. Shikam took great notice to this and offered him the position. A skinny, speedy seventeen-year-old, Mulhan swore his life to the people and their king that day and remained loyal. Even Obed, who was twice his age, commended such responsibility in one so young. Yet Mulhan had heard about Serena, who was not viewed too lightly by the Akronians.

"The Evil Whore," he said, approaching with four of his men. They were all clad in armor, spears and swords drawn. These were the king's top honor guard. These were knights. He approached Julius, a look of disgust on his face. "Julius, how dare you soil our sacred ground with the presence of this evil woman! She is vile, disgusting! The fact that you are next to her shows you have no honor! You're as filthy as she! Our king ordered you to bring a dead corpse before him, not a live snake!"

"Serena has no power anymore. She lost them at the hands of her own hate in the Forgotten Ruins. I assure you, she poses no harm. She even bleeds."

"If you cut off a serpent's tail, it's still a serpent. If a liar loses his tongue, he's still a liar, and if a coward puts on armor, he's still a coward. I should end this whore right now myself since you don't have the courage. You're a disgrace to what a man should be!"

"Don't bother with Julius, Mulhan," said the guard next to him, who was twice his size. "The slut probably gave him some action and now he's like a puppy getting some love." The other guards snickered.

"This woman is your wife?" Mulhan asked.

"Why, yes!" Serena said, smiling. "I must say being married to a knight has so much prestige to it. He saved me from being attacked and gazed upon my lavish body!"

"Serena!" Julius yelled.

"You slept with this snake?"

The Perfect Portrait

"Oh, yes! Being alone in the woods can do something to such a young lovestruck couple!"

"This is disgusting!" Mulhan said. "You best leave before I kill you both."

"We won't," Julius said. Mulhan and his men pointed their weapons.

"I am not playing, Julius! Leave or have more blood spilt on these floors."

"No, it's more like leave or have your intestines ripped out and choked with them, you pompous little shit-eating bastard of a child!" Serena screamed.

Mulhan and his men prepared to strike. The door the king's room opened and more of the king's men appeared. "You six! In here! Now!"

The six of them walked into the throne room, King Shikam waiting on his throne, obviously angry. They stood before him like kids in front of a parent. "Julius, what is the meaning of this?" said the king. "I sent you to rid us of dirt, not drag it into our kingdom!" Serena looked to Julius.

"Oh, so you were going to kill me, huh? You low-life son of a—"

"Silence! You are in my presence now, wench!"

"Sir, if I may speak?" Julius said.

"It better be good! Go ahead."

"I did not kill her because I wanted to bring her here. I think it would be wise to put her to use. Make the snake work for you. Killing her outright would not do much justice. Humiliate the snake, make it see just how powerless it is."

"What?" said Serena. "You ass…!" The guards held Serena's hands behind her back.

"Sir, the snake can be made to work for us. We are the Akronians, and conquest is in our blood! Let us conquer this snake as it once did many others."

"He's lying!" Mulhan yelled. "He's been to bed with her and he's covering for her!"

"I am not. All I am proposing is the servitude of her."

"Sir, Julius is suggesting we allow the serpent into our home which could doom us all!"

"Hmmm," said King Shikam. "Is this true, Julius?"

"Yes. She lost her powers in the Forgotten Ruins. I witnessed her powers being drained by a child." The other guards started murmuring.

"Really now? Is this true, snake?"

"Yes," said Serena. "I was attacked by the little bastard. I lost my power and begged knight dickhead to kill me, but he wouldn't. He told me I was better off earning my way in life."

"And where is the child now, Julius?"

"We don't know, sir. I told it to leave Serena be and it disappeared."

"Hmm."

"Sir, I think it would be a good idea to check the surrounding area," Mulhan said. "See if Julius and the serpent are trying to play us for fools."

"I assure you I am not, sir," Julius said.

"An intriguing argument. Do we know what this child looks like?"

"No, sir. It's hard to explain. Let me ask if Serena had her powers, she would not be so easily restrained now. The fact that she is still grounded with no wings is proof enough."

"Enough. Mulhan, you and your men take the fallen bird to a cell. Julius, you and I need to talk. By the way, I will have my decision when I am finished with her so keep an ear on standby."

"Yes, sir," Mulhan said. Serena gave Julius a wink as she was escorted out.

King Shikam shook his head. "Julius, what in the hell is this all about? Your orders were clear: kill her. You know of all the people in this kingdom, I viewed you the closest. You showed all the attributes and then some. Do you remember what you told me that day awhile back?"

"A true leader sticks by his decisions no matter what," Julius said.

"It wasn't that you told me that but you looked me dead in the eye. I respected you for that, as a man. You said you would do as I asked and put the greater good above your own needs. You think the fact that Serena is your wife excuses the duty or the fact that she caused several to go without? No, if she were my wife I and I did that, I would have her head on a platter. Being a woman with an alluring body does not excuse what she has done. And you want me to allow her to be in the same place as our people? Our children? She's not the woman you married, Julius! Let me tell you something. Maybe in another world, people sit idly by and hold their hand out, waiting for the angels to give them just that, a handout! Governments sit idly by and watch the masses starve and walk blindly, telling them everything is fine. You told me about a world where children pray to empty air hoping for a brighter tomorrow. I see my people and how they pave the way today. We built our heaven by our own works, and we do what we have to. Not to just survive but thrive! And you think I am going to allow some rogue woman to soil what I and my people have worked for? I am not buying the angel crap! I am not a majority of your world who hope when they can be the hope. My people will not bow to nothing and expect everything. I am not that kind of king. You can pray for change all you want. I am and the people of Akoran are the change! She will put to death, and you will be stripped of your title. That is what's best for the people. Also, you will be the one to put her to death, as punishment for defying orders."

"Sir, I can't," Julius said.

"Refuse and not only will she be killed but you as well. My decision is final. Now get out of my sight!"

. . .

"This is bullshit!" Serena yelled. "Get your fucking hands off me!" Mulhan watched as his men tossed Serena in the dark, dank, musty cell. The halls of the gallows were dimly lit at best.

"Julius can't get you out of this prison," Mulhan said, a chuckle following.

"I swear you will pay for this!"

"Yeah, yeah. Let's leave the bitch to rot, guys. King Shikam ordered a special occasion for tomorrow." The guards left Serena in her cell. She was furious beyond belief.

"This is bullshit! I swear if I had my sword…! Damn it! This is not how my portrait was supposed to be! My angel friends have deserted me. Broun's fat ass is gone! Shit!"

Serena could hear footsteps approaching. She prepared for another verbal lashing. Then she saw it was Julius. "Julius! Thank the heavens! Please tell me you worked out something." Julius hung his head low, silent. "What is it?"

"King Shikam would not hear me out. He's agreed, no, decided to have you killed at first light." Serena felt her heart sink.

"What? No! You're lying!"

"Serena, I am serious. He wants me to kill you in front of everyone."

"You will not, you foolish bastard! I am Serena Vega! Creator of this world, leader of angels and men, and bitch beyond and bitch! I will not be put to death!"

"Serena, listen! Your pride isn't worth shit now!"

"It's all I have! No, you can't do this! There's got to be something we can do."

"I am not the one who's about to die."

"You let me die and I swear on our son's life, I will haunt you until the day you rot just like my father!"

"It's over, Serena."

"Fuck it is! You have connections."

"No one here will help me."

"Dumbass, I mean connections from above. You can get Broun to get me out of here. Can't you see, Julius? They are keeping us from our son. He's lost out in a dark world, walking blind. Do this for me. Do it for him. I didn't have my mom and dad. Give him a chance to enjoy a family. Wouldn't you do anything for family?"

"Serena, I…"

"Please, please!"

"Serena, this could get us both killed."

"Julius, there is something you must know."

"Yes, Serena?"

"When we were in the woods that night. I dreamed of us. Our family. Imagine living in elegant life being an angel, her knight, and son, a prince in the making. People respected us. They envied us. We were their light. I promise you something good is coming and I want us to enjoy it as a family. Aren't you tired of fighting? Don't you want to be in charge instead of taking orders? DON'T YOU WANT A FAMILY?"

The Perfect Portrait

Julius was shocked at the change in Serena's voice at the end of that sentence. His heart started to race. "Trust me, Julius, I will show you how a world is truly supposed to be ran. Do this for me and I will get our son back. I will paint a perfect portrait and I will be all your and only yours. Do this for destiny!

Chapter 15

Serena's Christening

Julius stood there, beside himself, not knowing what to do. He knew what his duty was. He knew that he was supposed to end her. Yet, he hesitated, wanting so badly to believe his wife, whom he had met in the halls of his art gallery in a world so distant, could be saved. He missed hearing Serena laugh innocently. He missed that beautiful red sweater she would wear to presentations. But most of all, he missed the joyous look she and he wore that day they found out she was pregnant with their son, Jay. He had tried so hard to keep back the seeds of hate Serena had planted in her own heart. Yet, now, the recent events were the thunderstorm, and the seeds were sprouting.

"Come on, Julius," Serena said. "Do we have a deal?"

"This just feels wrong, Serena," he said.

"It feels wrong because you are just like I used to be, loyal to the world. Trying to fight for the approval of others. I wanted so badly for the world to approve of me. I painted the most innocent of portraits. Children playing, families getting together. I showed society a portrait I thought they would love. Yet, inside, I felt empty. I felt alone. Then, my trip to England showed me a different light. The angel holding her child was what I wanted. I wanted to paint my very own family portrait. Yet, I needed a hero, a man whom I could look up to. That's when I saw you. You were charismatic, bold, to the point, yet you worked with me to become the best. I wanted so badly to repay you, but I knew money wasn't the answer. Then I found out after we married I was pregnant with Jay, our son. I was so happy for us, our family. The proud look you wore on your face was priceless. We had done something together, yet when he died, a part of me died with him. I was broken on the inside and pushed everyone away, even you. You were only trying to help me. Yet my rage would not allow me to forget. I went into the darkest recesses of my mind and thought, what if it didn't have to end like this? What if I could undo it? My answers led me back to England, where I met a woman in Darbyshire. The woman who could undo even the twisted hands of death. I met this woman and told her what I wanted. I wanted my son to live, to enjoy life, but this would come at a cost.

"She told me she could do it, but it would require more than just a soul for a soul. In doing this, I inadvertently linked mine and Jay's forever. He lives because I live. I finally took the angelic form to show a manifestation of justice in its ultimate form. I would create a new world with order and wipe away all the pain. In doing this, I would create a heaven worth believing in and you and I would have our son. This is why I asked this of you, young knight. They want to end our dreams. Please don't let them do this."

"You realize what you have done, Serena. I just have a bad feeling about this."

"That's doubt, Julius. Don't let it come between our family."

"If I do this, promise me you will never hurt again."

"I promise. I will undo all this and can to any place as a family. Paris, France, sure would love us."

"Okay, Serena. I will do this, but only for our family. Will you be okay until I get back?"

"Yes, my love. I will." Julius left to go summon Broun. Serena smiled, a glint of evil in her eyes. "That's right, Julius. Thinking you could protect people; you just sealed the fate of so many souls. You will in the end, just as I have had so much blood on your hands. You will see what a perfect portrait looks like."

The skies were clear that evening as Broun flew through them. "Such joy," he said, gazing upon the sun shining brightly in the distance. He looked across the landscape and saw a shining flash of light coming from the shoreline.

The Perfect Portrait

"Hmm." He flew closer and realized it immediately. "That's the light from the Sword of Life. That's Julius!" He flew down to the location where he was standing. "Julius!" he said, walking over to him. "I saw you summoned me."

"Yes, I did. Did you deliver the news?"

"To Vega? Yes, yes! Although I am an archangel, I still love delivering good news among people. How is Serena doing?"

"Not good. In fact, she is going to be put to death tomorrow."

"What? Oh my! Did she do something?"

"No, not this time. I told you to lead her to me, which you did. Yet I was supposed to end her, but I couldn't. The people of Akoran, of course, met us with resistance, and the king ordered her death by my blade."

"Oh my, that's horrible! Even if Serena could be such a hmmm…"

"Bitch."

"Yes! She still was one of the few friends I ever had, and she did call me fat more than once."

"I know. What I need is a favor of you."

"Yes. Of Course!"

"Help me get her out. I surveyed the land and a few miles away is the village of Malesh."

"But sir, that's the village of once evil rituals!"

"I know, trust me. But it provides cover until I can get us both out of here. Serena's mortal and I carry the Sword of Life and light. We will be safe. For such a bold country, even Akorans don't go near it. It's the perfect cover."

"Don't forget, Serena may absorb the negative energy. She did orchestrate much destruction."

"I will keep watch on her. Don't worry."

"Julius, I really admire most of your decisions, but this…"

"Trust me, Broun."

"All right, but just remember what you're asking. A wise man once said some things are better off gone. So, how did you get out of Akoran?"

"I have my ways in and out. Serena is being held in the gallows in the palace. How will you get in?"

"First off, it's 'we,' not just me. Secondly, with me being an archangel, does it even beg the question? Get back in and I will meet you there."

"All right."

Julius went into the city through the back entrance, making sure to avoid detection. Luckily, the Akronians believed in sleep, and some of the guards were lazy. He saw Broun at the lower entrance of the palace. He beckoned for Julius with his hand. Quickly, Julius ran over to meet him. "Do you have a key?"

"No, I don't."

"No problem." He grabbed Julius and simply teleported them both to Serena's cell.

"Broun!" Serena said.

"Shh!" Broun said. "We can do reunions later. Julius and I are getting you out of here."

"Wait, won't they notice she's gone?" Julius asked.

"I will explain shortly. I actually did some talking with a fellow angel of mine. I anticipated this, just not the cursed village. She has agreed to come and take Serena's place. She's the got the eyes, hair, and everything."

"Enough chit chat! Let me out of here!"

"Okay, you two, touch my hand."

Serena reached through the bars and touched Broun's left hand, while Julius grabbed the right. Just like that, all too easy for an angel. The three of them stood outside the gates of Akoran. Serena smiled. She was free now, free to explore, free to reign. "The smell of that place was horrible! Yet it matters not. Now, Broun, tell me who this angel is that agreed to take my place."

"Why, Serena, that angel is you," Broun said. Serena looked puzzled.

"I don't understand. I am here fool."

"Let him finish, Serena." Julius said.

"When you went into the Forgotten Ruins and the room with the paintings."

"Oh, yes. I remember. That so-called innocent version of myself," Serena said.

"You thought you killed her, but you didn't."

"What do you mean? I stuck my sword right into that bitch. She's dead."

"She isn't," Julius said.

"You apparently failed to see why she was there. She represented the good that I felt was still in you. Being the owner of an art museum, I was keen to spotting potential in people. Some people had it, while others wasted it. I saw you were going through an inner struggle as your paintings depicted. While some did not get the message, I did. Yet there was one thing I noticed, and it was this: anyone can do anything. Any child can pick up a pencil, scribble some drawings, and call it art. Yet few truly have a passion for something. I felt that an artist's worth shouldn't be measured by the words 'pay to the order of' but in the amount of effort they truly put into something, with each painting, a part of you was instilled, a part of that intrigued me, and I am a man hard to intrigue."

"Aww, thank you."

"Now, Serena, I think we should find Jay," Broun said. "Forget the power and focus on the true treasures."

"He's right, Serena," Julius said. "This is our chance to rebuild our family."

Serena stood there, laughing.

"You're right," she said. "This is our chance to rebuild. My chance for revenge on those assholes for throwing me a piss-scented cell. I told you two I am nobody's bitch."

"Stop this foolishness, Serena. Forget the damn past and move forward!"

"I will move forward, but there is a score to settle first."

"Broun, get us out of here."

"I can't force Serena to do anything, sir," Broun said. "Humans have free will and I can't force her to stop this."

"Serena, let's go." Julius reached for her arm.

"Hell, no!" she said, snatching it away. "You have led me like a dog on a leash since we left that forgotten shit hole! No! It's time for me to take back what is mine! It is time to create a work of art!"

Sumurka Village Teaching

Without a body to reside in, hate is just a word. Without a mind to corrupt, hate is just a word. Without a soul to tarnish, hate is just a word. Without any action behind it, hate is nothing. We can be slaves to emotions or masters of them. The choice is yours.

Chapter 16

An Evil Emerges

The light had not been kind to his soul. The sun's rays seemed to burn into his very being. Despite the fact that this entity, this being of pure evil held a powerful sword and a bitter heart, the light still hurt him. Yes, it was he, who resided in the mind of a woman, only to twist it. He, who lived in her heart, only to corrupt it. He, who coursed through her veins, only to turn her blood black. He was at home in her body for more than three decades until the light shined that fateful day.

He was dry, cracked, and on the edge of oblivion. Blisters had formed all over his body, often bursting, allowing puss to drench him like a foul rain. He smelled of filth, bile, and the lowest waste possible. Without a body to reside in, he was nothing. For something that had existed since one man killed another, he was powerless now. The beauty of the world had cast him out like an angel out of heaven. He wandered over this new world; a world where flowers bloomed brightly and people prospered. Yet, he still remained for his host, who still held some longing for him like a lover waiting, hoping for their better half to show. "T-this sword!" the vile boy said, straining to drag it. "Why the hell is it so fucking heavy?"

He had dragged this sword, whose blade was as tall as he and fashioned from the purest mix of steel, gold, and silver and a blade as black as night. He carried it over countless worlds, not being noticed by anyone for he had no purpose. He stopped for a moment, catching his breath. Although he had no eyes, he could still sense, in his mind, something was near. Through the heat and dry air, he could feel the cold yet gentle kiss of his "mommy," the woman who had birthed him. "She is close. Why do I feel I still feel the burning of the sun? The air should be getting cooler."

In his mind, he failed to see that what he represented would never go away. Even if the sun was not shining, it was the light of a prosperous world that burned him. The dark will always hate the light. "I sense you are close, Mommy. You owe me, bitch!"

Broun stood there, shocked. He could see Serena was hellbent on getting her powers back. He saw darkness would be setting in soon. "If you truly wish this, Serena, then I won't stop you. It's your call."

"That's what I like to hear," she said. "My call!"

"Julius, will you stay behind? I mean, are you staying behind?"

"I am in this to see my son again," he said. "Even if Serena has given up, I haven't."

"Given up? Smh! You mean given in!" Serena said. "Aww, look at the light slowly fading away and the alluring embrace of the night approaches."

"As you wish, Julius," Broun said. "I must go. Darkness and I don't get along too well. If you need me…"

"I know. Thank you, Broun." He nodded and flew off. Julius turned to see Serena smelling the air and taking it all in.

"Now, where is that village I seek?" she asked.

"Don't be hasty when you know you've screwed yourself. We could have ended this charade, Serena."

"No, you wanted to end it. I was just playing along. Now, before we continue, I am getting out of these peasant clothes. The people in Akoran really don't even dress like this, so you fucking lied to me. I hate liars." Serena took off the clothes and stood there, naked. "Now, as I once said before, lead the way, darling!"

The village of Malesh was desolate, its buildings and few huts worn and decayed. There wasn't a single soul left. Maybe it was better that way. Three centuries ago, it was a thriving village that specialized in occult magic. Rituals to gods, goddesses, and even the elements were performed. The people here believed that darkness was not a bad thing but something to be embraced. They believed that the evil in the human heart served just as much as the good. The leader of the people was a woman named Lady Mihari who was skilled in ritualistic and dark magic.

At one time, it was rumored that she took a newborn infant and slit it from its neck down, saying that sacrifice was needed for its soul. The mother ironically agreed, for she was ill and was unable to care for the child. It wasn't also surprising to say Lady Mihari also condoned some of the most disgraceful acts. During the warm, humid summer months, she initiated what be known as "Mitako," or the ceremony of shared bodies. The villagers would make sexual advances among themselves and share themselves with each other. Lady Mihari would watch, her eyes rolling in the back of her head and chanting in strange tongues. She offered herself to others and became as such to others. "We must appease the skies, for we are to procreate and spread our seeds on this land so that it may be fertile for our children," she would say.

Such were the practices of this village, and such were its people. Yet their customs had drawn attention from the Akronians to the north. They viewed the people of Malesh as sinful and animalistic. Under Shikam's rule, he ordered that every man, woman, and child be killed. "We will rid the land of this filth and rebuild!" he said. Yet even the Akronians, as strong as they were, had to respect the fact that there was something more than just Lady Mihari watching over these people. Ironically, it was not an act of man that laid this village to waste. No, it was simply an act from above. That act was Serena.

She surveyed the area as Julius watched. She seemed to embrace the foul air that still permeated even after all these years. "Now this," she said, "this is one portrait I am capable of. These people didn't offend me with what they did. It was who they worshipped, which wasn't me. I tried to make my presence known but they attributed it to their gods. There is only one and can be only one."

Julius shook his head. Here he saw his wife turning into a shell of her former self. She wasn't innocent. She didn't laugh, or even say she loved him. He thought what happened in the Forgotten Ruins would have sparked something, but it only fueled the fire that was already burning. "This place is evil, Serena," he said.

"What you call evil, I call beautiful," she said. "Oh, how the air caresses my body and makes me feel whole. I must say this is where I will be reborn, like a phoenix, you know?"

"A phoenix is a heavenly bird. How dare you compare yourself to something majestic!"

"Oh, Julius. You just don't understand. I have put that part of my life aside to get here. I will show you what the real picture looks like. You should consider it an honor to bear witness to this. I might even have a job for you."

"Don't patronize me, woman! You are not the woman I married!"

"No, I am better than the woman you married. I am beautiful! Perfect! I am truly… Serena, the Vengeful."

"Serena, if you are planning something, I will have no choice but to stop you."

"You and what army? You lied to the king of Akoran, so you are no better than me. To be honest, you never were. I led you along, making you believe I was so sweet and innocent; a lost lamb who was looking for a shepherd. Well, that seemed to have worked out. And now, here I am, about to become whole again."

"What do you mean?"

"You can't feel it? You can't feel him?"

"What? Him? You don't mean…?"

Serena pointed and Julius turned to look. In the twilight, where the last vestiges of light gave birth to darkness, a warped boy approached. He foamed at the mouth, his eyes crying blood. His hair was parched and missing in some areas. His skin was missing in places, revealing weakened bones. "See, Julius? This is why my eyes stay black. I am consumed by this, this is so beautiful feeling. I will offer my body to this child I birthed and make it mine!" Julius grabbed his sword.

"Not this time, old man!" the thing said. It used Serena's sword to halt Julius's movements.

"What the hell is this, Serena?" he asked. Serena walked over to Julius and rubbed her hand across his face.

The Perfect Portrait

"Oh, darling, you are so blind. Thinking you could save me. You have been the most useful entertainment and I thank you, but I have a portrait I would like for you to see, a perfect one in the making!"

"You bitch!" Julius yelled.

"You haven't seen a real one yet." Serena walked back over to the thing and picked it up. "What do you want my beautiful baby?"

"I want to be a part of you, bitch!" the thing screamed.

"Oh, but you have something of mine."

"You can take your sword back. Just allow me to become one with you again, Mother."

"That sounds just so…perfect. No, divine! See Julius? Our son has returned to us."

"You're sick!" Julius yelled.

"No, what is sick is how you didn't have the balls to stop what you saw coming. How pathetic! Now, I will show you what a true painting is." She looked back at the child.

"How do you want me to do this, Mother?" the thing said.

"Oh, son! Come into my being, for I hunger for what you have to offer!"

"I am much obliged, Mother. Here I come!"

Julius watched in horror as the thing opened Serena's mouth and became an almost black oozing substance. It forced its way into her, spreading all over her body. She wore a look of joy on her face as this putrid, rotting liquid re-entered her. As it finished, it left Serena drenched in a foul, putrid black liquid. Her hate had returned. Julius was shocked by what he saw. Serena's wings had come back, sprouting from back, and she now held her sword again. Yet she didn't look the same as before. Her face was now covered in black, pulsing veins that made her look like someone who was truly possessed.

Serena looked at Julius and smiled. She walked over to him and looked into his eyes. He was now feeling what she had felt that moment back in the ruins. She opened her mouth and vomited black bile on him, the touch of it burning him. Julius fought back the urge to scream, yet he could feel the pain.

John Paul Shuman Jr.

"Hello, Father," the thing said through Serena. "*Heaven's light can't help you now, huh? It's fucked up how you never really got a chance to smash this bitch. Oh, well! I will be giving her some, how should I say, heavenly loving!*"

The voice receded and Serena spoke again. "See, Julius? This is what I wanted all my life. To be in control, to be god of my own world. Oh, you're in pain? Well, as a token of my appreciation for letting me use you, I will spare you from death. It's kind of my payback to you." She took her sword and used its infused magic to heal Julius. "See? Even darkness can have healing factors. Oh, and before I forget, let me take that sword. We wouldn't want you trying to get rid of me, now, would we?" Serena reached and grabbed Julius's sword. "Ah, light and dark. You know, it's a beautiful parody. Oh well, what to do with this? Oh, that's right!"

Serena held the blade in the middle and said the fateful words:

"*From the bowel of shadows of came the children of light. We now return the light back to its mother, the bearer of all. Ashes to ashes, destroy the light I must. To the ground you go and to it become rust.*"

The blade corroded under Serena's touch and fell to the ground, dissipating in the sand. "Now that's done, there is work to do. I will keep you around until I lay my brush down."

"You won't get away with this," Julius said.

"Sadly, darling, I already have."

. . .

"*The sea calls to me*
The ocean waves abroad
Waves pounding against the shore
Fish biting the end of my rod!"

The Logger's voice echoed with the waves that night. Wandering Leaf was listening peacefully, Sootshire was eating fish, and Catalina was looking over the side of boat in the distance. *Will someone please shut him up?* she thought. They

The Perfect Portrait

were close to shore, maybe another fifteen miles. Catalina noticed Wandering Leaf had been quite cheerful, even laughing with Sootshire and the Logger.

"We're getting close, you guys," the Logger said.

"Excellent," Sootshire said.

"Thank the fish abroad," Catalina said. "I am sure you're happy, huh, Wandering Leaf?" She saw he was crouched on the deck, his hands up to his head. "Wandering Leaf?"

"Hey, son, you okay?" the Logger asked.

"Wandering Leaf, what's wrong?" Sootshire asked. The boy continued to hold his head.

"It's not good," he answered.

"What's not good?" asked the Logger.

"It feels like something is stabbing my mind. It hurts!"

"What the hell is going on?" Catalina demanded.

"Oh no!" Sootshire said.

"What, rat? Spill it!"

"It's just like before. Serena has returned."

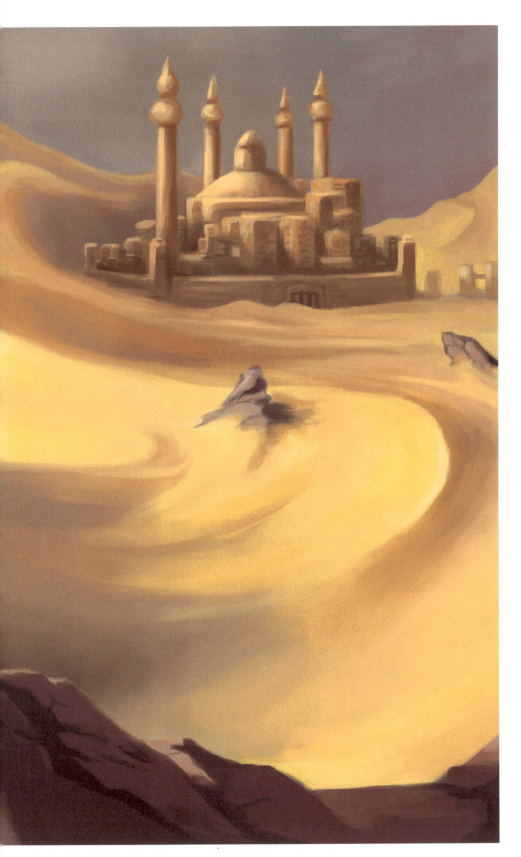

PART 5

A Philosopher's Question

There is great strength in a man's faith. His ability to see through the darkest moments when all hope seems lost. I have found that, although resilient, man lacks that strength in tough times. Faith is meant not to be questioned but embraced. The city of Rhodam has found such lost strength. We have built our existence on the mercy and grace of our beloved angel, Serena. To her we give thanks for this day and more days to come. Long live our Angel!

Simon
Priest of St. Michael's Cathedral

Chapter 17

The Quest for Truth

I have spent many days and nights pondering the concept of leaving my fate in the hands of another. The people of this providence, this city, believe in such a notion as blessings from the sky. I am only seventeen years old and already I question the future of this world. My concerns, to be more specific, are not with "will Serena do this" or "have we wronged her?" My concern is the fate of a people willing to offer their very existence to the whim of this so-called "Goddess on High."

My family, the Ruthmans, live in the village southeast of Rhodam. The village of Eden, not to be confused with the famous Garden. It is a simple village that lends its success and self- sufficiency to the will of its people. Yet even they ultimately give thanks to "her." My family consists of my father Milton, my mother Anna, and my ten-year-old little sister Mephilia, but everyone calls her Phyllis. My parents were hard-working people. My father had implemented a better way to care for the livestock in Eden. He suggested that insulation was needed to keep livestock warm in winter. As for my mother, she suggested that women should be able to hold a seat on the council, but her request was denied. I wonder if this Serena was aware of this injustice.

I, Neacen Ruthman, was different from the rest of the people in my village, my family included. For me, it seemed an odd place, any place to always give thanks to a being that had no involvement in its progression whatsoever.

John Paul Shuman Jr.

The foundations of places just as this were built on the wills of men, so why was the will of a higher being needed?

I spent a good majority of my youth forming theories as to the existence of this deity. I narrowed my theory to what I called "The Three Questions of Everyone's Mind." What is the will of a higher being? What is the will of men? Finally, what is the will of the world as a whole? I obviously didn't present my questions to anyone in Eden, for I knew they would fall on deaf ears. It was at that point I decided that my questions would be better posed in the heart of Rhodam itself. Added to that fact I was a complex child and the simple life wasn't for me.

At thirteen I did something well beyond my time. I decided to head for Rhodam on my own accord. I told my parents my reasoning was that I had many questions that Eden just could not answer. They understood and I was proud of how they had raised me on virtue. I told them I would keep in touch, nevertheless.

The city of Rhodam was in stark contrast to my humble beginnings. A city of a million souls, whose life revolved around that one word: faith. It was the central seat of power in the continent of Shrinedom, both in religion monetary funds. "A place where a poor man could find both wealth and hope," as the rumors did say. It was a city that had built its foundation on these two principles, and a city where disobedience was not tolerated.

I was not looked upon fondly as I entered this city of immense religious rule and prestige. This city, whose façade was laced in brick and scripture, coupled with a few wealthy families, did not take too well to a "peasant child" as I was deemed. Not that I cared what a few zealots thought of me. I was here for a reason, and being a fashion statement wasn't one of them. As I surveyed the city, I noticed that there were statues of an angel just about everywhere. They were on street corners, and, of course, at the churches. These people obviously had, for lack of a better term, a hard-on for this woman. The sight was pathetic, I must say.

Yet for now, I have spoken enough of this woman with chicken feathers. My first priority was, of course, finding a place of residence, which wasn't easy considering all I had were the clothes on my back. So, as such, with no money, finding work became foremost. Being as how I wasn't dressed in "holier than thou" attire. It wasn't until I came to a home that had a sign on it that read as follows: "Wanted. Help for logging, sorting, and editing books. Pay is open for discussion."

I was intrigued by this. I knocked on the door and the man that answered did not look like he needed help. He looked to be in his late thirties, blond hair that was pulled back in a queue, an wore a green blazer, with matching pants and black shoes with gold buttons on them. This man needed help? "May I help you?" he asked.

"Yes. I am here about your sign you posted."

"You look like you are lost, child."

"Sir, I assure you I am smarter than my age my suggest."

"Hmm. I see. Come in."

Upon walking in, I saw that his house was littered with books. Although it did look nice, as far as the furniture was concerned. There were paintings of castles and himself writing something. Chandeliers hung from the ceiling, and there was even an elegant-looking clock on the wall. "Forgive the mess," he said. "It is not easy collecting and sorting all this, added to the work I do."

"You collected all these books?"

"Why, yes. I even have a few I have written and published. Yet I must say that being occupied by ROOTGOR can be a strain."

"ROOTGOR?"

"Religious Order of the Government of Rhodam. It is no lie that the most powerful weapons in the history of man are faith and wealth. The council oversees secular and monetary dealings. It sees to taxing both in Rhodam and in surrounding areas. Basically, it's the heart and soul of the providence. Why do you ask, by the way?"

"I am on a mission to find the meaning behind man's devotion to this Serena character and why men, how do I say, put all their eggs in one basket."

"Hmm. You're the only person I have known to question the existence of a higher being."

"I honestly don't see why man puts his fate in the hands of an entity, if it exists that could end it if it wanted. What I am saying is this: we should focus on our own abilities."

"You have a point, child. Yet in a city and providence such as this, you might as well be planning your own execution. Serena is Lord in this land. Yet to be honest, I have never seen her or any member of the Council."

"Then you are deluding yourselves."

"To be honest, Serena is nothing more than a marketing tool to the Council. Tell the people, you are power and this woman, who probably sits on clouds getting a heavenly makeover, is watching them. Now that's control."

"So you have doubts?"

"I do."

"Then why are you on the Council?"

"Money, child."

"That's a lame reason, sir."

"I beg your pardon?"

"You will be begging for a lot more if you stay on a council that follows a ghostly woman."

"I must say I take offense to that."

"The truth hurts, I must say, sir…"

"Call me Hamilton. Joshua Hamilton."

"Mr. Hamilton, I believe you question things just as I do. I think that you disagree with this 'Praise Serena' speech you've been given. I propose a theorem to you: why do men give thanks to an entity that had no involvement in its affairs? Why do men see this entity in troubled times? All of man's troubles are earthly, from hunger to being poor to social unrest. To be honest, Serena couldn't care less about our toils. We, as intellectual beings, possess the powers to make our world better. Using Serena to get people to pay tithe and taxes to the council is hypocrisy at its worst."

"You strike an interesting point."

"Why should I ask a question you should have already posed to yourself? I am sorry I…no. I am not sorry. I will not work with blind sheep. Good day."

The Perfect Portrait

"Wait! You have presented a good point, young man. How would you like to work with me?"

"Why should I?"

"Because you seek answers and I know where the answers lie."

"I am not worshipping Serena."

"That's not what I mean. If you truly desire to see faith for what it is, walk with me into the lion's den."

I may have come from humble beginnings, but I was no fool. I told Mr. Hamilton I would go on this journey with him and that I was not in it for the money. I was simply looking for answers, but the first indication of a lie would end our arrangement. He gave me his word and I would hold him to that.

He first gave me a new attire, saying that in Rhodam, humble looks did not make for pleasant conversation. I asked him why was that the case and he said that in Rhodam, appearance was everything and a "peasant look" was a complete stain on a clean plate, as he put it. He showed me his wears and I decided on a white robe, a councilmen's robe. "Are you mad? You're not a member of the Council."

"I am seeking answers, and trust me, for even the sake of this, I will play the part. Get me in the door and I can handle the rest." Mr. Hamilton thought I was crazy. A boy from a simple village looking to join the Council after shortly being hired. I was not playing around.

In my new attire, I asked to see his collection of books, to which he obliged. "Are you sure you're okay sorting all this?" he asked.

"I will sort as I go. You collected and wrote some of these?"

"Why, yes. I found reading to be quite the hobby."

"Have you read *Edge of Divinity* by McSquire?"

"I am afraid I haven't. I have heard of it."

"It's a good read. You should look into it."

I looked through his collection and came across an interesting title. "*Letters to My Beloved*. By Joshua Hamilton."

"Hmm," I said.

"I wrote that when I was fifteen. I was actually courting a woman at the time."

"Gentleman caller, huh?"

"For lack of a better term, yes."

A knock came to the door. "Excuse me." I looked through more of his collection and saw that Mr. Hamilton really did have a thing for women in his youth. There were poems, love letters, and even trinkets. He came back into the room. "Something has come up at the Council Hall. I must make haste."

"Hold on. I am coming with you."

"Are you sure?"

"Of course. Let's go."

"Serena is Lord of this land, and the Council is her voice."

"What exactly does the Council do?"

"There are seven members on the Council, myself included. It mainly consists of wealthy men from the area. We see to the taxation of goods and the doings of the church."

"So it's like church and state."

"Yes."

"Shouldn't those powers be separate?"

"Not in Serena's eyes."

"Oh my goodness. Has Serena actually attended any meetings? I mean everyone here worships her of course."

"No, none us have seen her."

"So, you're following a voice you can't even hear? To be blunt, that is stupid."

As we approached the Council Hall, I saw that it had gates around the exterior. "Are the gates really necessary?" I asked.

"For them, yes," said Joshua.

Two guards approached us, both of them carrying swords at their sides. "Halt!" said one of them. "Who is this with you, Mr. Hamilton?"

"This is my cousin. I called him here a few days ago."

"Yes," I said. "My name is Nealen Dougan."

"Outsiders are not allowed inside the hall."

"It's been approved," Joshua said. The guards looked at each other.

"I am doing research with the Council," I said.

"All right, Mr. Hamilton. You two may proceed." They unlocked the gates, and we went towards the hall. I noticed a statue of Serena was on the front courtyard.

"I must say I hate lying like that," Josh said.

"Many people in this city have heard of my family," I said. "There was no way I would be getting in using my real name."

"The meeting room is on the second floor."

"Good. I am looking forward to hearing what urgency of this could be."

On the second floor was a room with six men of wealth. Religious text and documents concerning the affairs of the city as well as six men in coats gathered at the table. "You summoned me?" Joshua said.

"Yes," said the chairman. "Who is this with you?"

"My name is Nealon Dougan. I am a relative of Mr. Hamilton and I am doing research on the laws of Rhodam. I was hoping to gain some insight during this meeting. With this being the center of the providence and the holy center of Serena's proclamations, I find it worthy of my attention."

"I see, young man. Please sit."

"What is the concern?" Joshua asked.

"We have received word about the increase of tithe in the regional area."

"An increase in tithing? Who proposed this?"

"Need I say, Josh? Our records keeper here, Feldon, has received word from Serena herself."

Pure crap, I thought to myself.

"Serena has come forth with this?" Joshua asked.

"Yes," said Feldon. "She wants more to put into her works. She said that she will need more support from her followers to help mend broken matters."

"Matters such as?"

"The disagreements between the people of Rhodam and Akoran."

"That seems hard to do. The Akronians do not necessarily agree with our practices. Having the people of the providence pay more to the church to force two countries to hold hands? That seems odd."

"Do you doubt our Savior?"

"No, I don't. It's the issue of forcing ones will on another. The Akronians are not for that. I suggest we put the funding to improving conditions in Eden." The councilmen laughed.

"Really? That place?"

"Why, yes," I said. "I have visited that village, and the conditions are not up to standards."

"They eat, work, have their own system," said the chairman. "I don't see why more would be needed."

"Isn't it unjust that all of the providence isn't like Rhodam?" Joshua said. "For a society to thrive, there must be an equal distribution of wealth. The people of Eden should have the same privileges as Rhodam."

"Raising taxes and tithing here in Rhodam does nothing to benefit the continent as a whole," I said. "It's not a good consideration at all."

"To be so young, you know much about the affairs of the state," said the chairman.

"I taught myself," I said. "This proclamation is laughable at best." The councilmen looked at me, as well did Joshua. "What?"

"You might have just said too much," he said.

"If they and Serena don't like it, so be it."

Although my studies have lead me to many question, I have managed to come to a few conclusions. The first is that the Council had imposed the new legislation, thus meaning higher taxes and annexations in Akoran, as well as the province. It is no doubt that my family and others like them are feeling this burden. As for my meetings with the Council, only the voice of Joshua, whom I managed to speak some sense into, has kept me from a premature end, although he still plays to role of "Serena fanatic." Secondly, I have found no evidence of Serena's existence, yet many in Rhodam accredit the changing weather to her mood, if that ever made any sense. For the moment, I have not set foot in the Council Hall since

The Perfect Portrait

that day, save for some research under the Council's eye. I seek to learn more about Serena, yet I have hit a dead end. I need actual proof, yet for now it eludes me.

Neacen Ruthman

Chapter 18

Religious Resistance

The cool embrace of a dark night gave way to morning light. I awoke, my head still hurting. Outside, I could hear the birds of the ocean singing, and the sun being a welcome sight to my eyes. What had caused me to black out? I remember simply listening to the Logger singing, and then a sharp pain hit me and my pendants both felt warm. Did Serena have something to do with this? I wasn't completely sure, but it felt possible. Lately, the dreams have returned, and I struggle to sleep sometimes. The dreams of an abandoned church, a still world, still remain. Although I have come a long way since then, I feel like darkness is never too far behind.

Footsteps approached from upstairs on the deck. The Logger came into the room, the scent of fish on him. "Look who's awake," he said.

"Sorry I scared everyone," I said.

"No big deal, to me that is. Your girlfriend and Sooty were worried about you. Hell, she was yelling at me when you went out."

"Really? Wait, she's not my girlfriend." The Logger showed me the claw marks on his arm.

"She called me everything in the book and scratched me. She said if I didn't do something, she would kick my ass. Your lady is quite feisty to be her size. Hell, she even knocked Sooty off the boat twice."

"Again, she is not my girlfriend. Where are we?"

"We will hit shore in about fifteen minutes. Rest some more if you need to."

"No, I am ready to get up."

"Good. We all need to talk. I have us some breakfast ready."

"Thank you."

The smell of the ocean filled the air as I came to the upper deck. "Wandering Leaf!" Catalina yelled, coming and pouncing on me. She held me down with her paws.

"Good morning to you too," I said. Sootshire came over as well.

"You gave us quite a scare last night," he said.

"Yes, you did," Catalina said. "What was up with that?"

"Could you let me breathe?" I asked. She let me up and I got to my feet.

"What could be causing this?" Sootshire asked. "First you didn't want to eat, and then the event that happened last night."

"You scared me again," Catalina said. "First you act depressed and now this."

"I know it worries everyone," I said. "I am just as puzzled as everyone else."

"Please explain."

"How about we eat first," the Logger said, coming up with some fresh fish.

"We will talk and eat," Catalina said.

"Try not to get too comfortable. I can see the shore of Shrinedom up ahead. It looks a lot different than the last place."

"Considering there is a village nearby as well," Sootshire said.

"Ahem!" Catalina said, grabbing a piece of fish. "All right, kid, spill it!"

"It's hard to say actually," I said.

"Just say it, son," the Logger said. "You have no reason to hide anything."

"The world I am from is dull to say the least. Like the village we have been to, it's a simple place. You know, where everyone knows one another. I was cared for by a woman whom I came to believe was my mother, but she wasn't. I felt like an outsider in that world. I had no purpose, no self-esteem, nothing. Then one night I had a dream. In it, I was in this abandoned area with a church in the background. The area was cold and eerily silent. Then I heard a woman weeping in the background, her voice that I still hear now. When I awoke the next morning, I still remember that dream which was strange, considering I never really dreamed."

"Yeah, yeah," said Catalina. "What about the pendants around your neck?"

The Perfect Portrait

"These? The silver one was given to me by someone I don't know who it was. The second one is Serena's. The weird part is that when I feel something in the air, they get real warm, even hot, such as last night. I promised Serena's father I would give the angel pendant to his daughter."

"Wait a minute!" said the Logger. "That crazy bitch is his daughter?"

"Yes. Why?"

"I ferried Serena and her husband on my boat a while back. She was frisky and tried to flirt with me."

"I bet you liked that, huh?" Catalina asked.

"Her husband, Julius, was with her. There is no way I was falling for that."

"Serena and Julius, you say?" asked Sootshire.

"Yes. Why?" Sootshire's eyes widened.

"I will be damned."

"What?" I said.

"So the journals were true! Serena did marry!"

"What the hell?" Catalina said.

"No time for trivia!" Sootshire said. "We must make haste to Rhodam!"

"Hold it! I am not being the only one left in the dark here! Listen, rat, how do you know so much about this area?"

"I have been wondering the same," I said. "Since I came out about my involvement, you should do the same, Sootshire."

"We shouldn't have any secrets kept among us," the Logger said. "Spill it, Sooty."

"Can't this wait?" he asked.

"I am not moving until you talk," Catalina said.

"Me either," I said.

"Same here," said the Logger.

"As you wish," Sootshire said. "Wondering Leaf, do you remember the events that occurred in the woods?"

"Yes, I recall." I said. "It wasn't pleasant, but I remember it."

"I mean the woman that delivered the letter."

"No, I don't."

"That woman was Candice Vega, and her husband is the gravedigger you met when you first arrived." My eyes widened.

"Are you serious?"

"Yes. To be honest, this journey concerns you more than you could ever imagine. I have been down these same roads with the gravedigger Mitchell. We traversed these same roads and fought fairies in the Hallougen Woods, and even more. I know you for more than just a kid. I could tell from the moment I met you who you were and your ties to this entire thing."

"So what or who am I, Sootshire?"

"I cannot say right now. No, it's not my place to say. You need to hear it from someone closer to you. Now, if we are done sipping tea and chatting, we must find the researcher in Rhodam. A man named Neacen."

"You still have some talking to do, rat," Catalina said.

"All right, guys," the Logger said. "Let's move."

Sootshire, from the moment I met him, had a way of speaking that was almost cryptic. Every word, every detail, was always masking a deeper truth. I felt he also knew more about Serena, but I didn't question him at the moment. We came through the humble village of Eden, whose residents didn't take to Catalina very well. The Logger suggested that she buy some clothes and she swiped him, saying that a cat's body was pretty enough without human intervention. It was at this point that I realized that I had no funds, as neither did Sootshire or Catalina.

"How are we supposed to continue without any money?" I said.

"Don't worry about that," the Logger said. He reached into his pocket and pulled out a pouch and shook it.

"You son of a bitch!" Catalina yelled. "You had funds this whole time and you're just now sharing them? Is everyone hiding something these days?"

"A seafarer always comes prepared," the Logger said.

"Enough!" I said. "Let's just continue."

There was no denying the fact that they city of Rhodam was different from the other areas I had been to. It was a city of prestige, elegance, and a high devotion to Serena, as presented by the statues of her. "My, it truly is beautiful," Sootshire said.

"My home place is better," Catalina said.

The Perfect Portrait

"It never hurts to see the world," the Logger said.

"They have guards at a gate to the city?" I asked.

"Why, yes, they do," Sootshire said. "It won't be easy getting in. It is odd, though."

"What do you mean?" the Logger asked.

"Last time the gates were not here. I supposed a new law must have been put in place."

"Well, let's see what resistance awaits us here," Catalina said.

We walked up to the guards who stood in front of the gates.

"State your business here, you lot!" the first guard said, who was taller than his partner and stouter. His silver-plated armor appeared to bulge a little. Sootshire came to the front of us.

"Yes, we are here to see the researcher," he said. "It is very important," The two guards began to laugh.

"Don't be stupid!" said his slightly shorter yet equally stout partner. "You honestly believe we would let a raccoon, a naked freak girl, a peasant boy, and some guys who reeks of fish into the holy city? Get out of here!"

"Who are you calling a freak, you pig!" Catalina yelled.

"Calm it, Catalina," I said. "Listen, sir, I was sent here to deliver a pendant to Serena." The guards looked at each other.

"Are you taking us for fools, boy?"

"I am not lying. This angel pendant and letter in my possession have to be given to her."

"So step aside, asshole!" the Logger said.

"Would you look at that?" the first guard said. "They believe that just because they have Mr. Fisher here they can force their way through."

"How about I force my foot up your ass?" the Logger said. The guards withdrew their swords and held them on us.

"All right you four, you have seconds to be gone from my sight, or I will have you all taken in!"

"You think I am scared of your little toys?" Catalina said. The guard put his blade against her chest, and she swiped it away.

"That does it!" said the first guard. "You four are coming with us!"

"Like hell we are!" I said. The guards went to reach for us.

"Stop!" yelled a voice. The guards and us looked to see a boy, dressed in white robes, approaching the gate from inside the city. He wore glasses and carried a book in his hand. "Brutus, Casan, what is the meaning of this?"

"We caught these four scoundrels trying to get into the city, sir!"

"We have important matters here, you prick!" Catalina said. The young professor ordered the guards to open the gate.

"We will not allow them in!" said the second guard.

"Are you defying an order from a superior?" Dougan asked. "Let them in or I will report you two to the Council!"

The guards reluctantly withdrew their swords and allowed us in. Professor Dougan smiled as she saw the four of us, especially Sootshire. "It has been a while, Snowden," he said.

"Yes, it has," Sootshire said. "Fighting through fairies, babysitting these three mongrels. It takes a toll." Catalina swiped at the back of his head.

"Now, now, Snowden, you must learn that they deserve respect just as you do. No one is perfect, and my studies have shown me that. Who are your friends?

"I am the Logger."

"Catalina from Sumurka."

"I am Wandering Leaf," I said. Professor Dougan walked over to me and looked at me closely.

"Something about you seems different. I have never heard of anyone with that kind of name before."

"I don't know my real name," I said. "I am actually searching for Serena to deliver her something."

"The angel Serena? Interesting. I am currently doing a study on this hoddess on high that the city seems to worship."

"How has that been coming about?" Soothshire asked.

"Many dead ends until now," Professor Dougan said.

"Can't you just use your real name?"

"They know too much about my family in Eden. I couldn't risk compromising my own research."

"Another mask wearer," Catalina said. "Purrfect."

Chapter 19

Pardon

Professor Dougan kept looking at Catalina as we walked through the courtyard. "Why do you keep looking at me like that?" she asked.

"I have never seen anyone walking around in the nude before," he said. "It's quite intriguing to see."

"If you don't mind me asking, does anyone here know your real name?" I asked.

"Only the person I am staying with does, but that's because I have built a good standing with him."

"I can tell I won't be in good standing with these people," Catalina said. "They keep turning their heads. I know I am irresistible but really—"

"More like feisty," the Logger said.

"Shut up!"

"All right, you two," I said. "Professor Dougan…"

"For you three, counting Snowden already knows me, call me Neacen."

"Neacen, are there any rest pubs in the city, and I honestly need to change my attire."

"Grown tired of the homely look, young man?" Neacen asked.

"These were given to me by a close friend, and after trekking through villages, woods, and the sea…yeah."

"Ha, ha! I like you, young man. It's not often I come across a lot as unique as you four. There is plenty to wear at my residence. I am sure you're hungry as well."

"I'm fine with fish," the Logger, Catalina, and Sootshire said.

"Lately, we have been on a strict seafood diet," I said. "I am surprised I don't have fins growing from my body."

"Ha ha! It never hurts to change it up now and again. Fish was a delicacy back in my village of Eden. Mainly it was whatever was grown and harvested. Staying in Rhodam for four years has taught me somethings."

"Like how stuck up some people can be?" Catalina asked.

"Not all people are like that. Yet because of its reputation, Rhodams people tend to turn their nose up. I was met with similar resistance when I first came here. No one would talk to me. Then I inquired about a posting of a job as bookkeeper for the man I am living with now."

"You said you were doing research," I said. "May I ask about what?"

"It's several theories actually. The most prominent ones being the existence of this Serena that everyone worships. I have yet to find any evidence of her existence. I haven't seen her in dreams or anything. I have also questioned this insistence of man's will being a gift from a higher being. In no text, documents, or literature does it say that man was given free will by another being. If a divine being truly created man in their image, why are men so foolheartedly lost? Why can't man control life or death? In fact, the very text suggest that man is left to the will of gods and goddesses, helpless to help himself but more capable of destroying himself.

"Yet my research has hit dead ends, and the Council refuses to hear my arguments. They did impose higher taxes and tithing, which makes even my blood boil. My family and others like them back in Eden are having it rough, which is why I send my earnings to them."

"Then how do you live?" I asked.

"A good question, young man, with a very simple answer. I put faith in my works and myself. Being able to obtain knowledge is payment enough."

"I salute a man who provides for his family," the Logger said.

"The salute goes to you four. I am in no position to be vain. Yet let us go to my residence. Being out among so many lost souls does get to me after a while."

The Perfect Portrait

"Fish here we come!" Catalina purred.

Neacen's residence was quite the sight. It contained books upon books, paintings, antique artifacts, and a gorgeous living area. "Where is the man you are staying with?" I asked.

"Joshua? He's at the Council Hall doing his work. I occupy my mind while he is away with studies and readings. But to answer you, there is a bathroom upstairs. I will see to having you some fresh clothes and…"

"Fish!" said Catalina.

"Yes, even fish."

"You collect fine wine too?" asked the Logger.

"Joshua does. He gathered those on his many travels. I personally don't have the taste for such a thing."

"You mind if I?"

"If you must, but in stride, my good man."

"Hey, where's that rat?" Catalina asked. We looked and saw Sootshire in the study room. "Dork."

"It is not a sin to be studious, my lady," Neacen said. "As a cat woman you should know planning is key."

"Excuse me?"

"None needed. We are all friends here. Please, make yourselves at home."

It felt good to finally to be out of clothes that reeked of woods and fairy dust since my journey began. I must say I am not the most built thing on the planet and at times I feel as light as air. For the second time, I did feel right at home but something in the back of my mind kept telling me that this wasn't the end of my journey. There were still more things to do, people to meet, but yet most of all was the fact that Sootshire told me I was more connected to this journey than I could ever imagine. As for Neacen, he gave me that look others have given me in the past, as if I was some otherworldly being. Yet, why do I care?

I could easily make Rhodam my home and say screw it. At least that's what the old me would have done. Put a proposition in front of my eyes at one time and at one time I would have dismissed it as utter crap. Yet since that night in the woods, something in me changed. I started to actually pay attention. So far at least no one here has put the burden of proof on me. I have to personally deliver a necklace and a letter to Serena, whom I see in my dreams. Lately, she's been speaking to me. I haven't told anyone the full extent of my dreams, but sometimes I hear and see her. That long flowing black hair, those blank and pitiless eyes, and that black armor and sword. She tells me I am almost home, but what does she mean? What is home?

I noticed my new attire awaiting me as I got out of the tub. A shower wouldn't suffice, for I dearly needed to renew myself. A coat that was white with red buttons down the chest area, green tights, and dress shoes. "Really?" I said. I was baffled Neacen had selected such an unusual attire for me. "I guess it beats my old attire." I got dressed and looked in the mirror. "I look like a British soldier." A knock came to the door. "Yes?"

"It's me, Neacen." I opened the door and saw him standing there, a smile across his face. "Thanks for the outfit."

"I didn't choose that for you, surprisingly."

"You didn't?"

"No. Actually, Catalina, did." I was shocked.

"No way."

"Yes way. Anyway, I think it suits you well. A very nice upgrade."

"Thanks for the vote of confidence."

"You're welcome. Anyway, dinner is ready. We have steak, fish, salad, potato soup, and a casserole made from eggs."

"Going all out, huh?"

"You're my guest and I wanted to welcome you to Rhodam in the best way. Prepare to feast like a king tonight."

If I was to feast like a king, then the smell must have been heaven. Everyone was at the table with an array of dishes on display. "Looking handsome!" Catalina said.

"I didn't know you had such taste," I said.

"You know us cats, classy to the touch."

"I am honored to see you feel that way."

The Perfect Portrait

"Please sit and partake, my good man," Sootshire said.

I felt warm inside. I honestly felt as if I was seated among family.

"I found something interesting," said the Logger

"What's that?" asked Neacen.

"In all my travels, I never came across anyone who believed in a higher power."

"Why should they? People are more than capable to shaping their own destiny. To be blunt, we do not need these gods and goddesses. We are powerful enough to create and destroy. Religion is simply a tool used to control. No more, no less."

"You are very steadfast to your point," Catalina said.

"Yes, my lady."

"You can call me Catalina."

"I have been so used to formalities, but as you wish, Catalina. Picture this, let's say you have a country that solely believes in these higher beings. Now, if it was based solely on faith, what purpose would be for philosophy, arithmetic, the arts, science, and the like. These two conflicting points can't exist on the same plane. If faith is as powerful as people say, why are slums still in existence? Why are people growing less wise? Why is there no purpose outside of serving, man or otherwise."

"What about art that was inspired by faith?" I asked. Neacen looked at me, puzzled. "What? Some of the best art depicts acts of faith."

"That could be just inspiration," Sootshire said. "Just because they paint a picture of a divine being doesn't mean they truly believe."

"Wouldn't that be contradicting, though?" the Logger said. "Painting is just like writing; it stems from thought, or something that inspires the work. Inspiration can't be equated or deduced. It just is."

"But you can't hang a picture of someone and say that's who we all should worship."

"I didn't say that. Everyone has a right to believe what they want to. What they fuck up is when they try to shove it down someone's throat."

"True, but no one has seen her," Neacen said.

"I have," I said. Neacen looked at me.

"You have?"

"Yes. Several times."

"Where?"

"In the other world and in my dreams."

"Fantasies, my good man. Mere fantasy."

"I am serious. On the way here, I felt her in my head. It felt like pure anger and contempt. What she felt, I felt." The rest continued eating, save for Neacen.

"Your beautiful goddess on high is just a fantasy, young man. Serena is basically some child's wet dream."

"Enough, you two!" Catalina said. "I am not taking sides on this debate, but this much is true. If Wandering Leaf chooses to believe in Serena, that's his business. With all respect, Neacen, you can't shove your research in people's faces and expect them all to accept it."

"It's like the old adage," said the Logger. "You can make some people smile, but you can't make the whole world laugh. That's why I went on my own. I am under the whim of neither God nor man, but there still could be a chance. Wandering Leaf and his friends may be odd in their own right, but this journey did pique my curiosity."

"Well, then it seems I am outspoken on this issue," Neacen said.

"Oh my goodness!" Catalina said. "No one is outspeaking anyone! Your argument does have some points. People, as scum as they can be, can do positive things. Self-reliance is good, no doubt. My people are self-reliant, but they also believe in higher beings. The Elder and the one before him both have met Serena. Does that make them blind sheep, no, blind followers? I could tolerate a sheep. What I can't get is why you're shoving this in Wandering Leaf's face. He could be right, he could be wrong. Yet all of us are accompanying him on this journey because we all have something to discover. Now, you've mocked him enough, Neacen! Stop it!"

The Logger reached over and patted Catalina. "Calm down," he said.

"So you're on a mission to meet Serena?" Neacen asked.

"Yes," I said.

"Do you know where she is?"

"Not at the moment. We were hoping to get some answers here in Rhodam."

"Good luck with that. No one has seen Serena or would know where she is."

"There's got to be a way to find her," the Logger said.

"Tomorrow is Mass," Neacen said. "You could attend and see if there are any hints in the church."

"That could be a lead," I said.

"You're coming with us," Catalina said.

"To Mass? Certainly not!" said Neacen.

"Besides, I don't want to have to put my foot up those guards' asses," said the Logger.

"No one is going to pose you any harm, my good man."

"You're coming with us, Neacen," Catalina said. "That's final."

"Listen," I said. "You may not believe in Serena. That is your call. However, you seem to be respected in this city and I think it's best you come along with us."

"Hold on, Wandering Leaf," Catalina said. "I don't like this guy. He's too invasive with his mouth."

"He has a point, though," Neacen said. "A tempting offer but I will have to decline."

"You're studying her," I said. "What better way than to actually meet her in person."

"No. I have no time for long journeys to find nothing. This conversation is over."

"So much for Rhodam's great researcher," Catalina said. "What a waste." She got up and started to walk off.

"Catalina, where are you going?" I asked.

"Away from this stuck-up fool," she said, walking out the door.

"Excuse me," I said, putting my fork down and leaving as well.

"She doesn't like me, does she?" asked Neacen.

"You have a book stuck up your ass, that's why," said the Logger.

"We all need to go on this journey," Sootshire said.

"You have been quiet for a while now."

"I am just taking it all in. Is anyone going to finish that fish?"

...

I looked for Catalina through the city. Surely a nude half-cat, half-human shouldn't be too hard to find. I eventually sighted her in a park area near a bridge. She just stood there near a tree, looking out into the distance. "Sorry about earlier," I said, approaching her.

"It's not your fault," she said. "I just can't stand people like that, you know?"

"Hey, in the world I am from, people like Neacen exist all over the place. He does have good points. It's his way of driving those points into people that irks me."

"You and me both. By the way, I am sorry for acting rough with you back in the village."

"Hey, don't be sorry. It's just how you are. The Logger is how he is. Sootshire, me, Neacen. People are people."

"You don't mind my attitude?"

"Not at all. I was surprised you stood up for me back there."

"I wasn't going to let Neacen back you into a corner like that. Just like I wasn't going to allow that asshole back in my village to push you around. You're like a brother to me. You can be a little clumsy sometimes, but I can forgive that."

"You never bonded much back in Sumurka?"

"What do you mean?"

"You know…"

"Like a mate? I was focused too much on our survival. Love is one of those things I don't partake in too much of."

"I see."

"Why do you ask?"

"Curious, that's all."

"What about you?"

The Perfect Portrait

"No, none for me. I was a loner, a person who followed their own path. I never mated with anyone."

"Serena didn't flash you in your dreams?"

"Hey!"

"Just kidding! Lighten up a little. You're still young. You have a whole life ahead of you. I have been meaning to ask, what are you going to do? When this is all over, that is."

"I don't know. I may go back home."

"You say that like you will never see me again."

"No, it's not that. I just feel…"

"Out of place."

"Yeah."

"I can relate to that. You're really the only other person besides the Elder who took the time to connect with me."

"There isn't much connection between people these days. It's a pretty scary world if you ask me."

"I honestly couldn't care less about it."

"You cared enough about me."

"You and a select few are the exception."

"Are you going to Mass tomorrow?"

"By myself? No."

"You can come with me."

"You think Neacen should come with us?"

"If he wants to. That's his decision. I am searching for answers with or without his help."

"You have me with you, so you're not alone."

"It makes a difference knowing that. At least I am not alone."

"If you were anyone else, I would say you chose to be alone, but you're a different case. You truly did look like a lost soul when I met you."

"Now multiply that by twenty-two years and you have it. I don't even remember if my birthday has come and gone. It's like I really was a leaf in the wind all those years."

"We are all looking for answers. You know it would be scary if we lived a world where all that was true."

"If what were true?"

"If people were only made to pay debts to one another and lived only for a meager existence. I don't want that life. I want to be free of those chains, free of the worry. I want to know who I really am, Catalina. I am tired to being a leaf in the wind."

"You know, as the Elder told me, sometimes the truth can be just as shocking as a lie."

"I will take that chance. Whatever the cold truth is, I am willing to accept it."

"No regrets?"

"None. I used to hate the fact that Serena brought me here, but now I don't anymore. Maybe there is something she wants me to see."

"Sure there is."

"I am being serious here!"

"I know, I know! I told you to lighten up!"

"Sorry about that."

"Don't be. I love a guy who's himself. At least you're discovering things now. That shows growth in my eyes. I can't fault you for that."

"Now shall we return to dinner?"

"You mean lunch. It's only high noon."

"Oh."

"It's okay. Time is different in this world. Anyway, having this conversation was filling enough. Besides, Neacen and I kind of got into it because I wanted to eat fish raw and he wanted to cook it."

"Eventually, you will learn to deal with people like him."

"I doubt it."

"Hey, you warmed up to me. Everyone brings something to the table in this case."

"The only person I want at my table is you."

"You mean our table." Catalina swiped my cheek. "What was that for?"

"Because I like you."

The Perfect Portrait

"If that's love, I can only imagine."

"You mean if that's liking, you can only imagine love."

"Yeah, what you said."

"You're funny. I like the new you."

"Stick around. The fun's only beginning."

"Anyway, let's head back."

"Sounds good to me."

Chapter 20

One More Member

"Faith and taxes," Joshua said as he walked from the Council Hall. "We tax the citizens outrageously, worship an entity we haven't seen, and all this in the name of these two things. This world makes no sense. Yet it has me questioning my very position as part of the Council. Do I truly agree with the entire agenda? Certainly not! Before Necean took the position, I was already questioning it all."

Joshua arrived at his home. As he approached the door, he could hear talking on the other side. He opened it and saw four strangers in the living area. "What the hell is this?" he asked. He saw a man sipping his wine, a naked cat girl chasing a raccoon, and Neacen and a boy talking in the kitchen. "The hell!" Joshua shouted. Catalina and Sootshire stopped and looked at Joshua. Neacen and Wandering Leaf came into the living area as the Logger took another sip before setting his glass down. "Neacen, what the hell is going on here?"

"It's not what you think, Joshua," he said.

"It's a pigsty of nudity and perpetual filth!"

"Hey, we washed the dishes!" the Logger said, standing up. Joshua could see he was at least a foot taller than he and had more tone.

"Allow me to explain," Neacen said.

"I want these ruffians out of my residence!"

"Listen, jackass!" Catalina shouted. "You can go to hell with your preppy ass, loose tongued…"

"That's enough, Catalina," Neacen said. "There is a reason these four souls are here. Just hear me out."

"All right, Neacen. Explain."

"The reason they are here is because they are seeking Serena."

"Oh, really? Don't make me laugh."

"It's true. This young man, who is named Wandering Leaf, is traveling with his companions you see before you. Catalina, Sootshire, and the Logger. All of them have a meeting with her, but upon coming into the city, they were met with resistance by the guards. I overheard the commotion and saw they were being hounded. I put a cease to it and allowed them to reside here. My research had hit a dead end, but after talking with these four, I may have learned some things."

"Such as?"

"There is a chance that this Serena could be real. This young man was telling me about his dreams and the fact that he feels a connection to her."

"Am I supposed to believe this?"

"Believe what you want, but it's true. I am really curious as to what the results of this journey could do for my research. Trust me, Joshua, they mean no harm. In fact, they offer much to my research."

"I am tempted not to believe you, Neacen." Joshua walked over to Wandering Leaf. "Is there any trickery you are pulling, son?"

"Not at all," Wandering Leaf said. "We mean you no harm. There is a mission I have to complete and the people you see with me are my companions who are accompanying me."

"Then how do you explain that man drinking my wine and that half-human, half-cat chasing a flea-bitten raccoon all over the house?"

"I meant no harm," the Logger said. "I will gladly reimburse you for the wine. The girl is Catalina from the village of Sumurka, and the raccoon is named Sootshire."

"Pleased to meet you, Mr. Hamilton," Sootshire said.

"A talking raccoon?" Joshua said. "Normally a dish on a plate, or caught in a trap. This is the first I have seen of one that could talk."

The Perfect Portrait

"I am the first of many things," Sootshire said. "Yet it is a pleasure to be able to see this beautiful city once again."

"You four seek an audience with Serena? There's greater odds of a homeless man getting a scrap of meat from a queen. No one here in Rhodam has seen her. Not a member of the clergy. The statues of her are only depictions through fogged eyes and simple minds."

"Actually, you would be wrong, sir," Wandering Leaf said. "I have seen her for myself. I have looked into those darkened eyes and I will say, there is nothing benevolent about her."

"There is a chance you could be chasing an illusion. A mere ghost."

"For someone like me, who feels like a ghost, it's a risk I am willing to take."

"How bad was the pantry raided, Neacen?"

"It wasn't too bad. I did treat our guests to an exquisite meal, and they enjoyed every minute."

"It matters not. After the day I have had with the Council, my mind is exhausted."

Joshua took off his coat and sat in the living area. "So, your research still hasn't progressed?"

"No. I have hit more dead ends than leads," said Neacen. "That was until I met these four. Their story, although sounding completely ludicrous, could have some truth."

"We were hoping the church could hold some answers," Wandering Leaf said. "Texts, documents, anything."

"The church is always open to curious minds. I think there could be something there," said Joshua.

"It could be a lead," said the Logger.

"Sounds good to me," said Catalina. "We should go there now because, to be honest, I don't feel like attending Mass."

"Just to be sure, man," the Logger said, looking at Joshua, "we are good on supplies?"

"Yes, yes. I am beat right now. Sorry for my attitude. It's not easy being a member of the problem who thinks they can solve it."

"No sweat," said the Logger.

Neacen decided to accompany us on the walk to St. Michael's Cathedral. "I thought you didn't believe in this," Catalina said to him.

"I am not above investigating," he said. "Besides, I don't like for my mind to be idol."

"So have you decided?" said Wandering Leaf.

"To join you on your quest?"

"Yes or no, man," said the Logger. "We don't need dead weight."

"I will have you know I am not dead weight, sir!" said Neacen.

"More like dead brain," said Catalina.

"You know nothing of me."

"You're right. I know nothing of you because I can see right through you. You're scared to admit that maybe you could be wrong about Serena's nonexistence."

"My research is far from over."

"And so is your growing up."

"I have no time for arguments. Sootshire, why have you been so quiet?"

"Can't one simply take it all in?" he asked. "I am sure Catalina is enjoying my silence."

"Shut up, rat!" Catalina said.

We arrived at the cathedral a few minutes later. A grand symbol of the people of Rhodam's devotion to Serena. Grand walls, glass windows with pictures depicting creation and damnation. The façade being a symbol of man's futile attempt at perfect devotions and a perfect standard of living in the eyes of a being who seemed to turn a blind eye.

"In these halls rest countless books from abroad," said Neacen. "Various symbols of faith, scripture, artifacts. All these things reside in here."

"Well, let's quit gazing at Serena's and Rhodam's symbol of perfection and actually go inside." Wandering Leaf started to walk up the stairs when he felt something. "Aagh!"

"Hey, what's wrong?" the Logger asked, looking to him. Wandering Leaf could feel the burning sensation form the pendants again. It felt stronger than last time, and he dropped to his knees. The others came to him.

The Perfect Portrait

"What is it, Wandering Leaf?" Catalina asked, putting her paw on his shoulder.

"This place," he said. "It's emitting a great deal of energy. It's unreal."

"What the hell?" Neacen said.

"It's just like on the boat," said the Logger. "Young man felt the same sensation."

"Something is not right with Serena. This is her energy I am feeling."

"This is odd," said Neacen. "My research…"

"Damn your research!" Catalina yelled.

"Let's get him inside!" Neacen said. Catalina held Wandering Leaf close.

"It's okay. I got you," she told him. The two of them stayed behind a bit. "Do you want me to hold those pendants?"

"No, it's okay. I will be fine," Wandering Leaf said. The two of them went inside, where the others were waiting.

"You all right, man?" the Logger asked.

"Yes. I am fine."

They were approached by a bishop and two nuns.

"Bless the heavens!" he said. "How can I help you?" The Logger approached the man.

"We are on a quest to find Serena. Do you have any books or articles on her?" The bishop and nuns looked puzzled.

"Serena can't be seen with normal eyes," he said. "She is a divine being that many never see."

"Surely there are some books concerning Rhodam's history that involve her," Sootshire said.

"We keep a collection of her teachings in our archives. Yet only certain people can enter."

"Why?" asked Neacen.

"Because the books are holy relics. They must be handled with care and the church is strict on which individuals qualify."

"What if I told you we had someone who has seen her?"

"Don't be silly, young man."

"I am not lying," Wandering Leaf said. "I have laid eyes on her, and I am in tune with her. These two pendants around my neck allow me to feel her emotions."

"Are you serious?"

"He's not lying," Catalina said. "We have witnessed what the pendants are capable of and the effects they have on him."

"I still don't believe you." The Logger walked up to the bishop.

"With all due respect, we are on a tight schedule here. I have been around and I know a liar when I see one. This young man and his friends would not have come all this way just to sell a lie."

"The day that boy is telling the truth will be the day when the sky rains hell."

"You son of a bitch!" Catalina yelled. The Logger held her back.

"Forget it, guys," Wandering Leaf said. "It's sad when even men of faith will judge you just because of appearance. I hope Serena herself shows you the truth, then."

"Wandering Leaf!" the Logger said.

"Let's get out of here."

"What was that all about?" Catalina asked.

"Hold it," said Neacen. "I will come with you four."

"Why should we allow you?" the Logger said.

"I could be of help. Besides, there are things to see."

"Let him come," Wandering Leaf said.

"Really?" Catalina said. "Wandering Leaf, are you all right?"

"I am fine. Let's move."

"Let me at least let Josh know I am going."

"Fine. Handle what you must and make it quick."

The Logger pulled Wandering Leaf aside. "What the hell is wrong with you?" he asked.

"I am sorry," Wandering Leaf said.

"This is starting to get off as hell," Catalina said.

"It's the pendants," said Sootshire.

The Perfect Portrait

"Now look who speaks," the Logger said.

"If Serena is in complete control of this world, then that means that something or someone interrupted her abilities."

"You know, rat, I am about fed up with you secretly knowing shit!" Catalina growled.

"Let's not argue amongst ourselves," said the Logger. "We need to back track."

"Exactly," said Sootshire. "It's time we see Mitchell Vega again."

"Who is that?" asked Catalina.

"An old friend."

"If it can help us, anything works. I don't like the effect this Serena bitch is having on Wandering Leaf," said Catalina.

Neacen came back, a logbook in his hand.

"That's all you're going to bring?" Catalina asked.

"Yes, just my research book."

"Suit yourself."

"All right, team," the Logger said. "Let's go."

PART 6

A Light in the Darkness

Power. That fateful five-letter word has drawn so many meanings from the mouths of men. I think to myself, what is power? Hmm, let's see. Is it having millions of pieces of paper at your disposal? Is it one man's ability to see a dog back his own shit? You stand before me, Julius, a man who was stripped of all these things as well as my own father, whom I have nothing but the utmost contempt for. All I was at the time was a twenty-seven-year-old girl who auctioned off her own soul so one boy could live. I honestly think the adage about two dogs is fitting in my case. My hate grew the biggest, so I fed that one. My disdain goes far beyond that for my father. Don't give that puzzled look. You of all people know what I mean.

Serena to Julius

Chapter 21

Serena Reborn

"Black wings, check. Darkened eyes, check." Serena looked herself over and smiled as the rays of the moonlight shone beautifully off of her armor, now as black as the night sky above her and Julius. She turned to Julius, who was ironically now the one stripped of power. "Isn't it sad, Julius?" You now stand before a goddess, a perfect ruler."

"You're demented, you foul whore!" Julius thundered. "How could you lie to me about this entire situation?"

"Lie? No, I was being honest when I said that I was on a mission to recover my family. What I didn't say was how I planned to acquire all of this. To be honest, I feel greater than I have ever felt. To be reborn, to be complete. You know something, evil isn't bad when you have the right tools to handle it."

"You speak foolishness, woman!"

"No, I speak the truth, love. Now, if you don't mind, let us go pay the people of Akoran a little visit."

"I will not be a part of this anymore, Serena."

"You will come with me. Your stick of light is gone and you're in no position to be denying me. I have some unfinished business to tend to and you will bear witness, or I will be the one striking your blood."

"You bitch!"

"Thank you, love. I wouldn't have it any other way. Oh, and for your viewing pleasure, I want to show you what I can do with my new power." Serena opened her mouth, allowing a black mist to come from deep within her. Julius was horrified by what he saw. The mist formed a few inches above Serena's head and was carried away with the wind.

"By heaven's light, what have you done, Serena?" he said.

Neacen wrote in his journal as Catalina, the Logger, and Sootshire stood at the bow. Wandering Leaf was in the cabin, having not said much since the departure. "I am worried about the boy," the Logger said. "He wasn't himself."

"I know," said Catalina. "That's not like him to be so short with someone and withdrawn. Sootshire, you said something about Serena getting her powers back. What do you mean?"

"Apparently, something dampened them," he said. "She had lost them before, which caused the entire landscape to act more settled."

"I really wish you would explain in more detail instead of being cryptic," the Logger said.

"We will get more answers back at the starting point."

"Hey, Neacen!" the Logger said. "You've been writing for some time now." Neacen continued to write furiously. Catalina got a piece of wood and chunked it at him.

"Hey!" he said.

"Earth to Neacen," she said. She walked over to him and grabbed his journal.

"Hey, return that at once!" he said, reaching for it, Catalina holding it just out of his grasp. Catalina looked at the entry.

"Hmmm," she said.

To Estelle:

I am writing this letter to inform you that I will not be in the city for a while. I am embarking on a journey with a motley crew in search of this angel everyone keeps discussing. I will miss seeing you emerald-green eyes and reddish blood soaked hair. But not let me

The Perfect Portrait

ponder over such looks for I may tear. I hope to see you again once this is all said and done. Take care.

With sincere love,
Neacen Ruthman

"Really, Neacen?" Catalina said. "Who is Estelle?"

"She is a close friend of mine back in the city," Neacen said.

"Really?" Sootshire said. "I never knew you to associate with anyone, Neacen."

"A lot can happen in a short time,"

"So how did you meet the little angel?" the Logger asked.

"She's not an angel."

"Just tell us," Catalina said.

"It was shortly after I arrived in the city. I was starting to get acquainted with the locals, when I came across a beautiful girl in the park. Her hair was as red as blood, yet it was so graciously flowing down her back. Her eyes were as green as emeralds, and she wore the most beautiful white dress with velvet cuffs I had ever seen." The Logger looked to Catalina and she to him. "What?" Neacen asked.

"Are you sure you didn't dream this?" Catalina asked.

"Goodness, no! Estelle is real."

"Then why didn't we see her in Rhodam?" the Logger asked. Neacen looked away. Catalina put her face in his.

"Well, Mr. Lover?"

"Back off, you two," Sootshire said. "No need to explain further."

"Once again, Neacen isn't being up front," Catalina said.

"Enough!" Sootshire said.

"What is up with you?" the Logger asked. "First Wandering Leaf and now you?"

"I hear something coming from the cabin, you scoundrels!"

"Sounds like scuffling," the Logger said.

"I'll go check it out," Catalina said.

"Sure you don't need back up?"

"I'm just checking on him. Is there something I should find?" Catalina fluffed her tail and went into the cabin.

Catalina could tell something was not right the moment she went in. It was quiet save for the sound of a low murmur. "Wandering Leaf?" she said. She saw him writing something on the wall. His back was turned and the items in his bag were strewn about. Catalina could see the words "salvations behind damnation" being written over and over again. She got closer to him. "Are you okay?"

"Do not touch me, wench!" he said, turning around. His eyes looked like those of a crazed man, and from Catalina's view, that was not anything like she had ever seen.

"Wandering Leaf, what is wrong with you?"

"You could never fathom this work, this portrait! I told you people to stay away and not interfere, but no, you had to jump into matters that didn't concern you! Serena doesn't WANT AN AUDIENCE WITH SOME LOWLY CAT BITCH, A RAT, SOME LOVE-STRUCK GEEK, AND A WASHED-UP HAS-BEEN DRUNK!"

Catalina, who was shocked at the change in Wandering Leaf's tone, backed up and ran back to the deck. "It's Wandering Leaf," she said. "He's not himself!" The Logger and Sootshire both reached for a blade. "What the hell are you two doing?"

"It's Serena," Sootshire said. "She's back!"

"And I am always prepared for anything," the Logger said.

"Guys, this isn't needed," said Neacen.

"Like hell it is!" the Logger said. "Kitty, you and Soot, come with me. Book boy, stay here and man the boat."

"Really, people?" Neacen said.

"Just do it!" Catalina said.

"Fine!"

The three of them went into the cabin and were met by a horrific scene. The boy was standing on his bed, with his arms behind him, as if he was trying to carve something into his back. "Yo, son!" the Logger said, clutching his blade.

"Wandering Leaf, what the hell?" Sootshire said.

"MUST HAVE WINGS!" the boy said. The Logger took a few steps towards him. "GET BACK!"

"Look, this isn't you, son," the Logger said.

"Wandering Leaf, please! Let us help you!"

"OH, YOU ALWAYS HAVE IT, DON'T YOU, LESTER!"

"Lester?" Catalina said. "That's your real name?"

"OH YES! TELL US HOW YOU WERE CALLED THE LOGGER! ALWAYS LOGGING BACK DRINKS TO IMPRESS YOUR FRIENDS. YOUR WIFE WAS SO ASHAMED OF YOU THAT SHE LEFT YOUR ASS AND YOU COULDN'T TAKE THE PAIN. SO, LIKE A SCARED CHILD, YOU RAN OFF TO THE SEA TO HIDE FROM YOUR TRUE SELF!"

"All right, Leafy, that's enough!" Sootshire said. "We don't want to hurt you!"

"HURT ME? YOU, A RACOON, WHO WAS AN OUTCAST FROM NATURE ITSELF. YOU HAD SO MANY FLEAS YOU PUT A CAT TO SHAME! ALWAYS ACTING LIKE YOU'RE SO SMART WHEN EVEN A PACK OF PIG FAIRIES OUTSMARTED YOU. YOU'RE JUST HIDING THE FACT THAT YOU'RE SO WEAK! AND HOW CAN WE FORGET MS. CATALINA. ORPHANED AT SUCH A YOUNG AGE. ALL YOU HAD WAS THE TRIBE LEADER. NO ONE WANTED TO BE AROUND YOU AND NOW YOU THINK YOU DESERVE COMPANY WITH MY PERFECT SON?"

The Logger went to go for the boy. The boy held out his hand and the Logger stopped in his tracks. "OH MY! OH YES! IT'S BEEN SO LONG SINCE I DID THIS! DARKNESS BE PRAISED!"

Sootshire went in with his blade. The boy stopped him and lifted him up with his mind. "SO YOU LIKE FISH, HUH, RAT? FINE THEN! YOU CAN JOIN THEM OUT IN THE SEA!" The hatch window opened and Sootshire was tossed outside.

"Please, stop!" Catalina said.

"OH, LOVE, YOU ARE SO INTO THIS BOY, AREN'T YOU?"

"That's enough!" the Logger said.

"YOU KNOW WHAT, LESTER, I HAVE HAD ENOUGH OUT OF YOU!" The boy tossed the Logger out of the cabin door back on the deck and went and grabbed Catalina by her neck and lifted her up off the ground. She looked into the boy's eyes and saw they were not his. They were a lifeless, soulless, black. "GOT THE CAT BY THE NECK! OOOH!"

"Please!" Catalina said

"HOW PATHETIC! THERE IS NO OTHER WOMAN WORTHY OF MY SON'S LOVE EXCEPT FOR ME! I WILL NOT ALLOW SOME LESSER BEING TO BE WITH HIM! I COULD END YOU RIGHT NOW IF I WANTED, BUT SEEING YOU SQUIRM IS SO MUCH MORE FUN!"

"Hey, asswipe!" The boy looked and saw Sootshire was back. He was soaking wet and had a large seashell in his paw. "Seashell by the seashore, bitch!" He threw it at the boy's head as hard as he could. It hit him and even managed to draw blood.

"SOOTSHIRE, DID YOU JUST THROW A SHELL AT MY SON?" the boy said in a loud, distorted voice.

"In Heaven's name we pray." Everyone looked and saw Neacen standing there, a book in his hand. "In Heaven's grace I cast you out of this child."

"FUCKING NEACEN? OH, MY DARK LORD!"

"Leave the boy, go back to Hell. I cast you out in righteous light!" The boy started to growl. "Angel's mercy, give him strength, let him be at peace and in God's holy name, I send you back to the rotting pit of Hell!"

A black mist came from the boy's mouth, and he let go of Catalina, the both of them falling to the ground. Sootshire looked to Neacen.

"What did you just do?" he asked.

"I just saved our asses," Neacen said. Catalina regained herself.

"Necean, enough mystery. You will speak the truth about all of this! Now!"

Chapter 22

The Skies Turn Dark Again

"Are you all right?" Neacen asked Catalina.

"What do you think, jackass?" Catalina snapped.

"Hey!" said the Logger, "That's enough! Soot, how are you?"

"Wet, but fine," he said. "I checked on Wandering Leaf. He's resting now."

"The clouds are moving in, which means we have a storm coming. I got to fix that damn door."

"Fuck the door!" Catalina said. "Now, Neacen, you need to start talking. Enough games, no more avoiding questions. Answers, now!"

"Fine," said Neacen.

"And Lester, you stay. Everyone has talking to do."

"I began my research on Serena shortly after I arrived in Rhodam. I studied text about her and found out that she wasn't always an angel."

Sootshire interjected, "At one time, she was a normal person. A woman who was an aspiring artist at one time. She married Julius, the man who gave her a chance at one of his museums. They had a son, but he died shortly thereafter. Serena flew into a fit of rage and depression over this, pushing Julius away and withdrawing from the world."

Neacen continued, "I learned that one night, she made a deal with a woman who many in the city called 'Soul Shifter.' She said that if she could allow her son just one chance to live, she would bind their spirits and make a new world in her image. Thus she took the form of an angel, albeit a twisted one."

"Why an angel?" asked the Logger.

"Angels represent virtue, justice, and absolution. Serena wanted to be second to no one, and she created a world, a portrait, where she could be just that. I personally helped Neacen's mentor Joshua, which is how I know this."

"Really now?" said Catalina. "So, you three lied?"

"We didn't want to blow our cover too soon, especially in front of Wandering Leaf," said Neacen.

"So what if this is true, what is Wandering Leaf's real name?"

"Jay," said Sootshire. "His mother and father are Serena and Julius. I have known who he was since the day I met him. I just didn't say anything lest he know too much. I knew about the pendants around his neck and the fact that Candice, Jay's grandmother, was the woman who saved us from the pig fairies."

"As for Estelle," said Neacen, "she was the peace of my mind during those long hours of research. She was whom I envisioned would be my equal in love one day. A fantasy to some, but real to me. The green eyes for growth, the red hair for life and sacrifice, and the white dress for purity. She was the 'Serena' of my dreams."

"So you are a priest in training?" asked the Logger.

"Yes. Researching as just a rouse. I also took the pendants off of Jay's neck. Apparently, it links Serena and Jay together. A bond you might say."

"And to be honest, in a way, we are all her children," said Sootshire. "That is how she knows so much about us. I did wonder why you took easy to alcohol, Lester." The Logger rubbed his head and looked out into the ocean.

"I wasn't always a man of the sea," he said. "At one time, I was the life of the party, the guy who could turn heads the minute he walked into the door. Since my family was well known, I wasn't without resources. I had it all, but the most special treasure to me was my relationship with Bianc,a or Bee Bee as I called her, because she always loved to wear yellow. I was a good husband, when I wasn't turning loggers or kegs, hence why I am called the Logger. I wasn't too good with the alcohol, and I could become quite violent. Bee Bee didn't like to see that side to me. After one outburst too many, she left. To calm myself, I took to the sea, putting what money I didn't waste into a little fishing business. The sea taught me to be calm, let go, but most of all, forgive myself."

"And what about you, Catalina?" Sootshire asked. "Are you really an orphan?"

"Yes," she said. "One reason I don't trust people is because they killed my parents when I was little. They said we didn't deserve to live because of what we were. Out tribe leader found me in the bushes and took me in. I was little, but I developed a deep disdain for man. It is ironic being I am half human myself. Do I care for Jay? Yes, I do. Mainly because, just like myself, deep down inside, he is alone. Beneath this tough exterior is a soul waiting to be a part of something to be understood. I am guarded because I don't want to allow myself to be deceived or hurt."

"No mean to cut this off, but we got a storm approaching," the Logger said.

. . .

"Damn, it felt good to do that!" Serena said. "Julius, do you know how long it's been since I did a, how should I say, inhabit a body for a moment spell?"

"That's not funny, Serena," Julius said. "The sky is darkening, and the air is growing still."

"Perfect!" Serena said. "It feels good to be able to fly again. Well, it seems we are about to enter once again into the city of Akoran. I will find King Shikam and you will read my decree to the people. I think the terms are fair enough."

"I can't believe you are doing this."

"I can't believe I sold a dog back his own shit, but I did."

"I thought you hated Mitch."

"I do, but I can't help but nod to those crude tactics he used. It makes for success."

"He redeemed himself, Serena."

"I will be the judge of that. Now, here we are. Look sharp or you will be sharply torn apart."

Obed stood at the gate as the two entered. "Julius!" he said, walking over with his men. "I figured this! Akoran's most wanted in cahoots with Akoran's most hated. I figured that wench we executed wasn't Serena!"

"So you dumbasses do have some sense!" Serena said. The guards readied their spears and swords.

"Obed, listen," Julius said.

"No, you listen! I smelled traitor on you the moment you first came here! I smelled a foulness in the air for the last week and I knew this bitch was still alive! Did you really think I was that stupid?"

"You must have been to fall for that," Serena said. The guards began to move in. "Oh, please, this again?" Serena spread her wings and withdrew her sword, which glimmered, despite it being dark. "Little boys, please put your toys away, NOW!"

"Something is different about her," Obed said. "Julius, what is the meaning of this?"

"We will explain everything in the hall," Serena said. "Take us to the king or it is *I* who will be having *your* head!"

"You're sick!"

"Oh, honey, I could vomit shit on you that would melt your skin. Try me."

"Fine. Follow us."

The people of Akoran gasped in shock and horror as they saw a woman they thought to be dead walking among them. Obed and his men took Serena and Julius to the palace where more guards greeted them. "Is this trickery, Obed?" one of them said.

"No," Obed said. "It's just as I feared. Serena lives. We need to see King Shikam."

"Over my dead body!" Serena flew to the front and swiftly thrust her sword through the armor made of solid bronze into the man's chest.

"Invitation accepted," she said. She looked to the others. "Who's next?" They stood back, allowing them to pass. Once at the doors to the Hall, more guards arrived. "Little children, please just step aside. I know you missed me, but I can sign autographs later." The men drew closer. "Oh, boy! Fine!" She drew her sword again. "Here is a kiss for you!" she said, grabbing one of the guards and thrusting her blade into his mouth, breaking his jaw and coming out midway down his back. "A blow job for you!" she said, stabbing the blade in the crotch of another. "And lastly, you, sir, need to rest your legs!" she said, taking her blade and severing his legs. "Damn, I am a bitch!"

"Let's go," Obed said.

After more bloodshed, the group finally reached the doors to the throne room of King Shikam. A man with his guards met them with resistance. "Menede, please, don't try it," Obed said.

"This woman seeks to usurp the throne," he said. "That I can't allow."

"You sure about that?" Serena said, drawing her blade, which was now soaked in blood. Menede drew his own blade.

"I am not afraid of death. It is a corrupt society and a lawless land that terrifies me. If avoiding that means my death, then so be it." Obed walked over to Menede.

"Don't do this," he said.

"Obed, you swore an allegiance to our people and our king, and now you allow some girl with chicken feathers to compromise your ethics? You are a disgrace to King Shikam and our people. You are no better than Julius or her." Serena walked forward, her wings spreading over the men behind her.

"Look, boy!" she said. "I really don't have the time or the patience for this. I just want to get through. Now, if you value you and your men's lives, you will do as I say. If now, well, you were warned."

"I refuse," Menede said. He stepped forward and looked Serena dead in the eye. "I don't care what you are, angel or spot of crap on the ground. You're not getting through! I will cut your head off just as clean as day!"

"Really? Hmm. What say you, men?" Serena said, looking back at her small group. "Shall we test the theory?"

"Serena!" Julius yelled.

"Okay, fine!" Serena dropped her blade and knelt before Menede. "Go ahead, sir. Try it!"

Julius tried to step forward but was stopped by Obed. Menede raised his blade. "I do this for my king," he said before swiftly slicing off Serena's head. It fell to the ground, a black oozing liquid coming from the veins. "So much for angel on high," Menede said.

"So, it's over?" Obed asked.

"Now, all of you, leave!" Menede shouted. Then, all of a sudden, Serena's body stood up and contorted. The veins from around the neck reformed, forming a jaw bone, skin, hair, and finally, those devilishly black eyes. Menede, Obed, Julius, and the guards stood in sheer horror as the once decapitated angel now stood whole again. The head on the floor turned into a mushy black liquid and absorbed back into her.

"Hello, men! Did you miss me?" Serena asked in a mocking tone.

"It can't be!" Menede said.

"Ah, yes! Being renewed is the best thing ever. My little devil kid taught me that trick. He's so adorable!"

"You bitch!" said Menede.

"My son protects me, and I do the same. All I had to do was allow him to become one with me. It is amazing how evil keeps me alive. Now, good sir, it has been a pleasure. Now let me show you how this is done!" Serena took her blade and swiftly severed Menede's head. "That's for insulting my husband!"

Serena and her group of a knight, a head guard, and twelve men walked into the throne room of King Shikam. "Good evening, Shikam!" Serena said. The king was eating a feast fit only for a king. Three large pheasants, fish, apricot preserves, ham, lettuce, greens, seven vials of wine, and three pig heads. He looked shocked to see his men, a traitor, and a girl once thought dead before him. Serena led her men to the table hosting the grand feast. "Please, my good men, sit and feast! Today is a new day!" King Shikam sat, wiping his mouth.

"Serena," he said.

"In the flesh," she said. "Now, King, please enjoy your meal." Serena flew back and forth. "Now, I believe it's time to take this kingdom in a new direction, a better one. We need a new system for the people to abide by. This old business as usual thing just won't do. Now, first thing's first, change the goddamn dress code. Jeez, twenty-first century here people! We shall model this land after Rhodam. Ah yes! Architecture, intellect. Hell, it could even rival Rome. Anyway, an advancement for the people but mostly myself. Secondly, a firm belief in yours truly, the Dark Angel on high. The Shining Star in the Black Night. This kingdom shall be renamed Aubrelias."

"This is absurd," King Shikam said.

"Yes, but it's so absurd, it's brilliant! This land, this opportunity, and best of all, it will be…lovely. Now as for you, King Shikam, this will be your last supper and I rule death for you just as you did for me. Yet, please, enjoy your meal and let it settle. I want you to have a full belly when you are killed."

"You would kill me?"

"Oh, hell, I could look at you the right way and kill you, but it won't be me that kills you. I am just ordering your death. I am going to watch for I have had my fill of blood."

"You snake!" the king yelled.

"No, more like Black Widow!" Serena sneered. "I plotted, waited, planned. I led you all into my web of a damsel-in-distress act and the fact that you all thought I was dead. Well, all but Julius here who had the chance to prevent all of this but didn't."

"Julius," King Shikam said, turning to him.

"Forgive me, my king," Julius said.

"Aww! So sad!" said Serena. "Ha ha! How ironic! Anyway, I find this fitting and ironic! I am moments away from ruling a kingdom that truly despises me! How invigorating! But as I said, please enjoy your meal, gentlemen."

The feast was bittersweet, with Shikam's death serving as dessert, Serena's dessert. The king sat there, his belly full, but heart empty and hurting. "Don't look so sad, King," Serena said. "At least you can die knowing you will be succeeded by someone more fitting for the job."

"You are disgusting!" he said.

"I know my hair is and…" She smelled herself. "Oh, yes, I need a royal makeover and bath after you're headless. Anyway!" To Obed, "Did you spread the word?"

"Yes, Your Highness," he said sarcastically. Serena walked over to him and looked dead in his eyes.

"Don't push it, Obed," she said, smacking him slightly on the cheek.

"Now! Guards, please lead the former ruler King Shikam to the balcony in front of the masses. Julius, is your sword ready?"

"Yes," he said.

"Perfect! Lead my guards to the balcony, for I will fly above and deliver my version of a true declaration of independence." The guards lead the king out onto the balcony in front of at least three thousand people, all booing and screaming "Treason!"

"I can't believe this," the former ruler said. "Julius, don't do this." Julius couldn't help but turn away. There was going to be blood on his hand.

"Ah, my dear people of Aubrelias!" said Serena, who was a few feet above in the air, wings outstretched voice echoing across the land. "For the last millennia, you have been bound by old customs and sayings of old. Although it has kept you surviving, you haven't truly thrived, and that is a sin I cannot forgive. Yet now, I have a solution for all of us. A new age of prosperity for all of you and your children, so they won't have to suffer the same fate mine did. Yet the first step towards progress is to tear down the walls of the past. That being said I give you the destruction of your former selves in the form of Julius's blade down the head of your former king. You all will be reborn just like I WAS! Knight Julius, raise your sword!"

Julius looked into the eyes of his former king, sword raised. King Shikam shook his head.

"Why, Julius?" he said. "Don't do this."

"Are you ready, dear knight?" Serena asked.

"Julius," Obed said, looking at him with an ire of hate in his eyes.

"Now…STRIKE!" Serena yelled. Julius stood there, trembling. He could easily turn the blade on himself and end it all, but this wasn't his blade. "Julius! You have been given an order! STRIKE OR I WILL STRIKE YOU BOTH DOWN! DON'T YOU CARE ABOUT YOUR FAMILY? YOUR SON?"

Julius could feel the tears and inner struggle raging inside. "I WILL GIVE YOU UNTIL THE COUNT OF FIVE, THEN YOU WILL SEE WHAT HAPPENS! ONE!"

"Don't, Julius," King Shikam said.

The Perfect Portrait

"TWO!"

"What's more important?" Obed asked.

"THREE!"

"I love you, Julius."

Upon hearing those words, Julius looked and saw Serena as she once was. Sweet, innocent, and beautiful. She reached out her hands as if wanting to hold him. "I must be dreaming," Julius said.

"No, honey. I really miss you."

"I miss you too," he said.

"FOUR!"

"Now is our chance. Do it, for me, FOR JAY!"

"FINE!" Julius said. He swung his blade, severing Shikam's head down into the gallows below, his body, like his kingdom once was, falling down. The crowd stood in silence. Obed looked away, tears in his eyes. "Forgive me, my king," Julius said. Serena flew down to the balcony.

"Good job, Julius!" she said. "You have atoned for your sins and now you and our people are reborn."

"NOW, LET THE NEW WORLD ORDER COMMENCE!"

Chapter 23

Return to Sumurka

Mitchell Vega's eyes turned to the sky. A slight rain had started to fall, the heavens the color they were when he first arrived. He took out his pipe and lit it. "You always had a habit of putting something into your mouth when you're stressed," Candice said. "What is it?"

"The sky has darkened," he said. "Serena has gotten worse. You can't tell me you don't feel it, Candice." She sat her bag down, which contained only a few necessities: food, water, clothing, and one more thing. Kneeling down, she felt the leaves and the grass and noticed, even with this sprinkle, they felt lifeless.

"This world was full of color when I arrived. I don't hear any birds. The squirrels, even the insects are quiet. Something definitely is not right." Mitch went up to a nearby tree and tapped on it.

"Hmmm. Hollow."

"May I ask you something?"

"Yes."

"What did you mean when you said the world was ours? I mean, you were never the one to say something like that and not have a sense of direction."

Mitch took another hit of his pipe. "My time as a gravedigger is over, Candice. Those graves, that hut, that church, all in the past now. I am tired of living in the past. You know, before Jay left, I actually had some of the best sleep in my life. I dreamed golden dreams. Happy dreams. Peaceful dreams. I felt rejuvenated and felt a sense of purpose other than just digging graves. Life actually made sense again."

"So you will leave that hut behind?" Candice said.

"Look at what it represents, Candice," said Mitch. "Barely stable and teetering on collapse. The church in the background so obscure yet hauntingly always close."

"You never went inside of it, did you?"

"No, but Jay did. He did and he saw what we once saw. A glimpse into the past. A once happy portrait."

"Serena loved that word," Candice said. "Portrait. It's like her work became an obsession, and after Jay died, she became the face of her work."

"You mean her work became decadent along with her. Once bright pastel colors turned dark and foreboding."

"Mitchell, I don't want to lose my daughter. She is a part of me. Trust me, I have seen this play out in movies. People that go down this path only have two options: salvation or death. I don't want the latter for my daughter, my child."

"You are failing to see that she is *our* daughter, Candice. Don't slip back into that old way of thinking. Yes, I notice what's going on. Do you think I have like looking into eyes that are not the eyes of the girl we raised? Serena, who took the form of an angel, but acting like a demon."

"I don't think I could face Serena now, knowing she is like this. I would probably faint at the sight of her."

"Don't be so dramatic, Candice. Her disdain is for me, not you. I am the one that left you two behind and I have already resigned myself to whatever awaits me."

"Speaking of that, where exactly are we going?"

"We are going to visit an old friend of mine. One I haven't seen in quite some time."

"Well, let's make haste. The rain is picking up."

A few more miles in and Candice stopped. "What is it?" Mitch asked.

"How do you simply allow yourself to get so soaked? I am drenched!" Mitch put down his bag and opened it, retrieving two umbrellas. Candice

The Perfect Portrait

could see the base was a branch with vines acting as the vines that held the top up. "Are these supposed to be umbrellas?"

"Man's to make due. Deer skins for the cover. Vines to hold it up. I coated the base with tree sap and hardened it over a fire."

"Sounds like you met a nice auburn-haired wench with big boobs only held up by a scantly tight bra and you instantly wrapped that hard, hot wood of yours in a rubber."

"There's no Baytree Avenue whores out here. Just a lovely woman named Candice Vega and Mother Nature. Both of whom took to me nicely."

"You sly dog! Let me have one of those before I catch my death of cold." Mitch handed one over to Candice. She could see he put a small wooden latch like the piece that one would push up on an umbrella to open it.

"Opens just like a normal one," Mitch said, opening his. Candice followed suit.

"Impressive," she said. "By the way, you know what these woods hold."

"The Hallugen Woods. Flowers that emit an aroma so strong they make one hallucinate."

"Exactly, and also pig fairies."

"The rain has dampened their abilities somewhat. As for the fairies, I haven't seen any yet. I know they love to play games."

"I had to save Jay and his little raccoon friend from them when I came through here a while back."

Mitch took out his pipe and lit it. "Raccoon friend?" he said.

"Yes. I have never seen such a thing as a talking raccoon in my life. He sounded quite intelligent to say the least. Do you know him?"

"Yes. As a matter of fact, I do. It's been so long though, ever since way back when."

"Hmm."

"Anyway, Candice, let us continue. I am sure you brought your bow back."

"Back? Hell, I never forgot it. I always say shoot a pig through the heart, roast him over a fire, and fillet gently yet hard to the core."

"I have had thirty million reasons to learn that lesson. Trust me."

. . .

Her wing broken, on struggling to hold up a delicate yet ugly body, and a pride busted. Pixana and her flock were looking for revenge. "That woman!" she said to the others. "She has disgraced us! Me! We had what we were wanting. We wanted to simply play, but apparently that woman didn't want us to have fun."

"What should we do, Highness?" said one of the others. Pixana flew back and forth, before finally stopping and holding her snoot in the air. "We get revenge!" she said. "I can smell a human approaching from the Hallugen Woods. That woman will pay for this! I will not be beaten by…that woman!"

. . .

Mitch and Candice stopped by a river to rest for a moment. He stayed by the edge, catching his breath. "T-twenty miles," he said. "I didn't think twenty miles could be so long."

"You're not young anymore," Candice said. "This isn't the easy streets you once walked down."

Mitch reached in his bag and pulled out a flask of water. He smelled the air. "Flowers are getting stronger."

"Figures," said Candice. "It's like these woods are a trial. A…long trial!"

"Don't get sleepy on me," Mitch said. He reached into his bag and retrieved a cloth. "Here," he said, handing it to her.

"You know, I see the beautiful ocean is calling," Candice said.

"Candice, take this! Hurry!"

"It's so lovely and colorful!"

"Shit!" Mitch said. He had been through these woods before, but that was a while ago. Now here her was, holding up Candice from falling astray. He turned his ears to what he thought was a child's giggling. He looked and saw pink dust, a flock of fat, naked bodies, and one pissed-off Pixana before him and Candice. "Even the worst whore in an alley way doesn't look that bad," he said, facing Pixana and her flock. Pixana withdrew her staff.

"Oh, sweet, you haven't seen a real whore yet!"

. . .

"The sea is violent on this day
Wash away, wash away
The skies are dark with tears falling
The sea is calling"

"Oh, Lester, would you shut up?" Catalina said, leaning over the side, trying her best not to throw up. The wind was howling, the waters choppy and uneven, and the sky with clouds as black as the heart of the woman who created them. It was raining very heavily, and Catalina wanted so bad to go inside, but Neacen and Sootshire already had that covered. Someone had to watch over Jay. "It's bad enough I am wet out here with you but don't make it worse with that atrocious singing!"

"Lighten up. I have learned an old seamen's song helps ease the mind in times like this."

"Yeah, well, it's not easing my stomach."

"After the day we've had so far, a seamen's song is needed."

"How much further to we reach shore?"

"Oh, the sea calls!"

"Oh, boy!" Catalina said.

. . .

The skies have grown darker in this world. Serena's touch has already been felt. I have had to reveal my true identity in the wake of Jay's possession. Everyone is on edge, but the Logger continues to sing. The only thing keeping me safe is your guidance and light.

John Paul Shuman Jr.

Every moment I spend away from you is a breakage to my heart. I promise you, on my own soul, once this is over, I will never leave your side ever again.

With Sincere love,
Neacen Ruthman

Wandering Leaf was resting peacefully as Sootshire sat close by, eating some fish. "Writing Estelle?" he asked Neacen.

"Yes, Snowden. You have no idea just how much I miss her. It's like leaving a part of me behind."

"Imagine being surrounded by pig fairies. Now that is worth writing about."

"Snowden, you're missing the point."

"Then please explain."

"No. In time you will see just what I mean. I promise."

"At least Jay's at peace. Um, he can't hear us, can he?"

"No. He's out. By the movements of his eyes under the lids, he's dreaming."

"Of what, though?"

"I won't say. Be patient, my friend. Be patient."

. . .

Candice was falling deeper under the effects of the flowers. Pixana flew closer, her flock in suit. "Touch one hair of my wife's head and I will kill you!" Mitch yelled.

"Oh, Mitch!" Pixana said. "You must not realize that you're not the man you once were."

"Damn right I am not."

"Oh, honey! Don't get it, do you? You can't shoot a bow or arrow or wield a sword. All you know is graves and former glory." Candice started to cough and gasp.

"Candice! What the hell is going on, Pixana?"

"Oh, that's right, I forgot to mention. Continued inhalations of hallucinogenic flowers can cause breathing problems, hallucinations, and, ultimately, respiratory failure, which is fitting since you failed as a person!"

"You whore!"

"Thank you! My pleasure!" Pixana looked to her flock. "Now, ladies, what should—" She was interrupted by a loud snap and crunch. Once of her flock was caught by a mouth belonging to a gray-black-and-white-furred wolf with blue eyes. She chewed, crushing bone, wing, flesh, and grisle. "You fucking mutt!" Pixana yelled. "Ladies, let's kill this damn wolf!"

The fairies flew towards the wolf, but she stood her ground and tore into each one of them. One bite and they disintegrated until only Pixana remained. "You filthy beast!" she screamed. The wolf drew closer, teeth showing the blood of her fallen comrades. "I will kill you!" Pixana said. She charged and instead was met with the inside of the wolf's mouth, and the encounter of its teeth.

Mitch held Candice, who was still having a hard time breathing. He looked to the wolf and felt a peace coming from those crystal blue eyes. "Thank you," he said to the wolf. "But we need to get out of here and to Sumurka." As aged as he was, he grabbed Candice and hoisted her on his back. "I will feel the pain later. My wife needs me now! Come, wolf!"

The Village of Sumurka

Elder Mikel and the other villagers noticed the changes. "She has forsaken us," he said to Tonan, one of his closest warriors, whose loyalty and devotion was only eclipsed by Catalina herself.

"What should we do?" Tonan said, his short black pointy ears drenched wet. Elder Mikel looked dead in his green eyes.

"We must fortify the village. Gather the men and begin. We can't allow the sea to infiltrate."

"Yes, my Elder," Tonan said.

"I will gather the women and children to safer ground."

Then, they heard something coming from the woods. Mitch, Candice, and the wolf emerged. The people of the village acted guarded, except Mikel. Mitch looked at them and they met him with a look of…worry. "It's been a while, Mikel," Mitch said.

"Likewise," said Mikel, walking up to him, guards in tow.

"I could use some help here."

"You have come to right place, my friend."

. . .

Mitch watched as the Elder rubbed a gel made of local plants across Candice's nose, allowing her to breathe better. "She could have died," he said to Mitch.

"I know, Mikel," Mitch said. "If it wasn't for this wolf, I would have lost her."

"You found this wolf in the Hallugen Woods?"

"No, the wolf found us. We were in a pretty tight situation before."

"I know." He looked to his men, who were close by in case anything happened. "Leave us," Mikel said, waving his hand. "I will be fine."

Mitch took out his pipe and lit it. "I didn't know you smoked, Mitch," said the Elder.

"Only since I came here. Back then, however, I would have been making company with a stripper at Easy's."

"You still have that smart mouth of yours, I see. I take it Candice found you."

"Yes. I was coming home and saw her there with her bow pointed at me. I honestly didn't blame her for being upset with me for all that happened. To be honest, I still feel like this is somewhat my fault for not being the parent I should have been."

"Don't blame yourself, Mitchell. What happened in the past was in the past. You are a better man now than you were back then. Candice has forgiven you. You need to forgive yourself."

"But Serena, my child, she's still consumed by hate. I couldn't, no, I—"

The Perfect Portrait

"Mitchell, your daughter chose this path and now she is feeling her own negative energy. I know she is your child and you and Candice both still love her, but in the end, she chose, SHE chose, not you, not Candice."

"I don't want to bury my daughter, Mikel."

"Mitchell, Serena has already buried herself." Mitch shook his head. "Fret not, my friend. You must be famished and tired after such a long journey."

"I am. Eating natural only goes so far."

"Very well. You are welcome to use my personal tub in the back."

"Mikel, I couldn't."

"Please, I insist. Besides, for all you've done, it's good to know I can help you. I will have a nice stew ready for you."

"What about…?"

"I will watch Candice. Please help yourself."

"Thank you," Mitch said.

Mitch felt his body relax as he sat in the warm waters. He was surrounded by various plants and noticed Mikel even had a few birds flying around. It was peaceful compared to the horrors of the outside. He didn't even hear the rain or thunder. Just peaceful silence. "Ahh, this is Heaven!" he said.

"Oh, is it?" said a voice. Mitch looked and saw the water in front of him bubbling and slowly rose, that hair the color of darkened clouds, eyes that were soulless and empty. Wings as opaque as the primeval night and a body perfected yet twisted.

"You can't…" Mitch said, but stopped.

"Oh, I can, Father! I live in Hell because of you! This is all your fault!"

"Serena, listen!"

"No, you listen, Mitchell! I am perfect. I am law and you are a pile of wretched filth and now you are useless." Serena held her sword.

"Serena!" Mitch yelled. Footsteps were heard and Mikel came running in.

"Mitch, what is it?" he asked, poised to pounce on whatever was after his friend.

"She was here! Serena was here!" Mikel sighed and walked over. He sniffed the air and looked around.

"No, she isn't. Please don't allow your thoughts to consume you, Mitch. I promise you her dark hands hold no power over you anymore. Trust me." Mitch looked at the water and saw only blue liquid and steam.

"All right," he said.

"Finish up. We have dinner and much to discuss."

A man ravaged by the past smiled slightly, at least in the present. Candice was up, looking rejuvenated. "Candice!" he said, running over and hugging his wife tightly.

"Mitchell," she said. "You're hugging me like I was about to leave you."

"You were," said Mitch. "You don't remember what happened in the Hallugen Woods?"

"All I remember is seeing the ocean and that was it."

"It would have been had it not been for that salvation," said Mikel.

"Hmm?" Candice said. Mitch pointed over to the wolf who was licking a bowl of soup. "That wolf save me?"

"Saved us," Mitch said. "She had a fairy delicious meal."

"Ahem," said Mikel. "Let us eat and discuss what's next."

Mitch enjoyed every bite of the carp that was displayed in the homemade soup. "Oh my! This is heavenly!" he said.

"The last time you ate like that Mitch was on a business trip," Candice said.

"Too long ago," he said. Candice turned to Mikel.

"So, what's the next move?" she asked. Mikel sipped his tea and looked at her.

"You two will need to accompany them," he said. Mitch and Candice looked to each other.

"Who's them?" they both asked.

. . .

"Finally arrived!" the Logger said as the boat docked ashore.

"Thank goodness!" Catalina said.

The Perfect Portrait

Eyes that had been closed for a while finally opened. Wandering Leaf could hear rainwater crashing against the hull, and standing before him were Sootshire and Neacen. "Neacen, Sootshire," he said, sitting up. He grunted and put his hand to his head, where he felt the bandage covering a wound.

"You're awake!" Soothshire said, running over and slapping him on the face.

"Hey, what was that for?"

"What for? You mindless oaf! You nearly killed us all!"

"Enough, Snowden!" Neacen said. He walked over and sat beside Wandering Leaf. "I can tell you have been through hell. We all have."

"What do you mean? Did I do something?"

Footsteps were heard and the door opened. "Hey, we…" Catalina said before stopping mid-sentence. She instantly ran over and grabbed Wandering Leaf and slammed him to the floor. "You bitch!" she yelled, getting her claws ready to strike.

"Hey, hey!" Lester said, running in behind Catalina and grabbing her.

"Let me go! Lester, let me go! This bitch almost killed me! Now what, Serena! Huh?"

"Peace be unto you," Neacen said, standing up and putting his hand on Catalina's head. She stopped scratching and calmed down. "Let us go see Elder Mikel."

. . .

"Elder, who could you possibly mean?" Candice said. The door was knocked upon.

"Yes, Tonan. Please, let them in." The door opened, and there in front of Candice and Mitch stood Jay and his companions, wet but alive. Mitch and Candice stood and walked over to Jay and team. A smile of satisfaction came across Mitchell's face as he looked in Jay's eyes. They were stronger now, confident, and hopeful.

"My, it has been a while," he said, embracing the boy.

"Mitchell," said Wandering Leaf. "Likewise. I have made some friends along the way." Wandering Leaf looked at the woman that was with Mitch.

"Hello," he said. "My name is Wondering Leaf." Candice rubbed the boy's face and instantly started crying and turned away. "Did I…?"

"No," Mitch said. "She is just glad you're alive."

"Everyone, please sit down," Mikel said.

"Mitch," Wandering Leaf said. "I would like for you to meet my friends. This is Neacen." Neacen was sipping some tea.

"It's a pleasure," Mitch said. "Where are you from?"

"Originally, I am from a village called Eden. It is outside the main city of Rhodam."

"Interesting. Um, where is Candice?"

"Bathing with the wolf," Mikel said.

"I think we could all use one," Lester said. "No offense, Elder, but I think the intros can be saved for the open ocean. Time is critical."

"I agree," the elder said. "There are hot springs nearby. One for men and one for women. Please, be welcomed."

"Thank you, Elder Mikel," Wandering Leaf said.

Wandering Leaf and the other men sat outside in the hot springs. The rain had ceased, and the sky had begun to clear. "Whoever would have thought that a raccoon would bit sitting in a tub?" Lester said.

"Even I had to get the scent of saltwater and woods off of me, you ox!" Sootshire said. He turned to Wandering Leaf. "How are you feeling?"

"Fine, at least now, that is. I feel like my head is about to explode. How long was I out?"

"About four hours at least," Neacen said. "You slept like a baby."

"Neacen, my I ask you something?"

"Sure, J…just ask away."

"Just ask away?"

"The question, please."

"Back in the boat, when Catalina attacked me, she called me Serena and furthermore a bitch. What was that all about?"

"Wandering Leaf, don't you think that's a question best posed to someone more experienced?" Sootshire asked.

The Perfect Portrait

"True, but also add the fact that Neacen said 'peace be unto you' and touched her, instantly calming her. I mean, she came after me like I was not myself or something." Neacen looked to Lester.

"Hey, man, he's asking you the question, not me," Lester said. Neacen sighed.

"It was…" Neacen started to say.

"The pixie dust!" Sootshire interrupted.

"Really? How?" Wandering Leaf asked. "I thought I was over that."

"It was in your bag. Residue, I mean."

"O…kay? Then why did Catalina call me Serena, then? Are you three hiding something from me?" The others looked at each other.

Damn! Neacen thought. *Even without the pendants on, I can still feel something coming off of him.*

"Something like what?" Wandering Leaf said. Neacen, Sootshire, and Lester looked shocked. "Guys, please, just be honest. It's not like I am going to kill you." At that moment they started scrabbling out of the tub. "Okay, stop! I'm just playing. I could have been sleepwalking or something. No big deal."

If you only knew, Neacen thought.

"Knew what?"

"Nothing, Wandering Leaf," they all said.

. . .

Catalina was on edge, not from the water, but from the sight of the wolf sitting close nearby. "He won't harm you," Candice said.

"I have learned never to take chances," Catalina said.

"What did you say your name was? Catalina?"

"Yes."

"That's a beautiful name. My name is Candice Vega."

"So, you're Mitch's wife?"

"Yes."

"Are you two married?"

"We were at one time. We divorced over twenty years ago. I ran into him while traversing the lands. Now we agree to disagree."

"Did you two have a child?"

"Yes. A daughter we named Serena."

At that moment, Catalina remembered the talk she had on the boat with Neacen and Sootshire. "I will be damned," she said.

"Beg your pardon?" said Candice.

"Nothing. Just talking to myself."

"Are you mated to anyone?"

"Me? No!"

"No prospects? Come on, Catalina. I was a young girl too, and I raised one."

You raised a demon bitch, Catalina thought. "Okay, I have one," she said.

"Who?"

"Someone far away. It's not a big deal."

"You mean far away from your mind but close to your heart, right?"

Damn, she's good! Catalina thought. "N-no...no!"

"Catalina..."

"Yes, okay? I do."

"I knew you did. So, who is he?"

I swear if... Catalina thought. Her claws begging to come out.

"The closest one to you is probably Jay."

"Jay? I don't know any Jay?"

"The one you call Wandering Leaf. That's mine and Mitchell's grandson. Jay."

"Okay, and?"

"You kept smacking you tail against his butt when I first saw you guys in the Elder's home. I think you two would do nicely together. You seem to have that feistiness which compliments his thoughtfulness. He needs a tough yet loving woman in his life, and from woman to woman, you have my blessing."

"Thanks..." Catalina said. "Elder Mikel always told me I wear my emotions too much."

"I know the situation is dire right now, but please, try not to hate my daughter."

Hate? Catalina thought. "The bitch tried to kill of us off!"

"She's just lost."

"Lost in the echo of her own madness!"

"And…"

"She…"

"I still."

"Will be."

"Love her."

"Dead as dirt!"

"I am sure you understand from a family perspective," said Candice.

"Yes. Yes, I do," Catalina said. She thought to herself, *And I understand your daughter is one dead bitch!*

"Thank you, Catalina."

"The pleasure is mine, Ms. Vega."

"Candice. Call me Candice."

. . .

Neacen, Sootshire, and Lester sat around a fire under a canopy that night. Jay, Candice, Mitch, and the wolf were sleeping inside while Catalina was with the Elder. "What a weird last few moments," Sootshire said.

"At least the rain stopped for a little bit," Lester said.

"We almost blew our cover too soon," Neacen said. "Serena must have done something to Jay while she possessed him."

"It is odd that he read your mind, Neacen."

"Yes, but it was only mine! I know you two were thinking something, but he didn't read yours."

"That's a tough one," said Lester. "It would seem Serena has an intense hatred for you."

"Because of what I can do," Neacen said.

"At least she didn't try to possess you," Sootshire said.

"Snowden, once again, you miss the point."

Lester stood up. "You two can argue points on the boat tomorrow. I am bushed after three days on the open ocean."

"I am tired as well," Sootshire said. "You coming, Neacen?"

"Just a moment. Go on ahead."

As the two of them walked off, Neacen looked back into the fire. "What did you do to Jay, Serena? What is your plan?" He looked to the sky. "Sweet *Estelle*, please, watch over us and keep Jay safe. Amen…"

. . .

The sky was an indifferent gray as the new day began. The birds were silent, and the only sound was the villagers of Sumurka going about their daily lives. In the home of Elder Mikel stood seven souls. Neacen Ruthman, the boy who is masquerading as a member of Rhodam's Council. One, who is gifted with spiritual prowess and a strong sense of hope and his beloved Estele. Catalina, a cat girl with a feisty attitude and strong will. Her only soft spot is that for a boy she is still getting to know.

The Logger, or Lester, as he is actually known as. The man with a love for the sea. A man who distanced himself from his past to try to start anew. Sootshire, the one and only Snowden Sootshire. A talking raccoon of the forest, with an immense love for fish. The first point of contact for Wandering Leaf as he began his journey.

Mitchell and Candice Vega, father and mother to Serena, their daughter who created this world. The former, although seeking redemption, is still haunted by his past mistakes, while the latter is trying to understand what her child has become. And lastly, Wandering Leaf, known as Jay to everyone but himself. The one soul caught in the middle of it all. A boy trying to figure out who he is and where he is going. The centerpiece of a complex portrait nearly completed by a vengeful mother and distraught father. "I am sure everyone is aware of the situation," Elder Mikel said.

The Perfect Portrait

"Mostly," Neacen said. "We know that Serena must be stopped."

"And that she is making her presence more known," Sootshire said. He looked to Candice and Mitch. "Are you two sure you're okay being along for this journey?"

"I have dreamed of it," Mitch said.

"So have I," said Candice. "I need to see my child."

Elder Mikel walked over to Catalina and Wandering Leaf. He spoke first to her. "You have grown so much, Catalina." Catalina looked away, for she knew why, but still...why? "Listen to me, child. You must learn to understand that I will be fine. I have watched many a youth grow into fine warriors and you have exceeded my expectations. You are the manifestation of our people's strength, and now it's time for you to use that to help others in need." As he said this, he looked to Wandering Leaf. "And you, young one. Whatever awaits you for the remainder of this journey, I urge you to face it without fear but with courage. You, like Catalina, have grown so much. Find your true self and embrace it."

"I will," Wandering Leaf said.

"Good. Now, where will you seven be off to?"

"Rhodam," Neacen said. "This will be where this all concludes."

"How do you know?" Lester asked.

"Let the boy be," Mitch said. "I trust him."

"As do I," said Candice.

"And me," said Catalina.

"I do," said Wandering Leaf. "Hey, do you, Sooty? Sooty?" They all looked and saw Sootshire eating a piece of fish.

"Oh, yes! I do!" he said.

"Well, then," said the Elder. "Go forth and save our world!"

The others walked out, along with the wolf, which left Catalina there for a moment with Elder Mikel. They stood there, their eyes interlocked. The Elder simply nodded and Catalina nodded back. As they arrived at the boat, Lester stopped and turned to face them. "All right. To those of you new to this journey, I have one rule and one rule only! Respect *Estella* and I will respect you. Also, clean up behind your wolves, please." They all turned and saw the wolf behind them, eyes eager to see a new world.

"Whose wolf is that?" Wandering Leaf asked.

"She came with Candice and I," Mitch said. Catalina came and rejoined them, having said her words with the Elder.

"Fair enough," Neacen said. "Shall we go?"

"I am ready," Catalina said.

"All right, everyone!" Wandering Leaf said. "Let's do it!"

To Estelle,

At long last we have gathered our crew of seven on the road to you. You have been a beacon for me since I was old enough to understand and I know you will protect us. I can't wait to see your beautiful eyes again and hold you one more time…

With love,
Neacen Ruthman

Chapter 24

Back to Rhodam

Mitchell was amazed at the city of Rhodam's beautiful exterior. From the front of the boat, he could see her majestic buildings drawing ever closer on the horizon. "The ole girl sure is beautiful," he said to Lester.

"I take it you have seen the city before?" Lester said.

"As a matter of fact, I have."

"If that's the case, then none of this surprises you."

"Why do you say that?"

"Ever since you met up with the rest of us, you haven't acted like any of this was new to you."

"All I will say is that I have been around. Now, I have a question for you, Lester."

"Go ahead and ask."

"How is it that you managed to stay up all night? The rest of us were tired from all the fish we ate. Secondly, how did you manage to fit all of us on *Estella*?"

"One question at a time, old cat," Lester said. "First off, I have found out the smell of the sea and the sun shining off the crystal-clear waves are to too beautiful to miss. However, even I had to get some sleep last night. As for your second question, *Estella* is big enough to hold a hundred people, figuratively speaking. The largest crew she's held is what we have now."

"You know, I noticed my wife Candice holding Jay close last night."

"Grandmother's love, old cat."

"You know we're Jay's grandparents?"

"Mitch, I know more than I let on. When I saw you two, I wasn't surprised. Only the old wolf back in there caught me off guard. Your grandson is a good man. He acts lost at times, but you know how kids are."

"Of course I know. I…Candice raised one."

"You two split up?"

"Yes. I wasn't the best father or husband."

"Still carry regret?"

Before answering, Mitch took out his pipe and lit it. "What man wouldn't. Especially since you feel you're the one that lit the fuse to the powder keg. It was all my fault."

"You have Candice now, but you're still missing Serena."

"Yes. Despite having my wife and grandson back, I still miss her. Her face as it is now haunts me like a demon. Imagine your own child wanting you dead. I have trouble sleeping sometimes because of this."

"I was suffering from something similar back in the day. I was what you would call a high-class roller."

"Big shit?"

"Yeah. I had it all, but I let it get to my head."

"Heh, I know about that."

"Lost my wife, most of if not all my so-called friends, and nearly my mind."

"What saved you?"

"The very sea we're on right now. It washed me clean, but most of all, it taught me to forgive myself."

"Do you miss your wife?"

"Yes, I will admit. I would be a fool if I didn't, but…you know."

"Can't change the past."

"I thought you said your daughter's mood influenced the weather."

"It does."

"Then how is it this area has color and the area we were just in didn't? The sun is out shining brightly, clear blue skies, but back that way, nothing."

The Perfect Portrait

"I can't say. Rhodam should be a dull gray, but she's colorful."

"We're about to dock soon. I hope everyone's wiping sleep crust from their eyes."

"What time is it?"

"Judging by the sun's position, I would say early morning. Send the word. We have arrived back in Rhodam."

Seven souls and a wolf stepped onto the wharf leading into the city. For Neacen, Wandering Leaf, Catalina, Lester, Sootshire, and Mitch, this was nothing new, but for Candice, it was like stepping into a dream. "It's like Heaven!" she said, walking further in. She stopped and examined the statues of Serena; however, she did not know this as of yet. "These look like they took some time to sculpt. Are these pure gold?"

"Yes," said Neacen. "Statues symbolizing the eternal faith of Rhodam and its belief in the Goddess on High, Serena."

"Serena? Hmm, she has the same name as our daughter. She looks so… majestic."

"I need to talk with those two bonehead guards. Come, Sootshire."

"I hope they have fish," he said, scurrying along.

Wandering Leaf and Catalina walked up to statue. She looked at it with a look of disgust. "What's wrong?" he asked her.

"This statue just gives me an uneasy feeling," she said. Wandering Leaf walked up and touched it.

"Doesn't affect me."

"That's because…"

"Well, because?"

"Nothing. Never mind."

"Catalina, you've been acting weird lately. What is going on?"

"Calm it," Mitch said. "I think you two should enjoy yourselves." The wolf came up and licked Wandering Leaf's hand. "She can come with you."

"What is her name?" Catalina said.

"Considering she saved me and Candice at the last minute, I was considering calling her Miracle."

"Miracle, Mitch?" Candice said. "How about Mira?"

"I got it," Wandering Leaf said. "We'll call her Snow."

"Snow?"

"Look at her. She's colored just like it."

"Um, Snow is pure white, Wandering Leaf."

"Yeah. She's mixed with grey and black."

"Snow will do for now," Lester said. "Now can we actually enjoy the city now?"

"Sounds good to me," Mitch said.

"I will take Catalina with me," Wandering Leaf said.

"And Snow," said Mitch. He looked to Candice. "Ready to enjoy the city?"

"Why, yes, I am." As they walked off, Wandering Leaf looked to Lester. "And what about you?" he asked.

"I am going to mingle here for a little bit. Don't forget I have to fix the door and patch up some things."

"I have been meaning to ask you about that. What happened?"

"Horrible…" Catalina started to say, but Lester cut her off.

"Bad storm, that's all. You two go on. It looks like Neacen has the way cleared."

"All right. If you need us…"

"No, little man. Take the time to actually *enjoy* the city. Don't forget, I have seen a hundred like her."

. . .

Neacen and Sootshire sat inside Hopewell's Café. "This is peace," he said, looking out onto Estelle, the rays of sunlight shining beautifully off her breast. Her eyes were a beautiful and lush as the day he first saw them.

"Uh huh," Soothsire said, eating some fish.

"Oh, Snowden. You couldn't even fathom what I feel right now. It's true peace, at least for now. Estelle is looking back into me, and like me, she is worried."

"About what?"

"That answer will be revealed very soon, my friend."

"You hardly touched any of your food."

"Seeing Estelle is plenty enough for me."

"Can I…?

"Go ahead, my forest-based friend."

"Ah hah!" Sootshire said, quickly grabbing the plate.

"Sometimes I wonder if you wouldn't marry a piece of fish."

"Wh..t?" Sootshire said, gulping a piece.

"Never mind."

. . .

"Absolutely stunning!" Candice said as she looked at the paintings in the museum.

"A hundred different places we could be, you pick an art museum," Mitch said.

"Of course. I am not seventeen anymore, Mitch. Did you expect me to beg for a fancy dinner or a ruby?"

"Well, no, but we actually don't blend in too well."

"Mitchell S. Vega, of all people, you are worrying about looks right now."

"Just saying."

"You can't tell me Rhodam doesn't beat that shack you were living in. Come on, this is a new place, and besides, it has been a while since I viewed works of art."

"How about I pose this question, Candice."

"Go ahead."

"You don't find it odd that Jay is…"

"Seeing a cat girl? Me? Odd? Goodness, no! Mitch, you must remember I was a veterinarian before. The woman who could work with any animal. I am sure Jay has feelings for Catalina just like she does for him."

"Did you and Catalina talk about this?"

"That is between us. Now, may I ask you a question?"

"Sure, Candice. Anything."

"Did you ever want another woman since you came to this world?"

"Seriously, Candice?"

"Well?"

"You always liked to squeeze my balls. To answer your question, no. It has been me and my will to survive ever since I came here."

"You don't miss how it used to be?"

"Financially, no. Family, yes. I miss seeing an innocent girl run into my arms. I miss seeing my wife still smiling after a long day of doing what she loves. But most of all, I still live with the fact of knowing I had a chance to hold on to that but blew it. Why do you still insist on torturing me, Candice?"

"Simple, Mitch. If we are to move on together, I don't want there to be any regrets or lies untold. It's more or less a confession."

"Don't play like Serena on me, Candice. The girl already wants me dead. Hell, she held a sword to my throat.

"Yep, that's Serena all right. It's been a long time since I've seen her."

"You don't remember?"

"What?"

"The statue that you first saw when you came here?"

"That was Serena?" Candice said, starting to chuckle. "No way! I know our daughter loves angels, but seriously."

"I am serious, Candice. I have seen her with my own eyes, and she isn't the one to be laughing at."

"Mitch, are you sure your time in this world hasn't played with your head?"

"Believe what you want, Candice, but it's true. Now, are we going to enjoy this moment or keep going down memory lane, which I have had enough of."

"All right. I will stop."

"That's music to my ears."

"Why is that?"

"Because silence is golden in this case."

"All right, all right. No more past talk."

"I hope so."

. . .

The Perfect Portrait

Wandering Leaf, Catalina, and Snow decided to go to Rhodam's Skyline Bridge. Such was it called because it sat at one of the highest points in the city, allowing a person to look across the cityscape and view the majestic Capshen Sea. "I thought cats were afraid of heights," he said.

"There are always exceptions to every rule," Catalina said. She felt Snow rub against her leg and lick her heels.

"Look at this!" Wandering Leaf said, taking a moment and noticing Snow getting acquainted with Catalina's legs. "Looks like Snow wants to get to know you."

"Very funny," Catalina said. "Can I ask you something?"

"Sure."

"Some time ago, shortly after we first met, you said you were not from this world. I have been thinking about that, but I haven't said anything, at least until now."

"Originally I am not," Leaf said. "I am from a world far beyond this one. Honestly, the world I am from is nothing like this one. To be frank, it's pretty boring. Sooty asked me a while ago why I was on this journey. At the moment, I couldn't answer him. I was just getting started out on this quest."

"Can you answer it now?"

"Honestly, no. Catalina, you must remember I still don't know myself. So badly do I want to know. I haven't told anyone this, but lately, I have been having nightmares."

"Oh, you mean wet dreams about Serena, huh?"

"Catalina, I am serious. Ever since I passed out on the boat. I just haven't felt…whole."

"What happens in your dreams?"

"She just keeps telling me I am perfect. That soon and very soon, I will have the life and wings I so rightfully deserve. I also keep hearing Neacen's thoughts in my head and they seem like the mental ramblings of a worried mind."

"That sounds…"

"Crazy, I know…"

"It's not that. It's just…"

"And I can't find my pendant. I have looked all over the boat for it and I can't find it. That pendant has been a part of me since the beginning and I can't find the damn thing."

"Easy there. It will show up. Don't get upset over it. Please, enjoy the moment with me."

"Sorry. It's been a long journey. All I want to do is give Serena her pendant and be done with all this. I don't want to end up having to hurt anyone. You must understand, Catalina, I have never hurt anything, and I just get this feeling that I will have to make a choice."

"Please, Leafy, stop talking like this."

"All right. It just worries me, that's all."

"Then let the worry go. Enjoy this moment and let things take their course. Life is too short to worry." Catalina took her paw and put it on Leafy's hand.

"I just want to finally live, Catalina." She looked into the distance, knowing all too well that there was a chance before living would take place, there would be dying.

"Want to have some fish at the Fish in the Hole back in the city?"

"Catalina, we are in the city."

"I mean downtown. I saw it as we passed it on the way here."

"The Fish in the Hole restaurant. Sounds odd."

"I am sure it's good. Besides, you haven't really eaten much lately…"

"You're right. Sure. Let's go there. I am hungry. How about you, Snow?" The wolf wagged her tail and stood on her hind legs. "Good. Let's go."

. . .

"You have been through worst, *Estella*," Lester said as he gathered some nails and prepared to put the door back up. For Lester, or "Logger" as he was commonly known, the sea offered him a sense of peace and tranquility. The sea did not care if you were different, rich or poor, there was always room in the realm of the vast, mighty ocean. Lester smelled the salt in the air, a smell that had become a haven for his nostrils. "I hope the others are enjoying them-

The Perfect Portrait

selves. It feels good to see some color in a world gone dark." As he began to move the broken wood aside, he looked and saw a young couple walking down the boardwalk. The young man looked to be in his late teens to early twenties. His eyes were a greenish blue and his hair was cut real shore. The girl looked to be the same age, with her hair up in a bun, eyes akin to the man's. They both wore what looked to be clothing of the church, but was this strictly a religious center or something more?

Nevertheless, it struck a chord with Lester, as it reminded him of the time he once felt that same love. Yet, that was so long ago but it felt just like yesterday. Lester decided not to look back. That was then and this was now. At least now he served a purpose, albeit a person ferrying a few souls on a boat. Yet, every now and again, the thought of how life could have been different would cross his mind. "No," Lester told himself as he began working. "I hate what happened but that was the past. All I can do is move on. I just wish I knew how Serena was able to see into me?"

"The Religious Order of Rhodam," Mitch said. "You know I wrote a few entries in my own journal back in the village."

"I have read," Candice said. "You wrote all those journals back then?"

"Yes. You know I visited some of the best libraries in the country when I was younger."

"Yes, to hit on some."

"Really, Candice. You know, maybe you don't see it but I really want to start over. You know, see a brighter side to things. Stop hanging my past over my head."

"You really have changed, haven't you?"

"It's as I've said, I've learned my lesson. I am trying to start over, albeit at an old age. I figure you would be at least supportive of me as far as that was concerned. It's bad enough I have a daughter that wants me dead. Don't add fuel to the fire."

"All right, Mitchell. I will stop."

"Thank you, Candice."

John Paul Shuman Jr.

. . .

"Seven years for some of these fish to grow," Neacen said, examining the cottle in the stream. He and Sootshire were in Bronson Forest near the city. As Neacen put it, it was "time for the researcher to come back out."

"More like seven minutes to cook," Sootshire said.

"Are you always this into fish? From a cooking perspective I mean?"

"Why, yes, actually. Grill, fillet, fry. Three best ways for a fish to die."

"Ah, Snowden, you fail to see the elegance of life itself. Yes, we humans require sustenance, but let's not forget the raw beauty that exist outside of a dinner plate." He reached into his bag and pulled out a small net and scooped up one of the fish. He held it up in the light, allowing the sun to shine off its blue, green, and purple scales. "Now, what do you see?"

Sootshire looked and sniffed. "Dinner."

"No, no, Snowden. I am serious."

"I seriously see dinner." Neacen shook his head and sighed before placing the fish back in the water.

"That little fish could one day break a world record or could hold the cure to an illness. What I am saying is that there is possibility in all life."

"Neacen, why are you acting this way now? Hmm?"

"You know me, Snowden. I have missed the beauty of life, the glory of *Estelle*. When we were out in the dull grayness of the unknown, I clung so tightly to her. She is a beacon of light for me. Do you understand this, Snowden?"

"I understand fillet fish."

"Anyone that only sees a quick meal from pure life is a hog!"

. . .

"Oh, my! This fish is good!" Catalina purred. Leafy couldn't believe how fast she and Snow were eating piece after piece.

"Apparently, appetites haven't decreased," he said.

"You must be a light eater," Catalina said. "Even back in the village and when we first arrived in Rhodam, you didn't eat that much."

"I really haven't required that much in the way of food. I doubt I would be able to put on any pounds even if I did pig out."

"Surely, your parents watched how much or little you ate."

"Well, to be honest, I never knew either of them."

"You were briefly raised by a woman when you were young."

"Glenda?"

"Yes."

"I came to call her Mom. She was the closest thing to a mother if you wanted to be precise. Hell, I am not even sure she knows I am here."

"I don't see any phones around here."

"Don't worry, Catalina. I am taking this whole thing one day at a time."

"You know, when I first met you, you were a young smart ass. Now, you're young and smart."

"Everyone has to grow up, Catalina. To be honest, I was getting a feel for this world when I came here. Told by an old gravedigger that it was the manifestation of a tortured woman's mind. Serena's mind."

"I couldn't imagine living in someone else's dream. It would make me feel like an expendable fart, a thought in the winds of time."

"That's why I never believed in 'God' this or that. I mainly kept my thoughts focused on things I could actually see and touch."

"If that's the case, Leafy…you don't mind me calling that, do you?"

"I have been called worse than Wandering Leaf. It's fine."

"Okay. If that's the case, then why are you here?"

"In this realm?"

"Yes."

"Serena brought me here." At the sound of that, Catalina's eyes widened. "What? I was just minding my own business one day. I already explained some of this."

"Sorry. I just feel things are coming full circle."

"Really?"

"You know, with us all being together here in Rhodam, you're actually the only guy outside of Elder Mikel that truly accepted me."

"What about Mitch, Sooty, Neacen, or Lester?"

"I...to be honest, I have learned to tolerate them. But when I am with you, I feel a feeling I have never felt before."

"Which is?"

"You know that feeling you get when you've found someone you care for?"

"You lost me. In my twenty-two years back in the other world, I didn't really feel anything outside of nature."

"What about Glenda?"

"She put off powerful vibes, and I am not just talking about spouting about God this or that."

"Powerful aura, probably."

"I don't know anything about that."

"You sure?"

"Yes, why?"

"The dreams you told us about or the feelings you get from Serena at times."

"Yeah, I wish she would stop messing with my head. If there's something she wants me to see, show me already. All I can say is this, and promise you won't tell anyone."

"I promise, Leafy."

"Shortly after I first arrived here, I went inside an old, abandoned church near the hut Mitch used to stay in. It was dark, and I kid you not, as cold as it was, the front door was hot to the touch. I went inside and stood in the congregational area, and it felt as if I was seeing a wedding day play out in front of me. Serena's wedding day."

"Why would she show you this?"

"I don't know, Cat. Hell, it's just weird. I just started having these dreams not long ago, and to be honest there was one where I was..."

"Having sex with her?"

"No! I was looking into those dark pitiless eyes of hers. She kept telling me that I would grow up to be strong, smart, but most of all, perfect."

"Sounds creepy."

"Beyond creepy."

"I feel like this Serena might have a thing for you."

"You think? I don't understand why. I am only supposed to deliver two items to her. She looks to be young, but I am not looking for love right now."

"Leafy, that's not the point. What I mean is that it sounds like Serena has a plan for you."

"To send me home, I hope."

"Oh, brother. Leafy…"

"Kitty…" he said, putting his hand on Catalina's paws. Catalina began to hit Leafy on the back with her tail.

Council Mandate

"Order 73651," said the chairman. "The increase of the tithing and taxation of the people is set to pass in less than a week."

"Yes," said one of the others. "It is sure to stabilize the economy." Joshua sat at the far end of the table, blankly staring at his notes.

I can't believe this, he thought. *I haven't felt anything good the last few days. My sleeping has been thrown off, and I can't stop thinking about the people's safety.*

He heard the door open and saw Feldon come in and head straight for the lead chairman. He whispered something in his ear, causing a wide grin from ear to ear. "Please sit, Feldon," the chairman said. He stood up and tapped his spoon against the side of the glass. "Everyone, I have just received excellent news! Our dead Feldon here has just informed me of our Goddess's conquest of the city of Akoran!" My eyes widened and my blood instantly went from warm to boiling.

"That can't be!" I said, standing up, an outraged look on my face. The other members looked at me and started to laugh.

"Dear goodness, Joshua, you have been acting stranger than a fool on a hot bed of coals. You know Serena has the power to do whatever she wants. In fact, this act has just solved our trade problem with Akoran."

"Sir, I beg to differ. Soon, there will not be an Akoran."

"Of course not! Serena and her city will expand our provinces and consume that desert pit these people tried to call home for centuries."

"Sir, I beg you. Let me talk to her. This will not end well for anyone." The rest of the Council laughed.

"Sit down, Joshua, for you will do no such thing!"

Feldon had a shit-eating smirk on his face. "Don't forget, Joshua, we work for Her Highness. We belong to her. Remember the oath we took. You don't want Serena angry, now, do you?"

"Sir, I say we recess. It has been a long day."

"At a quarter to noon? Fine. At the request of Mr. Apprehension, we will break. We will adjourn back at one."

"Aye," the other men said.

Joshua couldn't believe what he had just heard. The city of Akoran was strongly built with a strong leader. Now Serena had taken hold of these people. He didn't see anything else but the fact that the Akronians, although experienced from stomping out the nearby occult village, were no match for Serena. "No! Listen to me!" Joshua said to himself. "What is going on here? Has my lack of rest taken a toll this great on my mind? I don't believe, or do I? Feldon has been known to stretch the truth in the past," He went to the inner-city courtyard and sat in a secluded area so he could think. "I don't want this to be true, but in a way…it could. I am conflicted with these thoughts as to how this could have happened. How did she get in? Did she play a hand of deceit and fool everyone?"

Joshua played with the end of his ponytail and noticed a group of birds nearby. "Two take off, leaving two behind," he said. "Hmmm. But whom would she take off with and whom would she leave behind? She's to be planning something. Something big. Has she played her hand too soon? Yet in all this, there is something deep inside of me that says everything is falling into place."

The Village of Sea Siren

The sound of waves crashing against the docks was music to Lester's ears. With only a few more adjustments, the door to the cabin would be back up, and soon, after a few more adjustments to other parts worn by the salty waves and humid air, Estella would receive a clean bill of health. "When you're out on the sea, time tends to slow down," he said. "I have seen various ports and docking points. Heard tales of being lost on the waves, and felt at this mistress's mercy. The sea truly demands respect."

Lester knew the sea was in him. For him, there wasn't a point to learning to love but learning to live with the ocean. The village of Sea Siren, so called that because it was a beacon of trade for nearby cities and ports, a place that lulled in merchants from all over. She was the seamen's version of hope.

Lester Mills was born to Canden and Madeline Mills, but his parents died shortly after, leaving him in the care of his grandfather, Jeremiah. From the eyes of the young boy, he watched as ships from ports in Rhodam and Akoran arrive, trading goods with the people. However, Akoran closed its treaty with Sea Siren, due to its trading with the occult village of Malesh and its leader, Lady Mihari.

The Veil Is Finally Lifted

As the afternoon gave way to evening, the motley crew of the seabound vessel *Estella* gathered in the courtyard. A cool breeze was setting in as the last vestiges of sunlight were fading. "You have been on that boat all day?" Mitch asked Lester.

"Yes. *Estella* is my baby, and now at least she's doing much better. How did everyone's day fare?"

"A back-and-forth verbal war," Candice said, looking at Mitch.

"Only because you fired first," he said.

"Contemplating life itself," Sootshire said, looking to Neacen.

"Only because all you see is food," he said.

"Getting to know and understand yourself and someone you care for," said Catalina to Leafy.

"Because that's the joy of having a friend," he said.

"Anyway," said Neacen. "It seems everyone, Snow included, enjoyed themselves. Shall we head back to my humble abode?"

"Sounds good to me," Leafy said.

Neacen took a deep breath as they arrived at his doorstep. "It feels good to be home. Here, I mean."

"Looks lively," said Mitch.

"It is lively, my good man. Let's go inside." Upon coming inside, Neacen noticed it was quiet, too quiet. "Josh should be home by now. Josh!" he called. He heard footsteps approaching from the dining area.

"Ah, Neacen," he said. Neacen grabbed him and embraced him. "I have never seen you this lively!"

"Good to see you again," Neacen said. "I have got more people with me this time as you can see."

Joshua looked at each one from Catalina to Candice to Snow. Yet when his eyes met Leafy's, a smile of joy came across his face and he nodded. "Please, everyone, let's go the dining room. There is much to discuss."

Chapter 25

A Call to Arms

"A guest should feel welcome," Joshua said, leading the others into the dining room. On the table were plates of fish, pork, seasoned chicken, onion gravy, shrimp, duck, sauerkraut, artichokes, greens, wine, grape cocktail. This was truly a banquet fit for a king. "Please, everyone, sit," he said.

"Josh, I didn't know you to go all out like this," Neacen remarked.

"I have had many years to learn. Please, everyone, enjoy." Leafy sat next to Catalina and began to reach for a piece of duck. Before his tong could grab a leg, he stopped and looked to see Josh looking directly at him. It was like he was staring straight into his soul.

"Hey, Leafy, that leg won't pull itself," Lester said.

"You all right?" Catalina asked.

"Y-y-yeah," Leafy said.

"Now, everyone, before we begin, there is one more person who will be joining our feast."

"Really?" Candice said.

"Who could that be?" Mitch asked.

Leafy looked around and saw no one else. Then he turned back and once again his eyes met Joshua's. He closed his eyes and the others in the room could feel the air began to change. Leafy looked and his eyes widened as Joshua's blond hair, pale skin, and blue eyes slowly changed. Neacen saw his friend turn into a young woman with short curly dark hair, softmedium brown skin, and eyes the color of ripe pecan shells. She wore a deep red shimmering dress that covered everything below the neck. On this dress were rubies, a diamond, and a velvet scarf across the front. The others, including Leafy, could not believe what they just witnessed. The woman looked at each of them and then finally at Leafy.

"It has been a while, Jay," she said.

The others looked at the boy. The one that they had been calling "Wandering Leaf" and "Leafy" was really a young man, under six-foot tall, short black hair, skin that was deep brown, eyes lost to the winds of time, and a heart that never got the chance to fully beat. This was Jay. He stood up and looked at his hands. These were his hands. They were uniquely lined, stitched by the hands of time. He looked at everyone else, not saying a word.

Candice and Mitch stood as well and walked over to him. "Jay," Mitch said, hugging him closely.

"Is it really…?" Candice asked.

"Yes," Mitch said. "Come, hold him." As they held him, Jay, yes JAY, could actually feel his heartbeat. They pulled back and Jay looked at the woman.

"How do you know me?" he asked.

"Jay, I have known you from before the threads of time wove you into existence."

"Who are you?"

"I have called many things. Soulshifter, mysterious…Glenda." Jay's eyes widened at the mention of that name.

"N-n.-no," he said. "Not the Glenda I know from the other world. Not the woman I called 'Mom' for all those years."

"Yes. That's me," Glenda said. "That is me."

"This is all too much," Jay said. "So, you are my mom?"

"To an extent," Glenda said. "Please, Jay, Mitch, Candice, sit, and I will explain everything. "

Jay sat and listened. Surely there was a lot of explaining to be done. "Twenty-two years ago, a woman came into my shop in Darbyshire. She was young, mid-thirties, stressed. I could tell from the moment she walked through

The Perfect Portrait

the door that something was stressing her, but more importantly, eating at her. She told me her name was Serena Vega, but she only wanted to be called Serena. She was an aspiring artist from a city back in the States, but her life had hit a terrible point. Her child, who was shortly born after this, died after birth, never having a chance to live. She had heard of me from around the area although I am not a person who wants their work plastered everywhere. I told Serena what I did and she proposed a way to, as she said, 'finish her perfect portrait.' I knew what I was doing would violate so many laws of not only nature but the spirit realm as well. The dead are meant to stay dead. I warned Serena of this although I went through the ritual. I told her I needed something from boy's, but all she had was a pendant she bought for him to give when he was older. I took this plus two vials of her blood. I used one to put on the pendant and put it over the candle flame to purify and strengthen, while the other, Serena's mortal blood, I kept as insurance."

"Insurance?" Neacen asked.

"Yes. I told Serena that I would serve as a bridge between her and the boy, a conduit as they call it. The boy would not be able to come from the dead but would exist as a spirit that would eventually be able to feel."

"Feel," said Jay.

"Emotions, desires, needs. The basic emotions all people feel. Yet, I told her not to cross that line, but as you can all see, that line was crossed."

"The obvious question is this," said Jay, "who is this kid?" Everyone in the room turned and looked at him. "What?"

"Jay," Glenda said, "that child is you."

"Wait, what? Me? T-that can't be!"

"Have you ever wondered why you felt like you were a ghost and that people couldn't, for lack of a better term, see you?"

"You mean that black-eyed angel, that voice that keeps speaking to me in my dreams, that was Serena, and she is my mother?"

"Yes," said Mitch. "Serena is your mother." Jay instantly stood up.

"No! No! I refuse to believe that! You all knew…knew I was wondering around lost all this time and you all hid this from me?"

"We didn't want to be the ones to tell you," Sootshire said.

"That's crap! You were the second one who met me, Sooty! No, the second entity I had contact with and you knew who I was the whole time?"

"Hey, Jay, let's calm it, man," said Lester.

"To hell with that! And you grandfather and grandmother, you both knew all along, and did you, Neacen?" Jay turned to Catalina. "Please tell me, Cat, that you knew nothing of this." She started to say something but turned away. "Glenda, you watched me lost for twenty-two years! Twenty-two years you watched me wonder like a blind man in the rain and you did nothing!"

"I was a bridge, Jay," said Glenda sternly.

"Bull!" Jay yelled. Glenda held up her fingers, as about to snap them.

"Jay, listen to me. I know this is a lot to hear at one time, but you must understand."

"I understand I was lied to!"

"Listen to me, boy, and you listen good! I love you like a child I never had, but as I told your mother, I could withdraw it and watch you both fall! Now, sit!"

Jay sat down and for the first time felt anger, his own genuine burning anger. "Listen!" said Glenda. "I wanted you to live, to feel, to experience life. I could have easily told you about that pendant you found in the closet, the dreams you were having but I wanted you to explore and learn for yourself. I knew once you put that pendant on, Serena would come looking for you. In fact, I felt her the whole time. Yet that pendant, that binding link, was a double-edged sword. It protected you, kept you safe from harm. It also allowed Serena to manifest her emotions through you. You wouldn't be able to explore this world alone. You would need the help of these six other souls here with you."

Glenda turned to each of them. "Snowden Sootshire, the talking raccoon whom you met when you ventured out. A representation of a true friend. Although narrow-minded with his obsession with fish, he kept watch for your safety, as with the dealings with Pixana and her fairies. Catalina, the fierce yet strong feline fatale from Sumurka. She was your voice, your strength, and she was the first person you ever felt true compassion and love for. Neacen Ruthman, who like you started from humble beginnings yet sought wisdom and understanding from within and the world around him. His belief in the human soul and the light of hope kept him safe and also kept you from falling into the dark waters of Serena's twisted mind. Lester Mills, the man who turned to the calming waters of the sea when all felt lost. A man who put himself aside to open up to you and your companions in your time of need. A man who has come to terms with his sins and repented. Mitchell and Candice Vega, who represent polar opposites in their union. One who has been redeemed, while the other is trying to truly forgive. Yet they both have a common ground not seen in all these years of marriage. A care and love for a daughter they both neglected and now want badly to forgive them. Lastly, me. The woman who opened the 'Forbidden Door' which allowed all of you to enter. The one who breeched the boundaries of life and death, light and darkness. In my hands I hold the greatest burden. I have struggled each day, wondering if I made the right decision that fateful night, and to be honest, I don't regret it."

"Yeah, and now my mom is in pain thanks to you," Jay said.

"Jay, you must understand, Serena chose this path. I have committed the ultimate sin of all and my forgiveness…" Glenda paused and looked to the ceiling.

"Well?"

"Will have to be answered one day."

"Glenda…" Candice stated to say, but Mitch put his hand on her shoulder and shook his head.

"To all of you," Glenda said, "Especially Jay…forgive me."

"I have something to say," Lester said, standing up.

"Lester," Catalina said.

"No, Cat. This needs to be said. Over these last few days, weeks, minutes, I have seen so much. I have lived on the water's edge, dealt with many people. I have stared evil in the face and looked into my own soul. I have seen the brightest days and the darkest nights. I know what it means to have your past come back to haunt you. To wake up, catching your breath to make sure you're still alive. I have wallowed in sadness, felt the burning hand of anger, and kissed the lips of joy. Most of all, I have learned that regardless of how many emotions

I have laid with, dealt with, and saw, ultimately, I had to face myself. I have wanted to hold the hand of my past mistakes, never letting go. I have not only sat in a pity parlor but sung in it. That was until the mistress dressed in a blue-green dress rescued me from that parlor's front-row seats. Now, we all make mistakes and we all struggle inside. But now we all have a chance to do things right. To make a new day free from the allure of past regrets. I have never been ready to finally face that parlor one last time and tear it down. I am ready to finally be a man, and I have you all to thank."

"So, what's our next move?" Sootshire asked.

Glenda folded her hands. "Earlier today, I received word that Serena has conquered Akoran."

"What?" Neacen asked.

"King Shikam is dead, cut down by the hand of your father, Jay."

"Julius," Jay said.

"Yes, and I have no doubt that she will make a move for other areas."

"I know," Jay said. "A part of Serena has always been in me. That's how I was able to dream as I did and hear Neacen's thoughts. How do we get her here?"

"First things first," said Glenda. She snapped her fingers. The others were amazed to see, standing beside her, white wings, a chubby body, and a cheerful smile.

"Archangel Broun at your service, my lady," said the joyous, jubilant, and benevolent baby-faced Archangel Broun.

"Angel?" Neacen asked.

"I remember you!" Jay asked.

"As do I," Mitch said.

"Broun has been watching and reporting to me the entire time," Glenda said.

"Yes, yes, my lady!" Broun said. "A lot has happened indeed."

"How would we all know?" Catalina asked. "We haven't seen what's been going on."

"There is a way," Glenda said. She turned to Neacen and nodded. Neacen sighed and reached into his pocket and retrieved Jay's pendants. He held Serena's pendant but gave Jay his own back. Jay looked at it and put it back on.

The Perfect Portrait

"Now each of you hold hands and I will be the link. Whatever you see will not harm you." All of them nodded. "Then let's begin." Each of them grabbed the other's hand, with Glenda serving as the conduit. "Now close your eyes."

. . .

After each of them did, a visual appeared of a black-eyed, dark-spirited Serena standing on the shores of Malesh. She looked triumphantly in the distance as she saw the Rotted Child approaching. "Now this is what I have been waiting for, Julius!" Serena said to her husband.

"Serena, how could you do this?" Julius asked.

"How? Because you didn't have the balls to stop it! Come to me, my child!" The rotted, grotesque form of an infant came to her. "What do you seek, my child?"

"Let me become one with you and I will make you whole again."

"Not this time," Julius said, drawing his sword.

"No, you don't," said the child, stopping Julius in his tracks. Serena opened her mouth and the child turned into a black ooze and went inside her. Serena's humanity, what was left of it, faded as the last rays of sunlight dissipated, inviting the eternal blackness of the night. Serena's body was reborn, and her wings completely restored as well as her armor, sword, and bitter heart.

. . .

"Stop it! Stop it! STOP IT!" Jay yelled, letting his hands go and breathing heavily. "That's not my mother!" Everyone else let go and opened their eyes.

"No," said Glenda, "that is a monster."

"She destroyed Julius's sword, or so she thought."

"What do you mean?" Candice asked.

"As long as there is darkness, there will always be light," Broun said as he reached into his sheath and slowly pulled out the Sword of Life. It emitted a light as bright as the sun, so bright, the others could hardly see.

"It's so bright!" Neacen said.

"This is the light of hope!" Broun said. "In the darkest hour, a spark is ignited and justice will be served!"

"Do you see the light, Jay?" Glenda asked.

"Yes!" Jay answered. "It's unreal!"

"No!" Neacen yelled. "This is hope! This is what Estele wanted me to see all these years!"

"Wait, how can you two easily look at it?" Catalina asked.

"As am I," Glenda said. "The Keeper of Hope, the Bearer of Hope, and Bridge connecting the two! Together we will see justice done and that monster will be sent back to the hell from whence it came!"

With everyone with a new perspective, it was time to plan.

"So how do we go about this?" Sootshire asked.

"Easy," said Glenda. "As Josh, I could talk to the council in the morning, but I will need the help of everyone here."

"Hmmm? How so?" Mitch asked.

"We will explain to the council that we have Serena's son here with us. We set up a festivity to be held in St. Michael's Cathedral three days from tomorrow."

"Sunday," Neacen said.

"Yes. We gather the people of Rhodam there and we will expose Serena for what she truly is."

"And what do we have as leverage?" Lester asked.

"The letter Candice gave Jay and the other pendant. Broun, can you deliver?"

"Archangel Broun at your service! This is what Broun can do for you!"

"Oh, Broun," Mitch said. Glenda motioned for Neacen to hand the other pendant to him, and Jay got the letter from his bag and handed it to Broun as well.

"But we still need bait," Catalina said.

"That is where Jay comes in. Jay, you know what you must do."

"Yes," Jay said. "My essence will serve as a calling signal. Serena won't be able to resist."

The Perfect Portrait

"Wait, hold on!" Catalina said. "Jay, this is extremely dangerous!"

"It's the best shot we have. Besides, I owe mother a kiss."

"We will wait close by, and I will have Neacen bless us, so Serena won't sense or see us," Glenda said. "Once Jay is in the church, we will wait for the signal."

"What is the signal?" asked Sootshire.

"Mother, your light is beautiful," Jay said.

"I will be able to listen in," said Glenda. "Once inside, the rest will be easy. It's the risk that's the hard part."

"Risk?" asked Mitch.

"Don't forget, Grandfather, mine and Serena's souls are linked," Jay said.

"Meaning if she goes…"

"You could leave too," said Lester.

"Jay, I will have what you need when the time is right. And when the time comes…"

"This is suicide!" Catalina growled.

"No, this is justice," said Jay.

"On the night before, we will all meet here," said Glenda. "I will do one last ritual with the Sword of Life. Until then, feast well, everyone, make peace, but most of all, remember who you are and where you come from and what you sacrificed to get here."

Chapter 26

Special Delivery

Serena looked at herself in awe in the mirror. Her hair, which had been flowing loosely since her birth, was now pulled in a chignon. On her body was a long, flowing black gown with her armor on top of it. Her breastplate was studded with diamonds. "I look perfect!" she said, spreading her wings. "Don't I?" she said, turning to Julius. He didn't want to answer or even look at this woman, this disgrace to their marriage vows. Serena retrieved her sword and slowly walked over to him until he could feel her soulless black eyes burning into his skull. She took the tip of her blade and slowly tilted Julius's head until his eyes met hers.

"Julius, I asked you A QUESTION!"

Julius could hear his own heart racing. That voice wasn't Serena's. "Yes…" he said.

"Yes?" Serena said, inching the tip a little into his chin.

"Yes, my queen."

"AND?"

"Yes, my queen. The salvation of myself and the people. Our perfected highness and light of us all."

"Perfect," said Serena, withdrawing the blade back. "You know you shouldn't show fear. It's not perfect."

"Yes, my queen."

"Now, let's take a tour of the new Akoran. MY AKORAN!"

As Serena flew above Julius, she smiled in delight at the new attire of the people. Everyone from children to adults were dressed in white robes. "Yes, yes!" Serena said. "Now this is perfect! White symbolizes purity, light, perfection. There is no need to be as dull as the desert hell around you. What society has women hiding their faces? One made of dirt and traditions not worthy of a dog shitting on, that's what! Of course, none of these women are as perfect as me. So, Julius, consider it an honor to be joined to perfection. Do you understand?"

"Yes, my queen," he said.

Obed, who was disgusted at this new change, saw Julius and Serena approaching. He and his men bowed before them. "My queen," he said.

"Ah, Obed," Serena said. "You look more like a man now than you ever have in your dirt-ridden life. You may speak."

"My men and I have fortified the defenses around the city. Imperfectors will be kept out, and only those who are perfect will be allowed in."

"Perfect, Obed!"

"Request for a break for us, Your Highness."

"Hmm. Granted. Remember, though, not a minute too late or…" Serena said, tapping the butt of her blade.

"Yes, my queen. Understood."

As Obed and his men left for the quarters, Serena spread her wings and smiled. "I'M PERFECT!"

. . .

Obed and his men sat in the quarters for about a minute without saying a word. They looked at each other, contemplating all that had taken place recently. Finally, one of them broke the silence. "This is not good," he said.

"You think?" said another. "We are wearing these disgraceful white robes like the people of Rhodam."

"King Shikam wouldn't have taken this," Obed said. "To think, I watched my king die right in front of me and I simply stood there."

"Our king," said the guard in the back.

Obed took a sip of water. "Menede was a true soldier. He stood for his beliefs and his people right up to his very death. How can I even call myself a guard?"

"It's not your fault, Obed," said one of the men, who was the tallest and skinniest of them. "It's Julius's. He betrayed our king and our people."

"More like Julius was being held hostage," Obed said. "I know that was his wife but even I wouldn't have stood for that. Hell, Julius doesn't hardly even speak to me, and we trained together. He just looks at me like a scared dog being chained by its master."

"Serves him right for what he did."

"Everything is never black and white. I'm just having a hard time figuring out what the shade of gray is."

"Well, I think I may have overheard something between the two of them," said the tall, skinny guard.

"Tihari, what do you mean?"

"Back when they first came here and Serena was put away, I heard her and Julius talking."

"Go on."

"Something about a kid and that the family needed to be together."

"So?"

"So, that could be a reason. It was something I couldn't help hearing in a silent as hell dungeon."

"Small talk," Obed said.

"Just saying, my liege."

"I am not your liege. That perfected bitch is…for now at least."

. . .

Julius and Serena stood near the coastline, the waves silent and still. "You should smile, Julius," Serena said. "I actually allowed some light in today. So stop looking like you just lost your best friend, or should I say king." Julius could feel his blood beginning to boil. "My has it been so long since I felt this kind of POWER!" Serena said, striking her sword in the ground and watching as a chasm split the earth into the very ocean itself. "You see? That is perfection at its finest. Hmm." Serena looked around. "Ah hah!"

She flew over to a boulder and stood in front of it. "By the darkest blade, perfection shall be made." She took her sword and multi-sliced the rock with ease. Then she took the pieces and held her blade over each of them. The darkened steel turned hot, causing each of the pieces of rock to shimmer. Soon, what was once clumps of dirt were now perfectly cut diamonds. "See, Julius? Diamonds are forever."

"Serena…" Julius said. Serena picked up one of the diamonds and held it.

"You know, Julius, there are two types of people in this world. First, there are those who can take the heat and become perfectly molded into beauty." She then took her sword and split the ground again. "Then, you have those that break very easily at the slightest touch. They are weak, fragile, imperfect. My father was as such. He could have been something great, but he allowed trivial things to cloud his judgement. Hmph! People in power are so weak at heart yet they are leaders in our world… no, MY WORLD!"

"Then, what am I?" Julius asked. Serena flew over to him and circled him.

"What are you?"

"Yes."

"What do you think you are?"

"What?"

"As you once taught me, you are what you think are. So, I ask you again, what do you think you are?" Julius paused at the question. "Julius, when you asked me this question, I instantly answered you, and now you can't come up with an answer yourself? HOW PATHETIC!"

"I…I…" Julius started to say. Serena landed and walked behind him. She put her lips to his ear, and he could feel his skin crawl.

"You people need to give your lives to an entity just to feel whole. You build your nations on pathetic ideologies and kill those whose rightful blood made the world. Even your money is useless. So tell me, Julius…who is the real monster?"

She then walked and stood before him. "And to think you called me a horrible being. Julius, have you looked in the mirror lately?" Julius could only hang his head. "My point exactly."

. . .

Joshua and Neacen stood in front of the council with Jay and company in tow. The chairman pulled down his glasses and looked at each of them with disgust. "Joshua, Professor Dougan, why are these unbelievers here in my presence, and why is the dog with them?"

"We have urgent news, sir, that demands your immediate attention," Joshua said.

"Really now?" said Feldon. "Joshua, the only urgent news you bring up is lunch hour and heart-felt sentiment." The rest of the council laughed.

"Never mind your wasted antics, Feldon," Neacen said. "We have Serena's son right here." He pointed to Jay. The chairman raised an eyebrow.

"Really?" he asked.

"Yes," Joshua said. "We believe we should a festivity in her majesty's honor to mark this occasion."

"I am direct blood line to her majesty," Jay said. "I am of Serena." He held his pendant and it gleamed in the light.

"I assure you it will be worth the time," Neacen said. "We should set it for Sunday morning. Gather everyone at St. Michael's Cathedral. I promise you, Serena will show up."

"And how will you contact her?" Feldon asked.

"We have a way," Joshua said. "Besides, what better way to mark her conquest and graciousness."

"And it will bring in splendid revenue," said Neacen.

"Hmm," the Chairman said. "Agreed."

. . .

Time drew out like a blade over the next two days. Finally came the night before the event. As mentioned, Glenda, along with Jay and company, gathered in the dining area. "The night has finally come," she said to everyone. "I hope you all feasted and made peace."

"We did," Jay said.

"Good." She lit a candle and snapped her fingers. Broun immediately appeared.

"I am here, my lady!" he said.

"Broun, the sword." Broun retrieved the sword and placed it in Glenda's hands. She then took out the vial of blood, Serena's mortal blood, and poured it on the blade and placed it over the fire. Jay and the others watched as it melded with the celestial tempered steel. "By blood we live and by blood we die," Glenda chanted. The sword emitted a flash of light, and so it was the bonds of light and sacrifice were needed. "Jay, come and hold the sword."

Jay got up and walked over. Glenda handed the sword to him and in the reflection of the blade, he saw himself. His true, real self. "Neacen," Glenda said looking to him. Neacen got up and stood before Jay.

"In Heaven's light, I bless thee and thy sword of divine radiance. May the goodness and mercy of truth and hope keep you forever safe," he said. Glenda looked Jay dead in the eyes.

"Jay, I am sure you're aware of what's at stake. When the opportunity presents itself, you must take it."

"I understand," he said.

"Now, Broun, take the letter and the pendant from the table and deliver them to Serena."

"Yes, my lady," he said. He took both items and was off to deliver.

"And now?" Jay said.

"Rest well, Jay. Tomorrow is *your* day to shine."

. . .

The Perfect Portrait

"Perfect, perfect!" Serena said, looking at herself. "Fabulous!" Julius simply shook his head. "Now, I…" Serena stopped as she gazed upon the fat, chubby face with the white wings. "Ah, fat stuff!"

"Broun at your service!" he said.

"And what brings you here?"

"I have this to deliver to you." He handed the pendant and letter to Serena. She looked at the pendant and put it on.

"Hmph!" she said. Then she opened the envelope and looked at the letter. As she read, her hands started to tremble and her eyes widened. "Julius, we need to go to Rhodam!"

Chapter 27

My Perfect Portrait

Mitch and Candice sat in the upstairs room that night, looking at that fateful last portrait of their daughter, a painting that was far from perfect. Serena's eyes were gouged out, hair in disarray, and blood rushing from her mouth. "How did we allow this to happen to her?" Candice asked.

"The real reason is why," Mitch said. "We weren't there for her when she needed us. I didn't show for her graduation, nothing. My life was more important than my own daughter."

"I am guilty as well," Candice said. "I didn't comfort her as a mother should after she lost Jay. It's morbidly ironic that now it's Jay who is alive and Serena who is dead. And to think I blamed you for all of this and held contempt for you all these years. How do I live with myself?"

"You learn to forgive. That's how I made it back in that dull gray hell hole. I took it one day at a time."

"Have you ever told her you're sorry?"

"Have you?"

"No."

"Besides, Serena wouldn't even give me the time of day anymore. At this point now, she would kill me without thinking twice about it." Mitch took out his pipe and…held it.

"Aren't you going to light that?"

"No…no. This is our time together. This pipe served its purpose, but now…it's empty."

"I won't allow Serena to hurt you, Mitch. I was too easy on her."

"How do you discipline an angel?"

"She might be an angel, but I am still her mother."

"I am not upset with you for the way you acted, Candice."

"Mitch, ever since that day we met back in that cottage, I could see you were a changed man. No, you are a changed man. I just wish I could have let go a lot sooner."

"It's never too late for change, Candice."

"Maybe we could create the—"

"No, Candice. Nothing's perfect, but we still can make a better one."

. . .

Catalina and Jay stood on the Skyline Bridge, overlooking the city of Rhodam in its nightly glory. "You know, this is the first time I have ever seen a cityscape this beautiful," Jay said.

"We have been here for a while now, Jay," Catalina said.

"True, but it's as if when you're—"

"Don't hurt your head, Jay."

"Do you miss Sumurka?"

"Yes. It is my home and always will be, but it is time I started living my own life. Can I ask you something?"

"Yes."

"What will you do when this is over?"

Jay looked up at the stars shining brightly in the night sky. "I have been meaning to ask you the same."

"Honestly, I want to settle down, have a life, you know. I want one where it's not this threat is coming or that."

"So do I."

"By the way, I am sorry for scratching you back when we first met."

The Perfect Portrait

"It's okay. I was amazed at how you pounced on me."

"You didn't show any fear. I love that in a guy."

"I thought you hated humans."

"I did at one time, but after being around you, I feel that hate has left. I will be blunt: I don't want anything to happen to you. You are the first person I have ever truly cared for, besides the Elder."

"So are you to me, Catalina. You are full of life, vivacious, and you have a grace about you that touches me in the deepest sentiment."

"Jay…" Catalina said, putting her paw on Jay's hand, and the two of them gazed into the distance.

. . .

Glenda, Sootshire, and Neacen sat in the study room going over last-minute details. "In order to save countless souls, one must die. This is not what I planned," Glenda said.

"You didn't know the risk," Neacen said.

"That's just it, Neacen. I knew the risk and I did it anyway. Serena could have changed the world for the better, but instead…"

"It's as you said," said Sootshire. "She chose this path. Now is not the time for regrets."

"I must ask the inevitable question," Neacen said.

"Yes?" said Glenda.

"Is there a way for Jay to survive this?"

Glenda looked away, eyes displaying the heartbreaking answer.

"Please tell me there is," Sootshire said. Glenda didn't say anything but only shook her head.

"How am I supposed to say the prayer if it will ultimately lead to Jay's …"

"Shut up, you oaf!" Sootshire shouted.

"We must remain focused," Glenda said. "Neacen, once you start saying the prayer, you CAN NOT STOP! Do you understand?"

"Yes," Neacen answered.

John Paul Shuman Jr.

"What will this prayer do?" Sootshire inquired.

Glenda smiled, not saying anything.

. . .

"I never thought I would be enjoying a view of the ocean with a furry femme fatale," Lester said, rubbing Snow's head. She looked up at him and smiled, showing those sharp teeth. "You know, Snow, the sea is beautiful, but at night, she's majestic." Snow let out a howl and wagged her tail. "It's hard to believe this journey's at its end. Seems just like yesterday I was meeting everyone. That Jay sure is a character worth remembering. Everyone is worth remembering. You know, I was thinking after this, you could go on the ocean with me. You would make a lovely 'Sea-Wolf.'" Snow howled again, and Lester embraced her.

. . .

The sun shone majestically off my glorious wings. I carried this sorry excuse for a man in tow as we soared through the heavens, my heavens. This world was mine, this life was mine, and soon, I would have my perfect portrait. "Ahh, Rhodam is up ahead. Julius, please look sharp and don't do anything stupid. Do I make myself clear?"

"Yes, my queen," Julius said.

As we approached, I could feel a strong essence. I looked toward the downtown courtyard in front of St. Michael's Cathedral and saw my son! I quickly landed, Julius behind me, right in the center of the courtyard. There, just a few feet away was my son Jay, the last piece of my perfect portrait. I walked up to him, dressed so elegantly and perfectly. He is my son! I spread my wings so he could be proud of his perfected bloodline. As I stood before him, I looked at him. His hair was short, black, skin a deep brown, and eyes that were bold, confident, and better than that disgrace of a father of his. "My son!" *I said, holding him close and tightly. I held him so close, I heard his heartbeat. I could actually hear his heartbeat.*

"Mother..." said Jay.

The Perfect Portrait

"Yes, yes, YES! I am…your perfect mother! Oh, my son! You are everything I dreamed you would be! Oh, so perfect! Julius! Don't stand there like a fool! Come! Behold, our perfect son!" Julius walked up to Jay and stood before him.

"Father," Jay said, getting a good look at Julius for the first time. Julius reached out his hand and rubbed Jay's face.

"Is it really you?" Julius asked.

"Of course it is!" I said. "Come, let's show Rhodam what real royalty is!"

We walked up the steps towards the door and I opened it. The people, at least ten thousand, turned and looked at us in awe. This was my city! MY PEOPLE!

MY PERFECT PORTRAIT!

Chapter 28

The Ultimate Battle

In my years, in my life, I had never wore a look of pride so boldly as the smile that radiated off my face at that moment. Finally, by my own hands, the perfect portrait was created. I could feel the people of Rhodam's eyes looking in awe as myself, Julius, and Jay took each step towards the front. These people worshipped me, adored me. I was their light, their perfected ideology manifested.

The three of us stood in front of the masses, my eyes catching sight of Heaven. Jay and Julius stood beside me, myself in the middle as the centerpiece. I walked forward, spreading my wings, my majestic wings, and took to mid-air, allowing myself to gaze down and see what it meant to truly rule. "My people of Rhodam, I give you MY PERFECT PORTRAIT!" I said boldly and loudly, my voice echoing throughout the church. The people applauded and said praises, but it was my time, so I withdrew my sword and silence was in order again. "What makes a true nation?" I said, flying back and forth, all the while holding my sword. "For years, I spent trying not only to obtain my perfect portrait but also trying to find the perfect place to display it. I built this city with two goals in mind. First, to showcase the display of perfection, but furthermore, to be a light to the rest of the world. A place where opportunity was plentiful, and in return for your steadfast devotion to me, I would share this glory with you all. You are all perfect in my eyes."

"Your glory shines as the brilliant sun, Mother!" my son said.

John Paul Shuman Jr.

. . .

Neacen, Glenda, Sootshire, and the rest of the crew were outside near a building. "That's our cue!" Sootshire said.

"Ready?" Glenda said to Neacen.

"Yes," he said. He turned to the rest. "Let's go!"

As they walked, Neacen could hear his heart racing inside his chest and his breathing grew heavy. "Stay calm," Glenda said, putting her hand on his shoulder. As they walked up the steps leading to the door, he could hear each tap of his shoes against the concrete. Destiny was right on the other side of that door. Neacen reached for the knob, his right hand shaking. However, he stopped just shy of it and stared at it. He saw his life flash right before his eyes.

Will I ever see my family again? he thought. *Or my beautiful Estele?*

"Neacen!" said a familiar voice. He turned around and saw Joshua, who wore a bold yet confident smile on his face. He nodded to Neacen, and so did he in return. "No fear, my friend." Neacen regained his composure. It was time. He grabbed the knob, slowly turning it, and opened the door.

. . .

"Within this realm, new life will be born!" I said. "I have conquered the kingdom of Akoran and my kingdom, THIS kingdom, will reach out its hand and touch every corner of the world!"

The people applauded again but were once again silenced by me. I had my back turned and looked at the glorious works of these perfected walls. "Alas, however, there is still work to be done, for not everyone has been enlightened. Isn't that right, Professor Dougan?" Everyone and I turned to see the motley crew of imperfect trash that had step foot into MY DOMAIN! "Dear Professor and company, please…COME IN!" The doors behind them slammed shut, the echo resonating throughout the still silence. I flew towards them, sword held ever tighter.

The Perfect Portrait

"To my good people of Rhodam, as you can see, there are still imperfections that need to be purged; furthermore, to the council and head chairman, how could you allow these lesser beings into MY CITY?" I flew and looked at each of these imperfections. "You allow a flea-bitten cat woman, a has-been drunk, a filthy rat, a helpless romantic, a gravedigger, and worst of all, a nonbeliever into MY CITY? Oh, yes, please tell us about your beliefs, Professor Dougan, or should I say Neacen Ruthman, of the Ruthman family from the peasant village of Eden!"

The church erupted in gasps and murmurs. I landed and walked up to that disgrace I had the misfortune of calling a father. "You are by far more detestable than Neacen, Father. How dare you tarnish my perfect city with your disgusting presence. You are not worthy of breathing the same air as me. You are better off in a grave yourself, you lowly piece of…"

Then I felt a hand smack across my right cheek, the sound echoing across the room. I looked and saw beside this disgrace was my mother. "Mother!" I said.

"You are no child of mine, Serena!" she said. I felt the sting on my cheek and looked at her.

"Don't be foolish, Mother," I said. "Can't you see? This, THIS, is my life's work! My perfect portrait! You helped me create this glorious work of art, and now you throw that honor away to stand beside this trash of a man?"

"Listen to yourself, Serena. I told you back when you were in school the affairs between me and your father did not concern you, but you had to have your word be final. I sent you off to become something great, but instead you became something I am ashamed to call my daughter. Your father repented of his transgressions, and I forgave him. He tied to talk to you as a parent who wanted to obtain forgiveness from the child he left behind, but all you saw was a stain on your so-called perfect portrait. You sicken me! I have put down animals that had more honor than you!"

"You are delusional, Mother," I said. "All of you are. I create this perfect masterpiece for you and this is the thanks I get? Mother, father, to all of you blind sheep. I am the only reason you even breathe! I own you! YOU ALL

BELONG TO ME! I looked at the pathetic heaps of trash before me and held my sword with the tip of the blade pointed at them. "I will create one last portrait. I will call it *A Sinner's Judgement*, and I will paint it with the blood of each of you."

"You will not harm another soul, Mother!"

I turned around in the direction of the voice and saw my son walking towards me. "My son! You have been through so much in your life, but do not think these lowly wretches care about you the way I do." He walked behind me and stood with the maggots.

"These so-called wretches have been more family to me than you ever were! Sure, they may not be perfect, but what is? However, through them, I was able to experience friendship, family, what it means to care for someone, to forgive, but most importantly, faith and hope."

"You speak the same foolishness your father and grandfather did," I said.

"Tough talk coming from someone who betrayed the family they claimed to love."

"Family? How dare you speak to me about family, you disloyal, ungrateful brat! The only family I care about is you and your father! I loved my mother, but since she sided with that incompetent shell of a man, one Mitchell S. Vega to be exact, she and he both mean nothing to me anymore!"

"Mother, have you looked in the mirror lately?"

"Have I? Oh, yes, I have, and I see perfection at its finest! I am perfect, and Jay, this could be you!" I manifested a portrait of himself with wings alongside Julius and I.

"I don't want that, Mother."

"What do you mean you don't want it? I sold my soul for you!"

"That makes you a sell-out, Mother. I would rather live in an imperfect world that still offered hope than your perfect world of lies!"

"And these lowly cretins are your hope?"

Then, Joshua, the hopeless romantic fool he was, began to change form. He became a face I thought I would never see again. "You?" I snarled. "I thought you would be dead by now!"

The Perfect Portrait

"I told you all those years ago not to cross me, Serena! Yet you crossed that line anyway, and all in pursuit of your perfect portrait!"

"Yes, I did and look at the pay off! I am light, darkness, life, and death. I am a true angel!"

"No, you are a disgrace to what a real angel is." The woman snapped her fingers and appeared that chubby, baby-faced white-winged loser.

"Broun?" I said. He didn't look happy but serious. "You call this oversized puff an angel?"

"He helped us, Mother," Jay said. "Where were you?"

"Pray tell, my son, how could he have possibly helped you?"

Broun reached to his back and slowly withdrew the sword I had not long ago destroyed, at least that's what I believed. It emitted a light so strong it hurt my eyes to even look at it. Now, here it was, redeemed and in the hands of this fat being, who called himself Archangel Broun. He handed it to the woman, and she presented it to my son. He took it and held it, gazing at the newly sharpened steel. "I…I destroyed that!" I said.

"Mother, has your time in this realm twisted what little sense *you* had?" said my son. "You can't destroy the light, and how fitting that I hold a blade strengthened as I have been."

"You would dare defy your OWN MOTHER?"

"Frankly, yes."

I stood there and gazed upon this disgrace to my perfect portrait. "HA HA! HA HA HA! Son, have you forgotten? Our souls are linked. If you destroy me, then you will cease to exist as well."

"To pave the way for a brighter tomorrow, I will gladly accept those terms. I raised my sword as did he.

"By blood we live," he said.

"And by my blade, YOU WILL DIE!"

. . .

John Paul Shuman Jr.

I swiftly swung my blade for the boy's head, but he dodged, barely missing an untimely demise. "You're quicker than the rest of these imperfect fools," I said. My son didn't say anything but charged at me with his sword and went in for a strike. I blocked, our blades, forged in light and darkness met, creating a spark. We pulled back, our eyes dead locked. "Enough games, Jay!" I said, spreading my wings fully and flying straight for his chest. He blocked in a timely manner, the edges of our blades once again touching.

I stood there, my blade pressing against his in a metallic struggle. He held strong, but I could feel his legs bending, almost touching the floor. He pushed back and took a quick swing, managing to cut the side of my face slightly. I licked the black ooze and went in for another strike. He dodged and took another swing for my head, but I pulled back. It was time for me to up the stakes. I focused my energy, and my blade grew hot. I struck the floor, causing a fiery chasm to appear. Jay dodged the fire by leaping out of the way.

"Figures," I said, swiftly flying and landing behind him. He turned only to be met by hot steel across his shoulder. He staggered back a bit, the cloth he wore being slightly burnt at the arm and taking some flesh with it. He took in the pain for a moment. "Give up, Jay!"

"Never!" he said, running and managing to sever my own gown at the lower torso. I swiftly retaliated and returned the favor with my own blade. He charged again and I blocked. He pushed forward this time, actually causing me to strain. With one leg holding me up, I took my free foot and jolted him in the chest with full strength, causing him to be lunged across the floor. I got up, took flight, and went in for a dive bomb straight at his chest, but he dodged at the last second. He reached up and grabbed my left wing and slung me, causing me to land straight through a glass window. I recovered and flew back in, more ooze dripping from various cuts across my face, legs, and arms.

Glenda looked to Neacen. "Now, Neacen," she said in a barely audible whisper. Neacen nodded and began praying.

I looked at my wounds and realized they were not healing. "What the hell?" I said. "How dare you defile my perfect body, boy!" I let out a loud roar that echoed so strongly the glass broke. I flew straight for him and grabbed

The Perfect Portrait

him by his shirt. "Time to teach you some respect," I said, putting my sword back in its guard for a second. I took my free hand and backhanded him across the face, causing him to fly back into the altar. I drew my blade and went in, but he dodged, AGAIN!

I could feel myself fly straight into the altar, the wood hitting my breast plate so hard it temporarily knocked the wind out of me. I got up, panting heavily. I gathered myself and went in for another lunge. He blocked. As our swords struggled, I smiled, revealing my razor-sharp teeth. "Jay, do you really want to know what happened to your bitch cat girl's parents?" I could see his eyes showing a look of concern at the question. "I killed them! That's right! Your own sourpuss's parents. Where's your convictions, Jay?" I could see his eyes start to grow with anger.

"Jay! Jay!" Jay looked and saw a light coming from his pendant. The voice was Glenda's. "She is trying to throw you off. Don't let her upset you!"

The boy pushed back and took his free hand and landed and punch right into my stomach. I fell over, crouching in pain. I coughed up black bile and had to catch myself. I regained myself somewhat and noticed some of the feathers on my wings were falling out. I got up and went to pick up my blade… only to find out I couldn't anymore. At this point I was done with this. This world. THIS BOY!

I roared and spread my wings, causing more feathers to fall out. I flew straight for him, but my body had started to grow sluggish. "I HAD EXISTED LONG BEFORE YOU WERE BORN AND I WILL EXIST LONG AFTER I SMEAR THESE HALLOWED GROUNDS WITH YOUR BLOOD!" I flew in for his throat, but as I got within inches of him, I felt a sharp pain in my chest. I looked and saw the tip of his sword in me. He pushed it in further and twisted, and pulled it out. A few seconds passed but nothing happened. "HA HA HA HA!" I laughed demonically. I could still win. "YOU SEE, JAY? I AM PERFECT! I HAD SUCH HIGH HOPES FOR YOU, BUT YOU TURNED OUT TO BE A DISAPPOINTMENT LIKE YOUR FATHER AND GRANDFATHER! HOW DARE YOU RUIN MY PERFECT PORTRAIT!"

John Paul Shuman Jr.

I went in but stopped when I saw him look down, and so did I. Black ooze started gushing from the wound onto my desecrated floor. "NO! NO!" I said as my body began to turn into a disgusting black slush. I took a look into the reflection of his sword and saw my true face. I was old, weak, but most of all I was NOT PERFECT! I turned to face Julius. "Julius, please! Help!" Julius walked forward and looked at me with disgust.

"From the moment I first met you, I told you I would NEVER baby you, Serena!"

And so I was as I had always been: weak, selfish, hateful, and saddest of all, NOT PERFECT!

. . .

Everyone in the church stood and noticed the ooze, the blackened remains of Serena on the floor. She was truly gone, a being who only wanted perfection. Neacen was breathing heavily, tired from his praying. Glenda nodded to him and so did he to her.

"Jay!" Catalina said, and everyone's attention turned to the boy, no longer a leaf in the wind, but a Hero, passed out one the floor.

Chapter 29

Jay's Awakening

Catalina ran, tears in her eyes, through the crowd to Jay, who was laid out on the floor, the sword still in his hand. She knelt down beside him and held him. There was no pulse, no breathing, nothing. She cried, the tears piling on top of themselves, falling onto Jay.

Candice, Mitch, and the others walked up as well, and Julius stood with them. "Glenda!" Mitch said, turning to her. "What happened? What in the hell has happened to our grandson?" Candice could feel the rains of sorrow falling from her eyes. She knew for she now bore the pain of losing a child.

"The link…" Glenda said weakly.

"Damn your link!" Sootshire yelled, tears in his eyes as well.

"When Serena went…" started Lester.

"So did Jay," finished Neacen. Julius looked down at his only son, lying there lifeless. For years he had been wanting to have his family and a life to remember. Once before, Serena had destroyed his sword, but metal can be rebuilt. Now, even in death, she was laughing at him, for she now had taken his son. He could feel his anger building for in his mind, he still saw those soulless black eyes and smirk staring him in the face.

"Serena!" he yelled, running towards the ooze, which had sunken into the floor. Her armor, sword, everything was gone. Lester ran and caught him, holding him back.

"Let me go, Lester!" Julius yelled. He struggled, but Lester held tight.

"Julius, don't, man! Serena's gone now!"

"She took my son! I'll take…"

"Julius, SHUT UP!" Lester said, letting him go, the two of them facing each other. "SERENA'S GONE! BE A FATHER FOR ONCE A PAY ATTENTION TO YOUR SON!" Lester pointed to Jay, who was still lifeless in Catalina's arms.

"Please, Jay, don't go!" Catalina cried. "I never wanted it to end this way. I loved you and I wanted us to be happy together. You were never a leaf in the wind. You were my hero! Please, Jay! I LOVE YOU!"

She held Jay closer, the tears falling on the pendant. Silence was all around the church. Not even a pin drop could match Catalina's tears hitting the pendant.

Then…the pendant started to glow. Everyone took notice as the pendant glowed brighter until the entire room was filled with light.

"And to those that believe in the light will never taste death but shall have eternal life," Broun said. "Amen."

The light faded and everyone looked at Jay. Catalina could feel his essence returning, his heart beating again. Slowly, Jay opened his eyes and gazed up at her. He reached up and wiped her tears. "I love you, too," he said.

"Jay!" Catalina yelled, a look of joy and astonishment coming across her face. She held him tightly, and the people erupted in applause. A true miracle had taken place in the city of Hope.

Jay slowly got to his feet and looked at everyone with the clearest of eyes. Sootshire, Neacen, his grandparents, and Catalina all hugged him and embraced him. "I thought I had lost you!" Candice cried. Glenda walked forward as they gave Jay a chance to breathe.

"A miracle," she said, facing him. "I believed all these years that you would go when Serena went, but the strength you received from family and friends, and your will to live, brought you back from death. Jay, you truly are a miracle."

The Perfect Portrait

"What do we believe in now?" asked the chairman. Neacen shook his head and walked to the front of the church.

"We believe in ourselves!" he said. "Don't you all see? All along we have held the power to change our world for the better. We are not blind sheep who follow nor are we reckless lunatics. We are a clear, free-thinking entity that is united by bonds we could have never imagined. So often do we spend time hating ourselves, blaming ourselves. Yet forgiveness is open to everyone. We all can start anew. Rhodam isn't just a city. It's hope! We have the power of hope in our hands. I took on that power when I first came here. Yes, I regret lying about who I was, but I never forgot one thing my father told me: If there is any chance to do better, ANY, take it! I took it, and from the graciousness of Estele, she showed me the light! We don't need gods, goddesses, fallen angels to tell us who we are. That power is in all of us. To the Council of Rhodam and to kingdoms all over the world, hear me!"

"They already can, my friend," Jay said, his pendant shining brightly.

"Believe in your people! They each have something to give! All of us are united and we all are a part of life's ever-flowing and everlasting circle! Do not oppress your people but bolster them. Help them see what light Estele has shown me. My we live AS ONE!"

The people applauded, and Neacen cried tears of joy. One of the people in the back opened the doors and the light from the outside filled the entire church.

"TO THE PEOPLE OF RHODAM! IT IS TIME TO TEAR DOWN THESE STATUES!"

Epilogue

As the statues of Serena crumbled, a new life was created for the people of Rhodam and the world. The sun shone brightly across the far reaches, and life was restored. Obed became the spokesperson for Akoran and decreed that he and the people would rebuild their heritage. Mikel, who now was one with his people in Sumurka, flourished from the waters nearby under a new and brighter sun.

Mitch and Candice decided to stay in Rhodam and mend broken fences over thirty years forgotten. Sootshire and Neacen became scholars, teaching the people about faith, hope, and the power of the human soul. Julius, whose heart was in pieces, found peace and forgiveness with Lester and Snow on the open and embracing waters of the world. As for Jay and Catalina, the boy who began as a ghost and became whole again, a new life started with Catalina by his side.

As for Glenda, she took back the Sword of Life but reminded Jay with a tap of the blade to his pendant that "If you ever need me, you will know where to find me."

After years of darkness, she and seven souls found new life in the light of a new, colorful, but most of all…HOPEFUL WORLD…

Printed in the USA
CPSIA information can be obtained
at www.ICGtesting.com
LVHW060107280923
758142LV00004B/14